I0684587

Seventeen stories that draw on a variety of fantasy themes and settings ranging from contemporary stories of magic to adventures in alternate realities, from the Old West to the present day or even alternate histories. There are parodies and humor and even a fairy tale.

Managansett Press

Don D'Ammassa is the author of:

Horror
Blood Beast
Servant of Chaos*
Caverns of Chaos*
Wings over Manhattan
The Gargoyle
That Way Madness Lies*
Little Evils*
Passing Death*
Date with the Dark*
The Devil Is in the Details

Science Fiction
Scarab
Haven
Narcissus
Translation Station
The Sinking Island*

Mysteries
Murder in Silverplate
Dead of Winter*
Death at the Art Gallery*

Fantasy
The Kaleidoscope*
Elaborate Lies*

Nonfiction
The Encyclopedia of Science Fiction
The Encyclopedia of Fantasy and Horror
The Encyclopedia of Adventure Fiction
Masters of Detection Vol I*
Masters of Detection Vol II*

*published by Managansett Press

# Elaborate Lies

# Don D'Ammassa

Managansett Press

"The Black Rose" first appeared in *The Book of More Flesh* (2002)
"The Knight of GreenwichVilllage" first appeared in *Adventures in the Twilight Zone* (1995)
"Foodworld" first appeared in *Millennium* (1998)
"Natural Law" first appeared in *Tales of Old* (2011)
"The Library of Lost Art" first appeared in *Tomorrow* (1993)
"The Kaleidoscope" first appeared in *Return to the Twilight Zone* (1994)
All other stories appear for the first time in this volume.

Managansett Press First Edition 2015

# Elaborate Lies

# CONTENTS

7

# TIMELESS IN A BOTTLE

One of the rare presents I received as a child was a ship in a bottle which my father claimed to have purchased during one of his business trips abroad, although I later saw many of nearly identical appearance in a curio shop near the Thames. It was undoubtedly a crude, inexpensive version created by inserting a collapsed model through the neck, then pulling on a string until the masts swiveled on a concealed hinge and stood upright. At the time, however, it seemed a marvelous thing to me, a miracle that I could see and feel rather than one of those cited in the parson's dry Sunday sermons. I rarely tired of staring into its depths, imagining a tiny crew swarming up the rigging, swabbing the decks, or battening the hatches to prepare for a storm. I even knew the names of some of the *Terpsichore*'s crew. There was stern but fair Captain Mansfield, Seaman Grundy with his tattoos and wooden teeth, the cabin boy, Jim Hawkey, and many others.

Eventually I succumbed to the inevitable fate of childhood. I grew older and somehow misplaced my imagination in the process. I cannot remember what happened to the bottled ship. I may have broken it, or given it away, or my mother might have packed it up in the attic. I also misplaced my plans for the future. I did not run off to sea and work my way up to captain of one of the new clockwork dreadnoughts. Nor did I join Her Majesty's Army and suppress rebellious natives in the Raj or the United American Colonies. I once met the daughter of a duke and she even allowed my roving hands a few liberties in the darkness, but I neither married nor was elevated into the nobility. The country did not acclaim me for my perspicacity and elect me Prime Minister, and my brief fantasy of becoming a surgeon vanished when I find myself lightheaded after seeing a man's leg broken when he stepped unwisely in front of a Brougham and four. The closest I ever came to replacing Henry Irving as the world's foremost actor was a brief engagement as general help at the Strand Theater, and the wizardry of Mr. Babbage and his steam powered mechanical brain were beyond my comprehension, let alone my ability to improve on his work.

My father's bankruptcy and subsequent suicide discouraged me from following in his footsteps, and left my mother and I eking out a precarious existence on her own income, a small inheritance from two aunts, neither of whom had ever married. I was able to supplement this somewhat by carrying messages back and forth across London and by means of other odd jobs, but I chafed at the constraints placed upon me and was initially rather relieved when mother followed father two years later. It was only after the passage of several months that I realized how much I missed her and, by extension, my father. I had no other relatives.

One spring morning I was walking along the line of docks, theoretically looking for day work, when I happened to notice a familiar name. The ship was a three masted schooner whose peeling paint suggested she'd seen better days, but the name *Terpsichore* was clearly visible on her bow. I felt a momentary disorientation because when I stepped back to gain perspective, I realized that this was indeed the ship I remembered from my childhood, down to the last detail. It was a moment or two before I saw the sense of it, that this was an old ship and was no doubt the original from which my model was made. I even thought to go aboard and inquire about work, more to satisfy my curiosity than because I actually wanted a position at sea, but there was no sign of life and I eventually turned away.

Although my father always insisted that he was prosperous in his business, my mother's worried looks and continual economies suggested otherwise long before his final fall. It is true that he had his small triumphs. We would eat well at times and my old clothes would be replaced by fresh new ones, but we continued to make do with the aging furniture my mother had salvaged from her childhood home, we never kept a carriage and rarely hired one, our Cheapside address never changed, and the periods of comparative wealth grew shorter and occurred at greater intervals as I grew older. Most of my childhood amusements were born and nurtured in my own imagination. There was an alley not far from Clerkenwell that was so

over-towered with tenements that I fancied it a cave, home to
Polyphemos whom Odysseus blinded, or bands of thieves with chests
of stolen treasure. Other children played there as well, though rarely
and never with me since we shared no language, literally or
metaphorically, and I christened them without their knowledge
Acastus and Patroclus and Laertes, adding the Argonauts into the mix
simply because I remembered more of their names.

There were other places in the city that I treated in similar
fashion. The theaters in Shoreditch became palaces where I was
assigned secret missions by the crowned heads of Europe and beyond.
The remains of the Great Fire of 1861 in Southwark became the outer
regions of Hell where I outwitted Satan himself. Lincoln's Inn Fields
was a mosaic of Africa, India, the western United States, and the lost
continent of Atlantis. There were many other fantastic locations I have
long since forgotten, as I ranged from Marylebone to Stepney and
from Highbury to Catford in search of playgrounds whose hidden
qualities were visible only to myself. There I was limited only by my
imagination and I triumphed over half naked savages, mechanical
soldiers, or hideous monsters as fancy led me. As I grew older, I shed
these one by one and by my twentieth birthday, as my mother sank
into her final illness, they all seemed stories I'd heard about some
other person, not memories of my own past.

I was sitting alone in the house one night when I realized
exactly one year had passed since mother's death. Suddenly I felt a
wave of longing and loss so intense that I couldn't remain there.
Despite the late hour, I grabbed my cap and set out to walk the streets,
no real destination in mind, and was surprised some time later to
discover that my restless feet had taken me south across the Thames
and into Southwark. Much of the blighted area had been rebuilt, but
there were still charred ghosts of structures that were gone forever.
The neighborhood had become a patchwork of rare survivors from
before the fire, the newer structures that had replaced those lost, and
the charcoal ruins of others still neglected. It was near one of these last
that I paused to have a smoke.

It was one of those rare, clear nights and even though there
were no gas lamps in the immediate vicinity, I could see quite clearly.

The building next to me had formerly been a private home. The rear wall was still largely intact, as was one corner where the remains of a staircase lead up toward rooms that no longer existed. There was considerable debris including a rag doll that dangled by one leg from where it was pinched between a railing and a fallen board. It looked to be nearly intact and, responding to some sudden impulse, I made my way cautiously over the uneven footing and pulled it down. Except for a scorch mark on the head, it appeared to have suffered little damage, but the charred cloth altered the sad expression, exaggerating it into a mask of misery and terror. I was so startled that I fumbled and dropped the doll. When I recovered and picked it up, I found that a sharp edge had poked through its side.

There was a ragged gash in the fabric. Smooth, pale sand poured out and fell to the ground.

I felt suddenly uneasy, as though someone was watching, and an uncomfortably warm breeze rose from nowhere. I tossed the doll back into the shadows, felt a twinge of guilt as though I'd abandoned a living child to damnation, and hastily made my way back home.

I have never been comfortable in the presence of the opposite sex, excepting my mother. I don't think that I'm unhandsome and as I grew toward manhood, my body filled out well. My complexion is good, my features regular, and while I cannot afford to dress as a gentleman, my clothing is respectable and well mended. Be that as it may, there appears to hover about me some impalpable force that repels women. Even the frowsy tarts in the pubs avoid my company, preferring to cajole others for their drinks. Men are more tolerant of whatever quality it is that isolates me, but even in this case, I cannot say that I have ever had friends in the sense that I could rely on others in times of trouble.

If self reliance is a virtue, then I am a virtuous man. But I am also at times very lonely.

I spent a week working for a Mr. Adderley in Camden who had acquired a row house in an estate sale and discovered, to his dismay, that the attic was filled to the rafters with the accumulated detritus of several generations. There were boxes of clothing, old paintings, broken down furniture, bundles of papers, and several cartons of penny dreadfuls that had deteriorated beyond hope of resale, old dishes and cups and odds and ends of house wares. He had offered me a reasonable fee plus whatever I could gain from selling off anything serviceable that I found, and I'd hired a horse and cart to carry it all away.

Adderley had promised a bonus if he was pleased with the results and if I could be finished by Friday, which I had done. He made a brief tour of inspection that morning, proclaimed himself very content indeed, and added an acceptable if not princely sum to what he had promised. Feeling well satisfied, I decided to indulge a whim and dine at one of the posh restaurants I could rarely afford, and then perhaps walk off the effects of such fine food in Lincoln's Inn Fields.

The park was much as I remembered it and I was happy to note that the grounds were sparsely occupied, so that I could imagine myself completely alone. The grounds were not as well kept as they might have been. Tall weeds crowded around the trees with an intimacy I didn't remember from my childhood visits and some of the shrubbery was in sore need of pruning. What youthful eyes had deemed magical and mysterious were now transformed into sloth and indifference.

I was walking beside one row of trees when I had the distinct feeling that I was no longer alone. I've never believed in the immaterial, not even the enigmatic God described by Parson Manners in the days when I felt obligated to attend church. I once read a book about theosophy and another that described religions of the Orient and considered them both to be rubbish. I've attended performances by mentalists which have only confirmed my skepticism of the occult. If their pretended powers were real, what need would they have to debase them in such fashion?

But that day I felt a sensation which seemed to have no basis in the five senses. I say "seemed" because I believe that we may sometimes react to a stimulus of which we have no conscious knowledge. A sound on the threshold of audibility, a slight movement at the edge of the field of vision, perhaps the hint of an odor – all of these might well waken the primitive, animal instincts which we have exchanged for our present civilized demeanor. Something at least told me that I was being watched.

I stopped where I was and slowly turned my head as though casually taking in my surroundings. I'm not sure what I imagined, perhaps a vagrant plotting to attack and rob me. It was broad daylight, but roguish attacks of this kind were not unknown, even in Camden. I looked about me for some makeshift weapon – a fallen limb, even a stone that I could hold in my fist. The ground had been littered with them earlier but the grass here was like a carpet. Still, I am taller and heavier than most, and thought I could face down most trouble.

Something stirred in the hedges to my right. I had not been looking that way, but now I turned my attention there. Indeed, several branches swayed or bent as something moved in obscurity, a large body, at least the size of a man. I thought that I might call out, but something told me to hold my tongue. Then I heard a sudden, brief sound as if air had been suddenly expelled from a large bellows. This was followed by a low rumbling that I identified as the panting of an animal, perhaps a horse. But if someone had decided to ride through the park, surely they would be visible above the low hedge.

I thought to call out, or whistle to announce my presence, but an unseen hand restrained me. Then I heard a cough, deep, throaty, and the hairs on the back of my neck stood up. The sound was quite literally beastly and a moment later there was movement again and I caught a flash through the rambling hedges – light brown hide or fur, smoothly curved muscles, the hint of something that might have been a mane. It could have been some large dog, of course, but at the time I was firmly convinced that I stood in close proximity to an African lion. I was paralyzed by shock and didn't move until long after my unseen companion had quitted the area.

When I emerged at the end of the row, there was no sign of anything amiss, just a family having a picnic and two young boys playing some arcane game with sticks. I felt profoundly embarrassed even though there had been no witness to the episode, and I hastened to leave the park.

I have made several efforts over the years to secure steady, gainful employment. I am not afraid of physical work, I read and write well, know my sums, and I believe in giving good value for my wages. Nevertheless, I've never held a position for more than a few months.

"I have no complaint about your industriousness, young man. But the other lads don't care to work with you. I'm sure you'll find something more suited in short order." That was Mr. Carswell, who'd hired me to help move freight in and out of his warehouse.

"I'm afraid you just won't do. You make the customers feel uncomfortable. There haven't been any actual complaints, mind you, but Mrs. Sturges told me that she won't come into the store unless there's another clerk to wait on her, and I've heard hints of the same from others." That was Mrs. O'Hara, where I'd been engaged to sell millinery supplies.

"This isn't working out, my boy. No reflection on your efforts, of course, but I've decided to make other arrangements. I will happily give you a recommendation." That was Mr. Carnaby, who had offered to pay me a substandard wage to clean the stalls in his stables. Apparently not even the horses cared for my company.

I was much more successful at odd jobs, day labor or a single short term task with a fixed time limit. Although I was able to survive on what was left from my mother's estate even after the death duties had been paid, I needed to secure additional income if I wanted to spend time at the pub, purchase new rather than used clothing, and eat as well as I preferred. Fortunately, there was no shortage of such work, and I was even able to turn down those offerings which I felt paid inadequately.

At one point I had occasion to find myself in Clerkenwell. I had been engaged to deliver a package to a small shop in that area and had somehow lost my way, probably through inattention. I attempted to correct my situation by the most direct route and found myself in a neighborhood that looked increasingly familiar. Many of the signs were indecipherable and I realized that I had strayed into the Italian district. Curiosity caught hold of me and I went looking for the dark alley that my youthful imagination had filled variously with blind cyclopean giants, the treasure of Ali Baba's forty thieves, or medieval dragons waiting to be slain.

I found it without difficulty as it had not changed to any noticeable degree. It was still impassable to wheeled traffic, piled high with unsalvageable rubbish, broken cobblestones, and filth of unknown origin. Above me, ropes stretched from window to window, from which depended a variety of clothing in various degrees of dampness. I passed a street peddler whose cart was filled with broken tools – hammers, staves, levers – and some unidentifiable items that looked like spearheads and arrows.  There was garbage intermixed with the other debris and a stench that discouraged me from penetrating any deeper, but I hesitated at one end of the alley, perhaps trying to recapture the sense of wonder I'd felt here as a child.

Something moved in the shadows, not in a furtive or menacing way, but I had learned to be cautious and I stepped back, measuring the distance to the more heavily traveled thoroughfare behind me. There was a sudden heavy rustling and I scrambled back, then paused when I saw a large ewe picking its way through the trash. I knew that some of the poor families in this part of town kept chickens or even swine, but I'd never seen or heard of anyone harboring sheep.  The evidence was incontrovertible, however, and I pressed back into a doorway as the animal trotted past, even though there was plenty of room for us both.

For just a moment, I thought I saw something half hidden in its heavy coat, as though a man clung to its belly. Then it was past me and when I emerged from the doorway, it had disappeared.


I will never know the cause of the fire that destroyed my home. It was probably an accident of some kind, although it may have been deliberately set. I barely knew my neighbors. In the past I had made some slight efforts to acquaint myself with them, but the properties to either side of my house were rentals and tenants came and went with unsettling frequency. Two days before the fire, I had surprised three young boys chucking stones at my windows and boxed one of them smartly on the side of his head. I had also exchanged angry words not long before with the housewife on the north side who had begun to make a habit of emptying her dirty wash water in my garden. I will never know the truth. What does it matter?

The fire brigade managed to save both adjoining houses, but they were content to contain the blaze rather than preserve my property. It burned itself out while I stood nearby, contemplating my choices for the future. That night I slept under one of the bridges over the Thames.

I still had my income, but no lodgings. Instinctively I knew that it would be difficult to find a landlord willing to accommodate me, and in any case, the rent would diminish my ready cash to the point where I could not survive without a steady supplement. I had heard that there was work available on the docks, so I set out to find employment as soon as the sun rose.

The rumor of work had grown somewhat in the retelling. The morning slipped past and the best I had heard was the possibility of something in "a fortnight or two". I ate sparingly to conserve my ready cash and renewed my search in the early afternoon. It was then that I noticed that the *Terpsichore* was either still at, or had returned to, its berth. The feeling of familiarity was reassuring and I walked to the end of the gangplank. Her barnacled hull was more welcoming than the faces of the factors and agents I had spoken to earlier.

I was about to go when I heard footsteps from above. I turned and saw a tow headed boy of perhaps fourteen years skipping down toward where I stood. He caught sight of me at the same time and moderated his pace. "Is it work you're here for?" It was a simple question, but I must have looked absurd as I gawked at him. It wasn't his words, of course, but rather the fact that this was the very same Jim Hawkey whom I'd imagined into existence as a child.

"Are you dumb then?" He stamped his foot impatiently.

"No," I managed, moistening my lips. "I wondered if there was a berth available for an unskilled hand."

"There might be, but you'll need to speak to Captain Mansfield and he's gone ashore. You can wait for him aboard if you want, but I don't know when he'll be returning."

"Thank you. I will."

I went aboard the *Terpsichore*. She had seen heavy duty in her time. Her fittings were corroded, her furled sails were heavily patched, the decks were stained and splintery, and her railings cracked and notched. Rope lay in untidy piles, wooden crates and bales were stacked up haphazardly in odd places, and she looked grey and drab, as if all the color had been leeched out of her over the course of years. There was a single sailor in sight, bent over and facing away as he made a half hearted effort to clean part of the deck with a long handled brush.

I didn't need to see his face to know it was Seaman Grundy.

I wandered the decks in a daze, wondering if I was dreaming, or simply allowing the present reality to supplant old memories. Was this in truth a reflection of the microcosm I'd created as a child, or were the images in my mind simply delusions prompted by my surroundings?

I began to feel lightheaded and looked about for a place to sit for a while. I finally chose a reasonably intact wooden crate that stood not far from the foremast. My feet were none too steady and I nearly tripped over an odd metal fixture attached to the deck, two short metal rails and some kind of spring and locking mechanism. I managed to keep my feet and staggered to the crate.

I sat with my head down for a moment or two, not even thinking, just waiting for reality and my perceptions of it to coincide once again. Then I was startled by a hand on my shoulder, jerked my head around to see Seaman Grundy standing beside me with a leathern flask in his hand.

"You look like ye've seen a ghost, mate. Here, have a pull of this."

He offered me the flask and, after a brief hesitation, I took it. The liquid was bitter, the alcohol strong, and I coughed as it went down. It did, however, steady my nerves. I took another long pull and this time I didn't cough.

"Have you served on the *Terpsichore* for long?" I asked, for want of anything better to say. My head was starting to spin as the liquor coursed through my blood.

"Aye, that I have. Couldn't say exactly in years, mind you. It feels like I've always been here. Oliver Grundy is the name. Seaman First Class."

I gave him my name, shook his hand, and searched for something else to say, finally glanced down toward the curious metal device embedded in the deck. For some reason it seemed important that I understand its function. "What's this contrivance?"

Grundy took a pull on the flask, wiped his mouth with the back of his hand, and screwed on the top. "That's the hinge, mate. The hinge for the mast. There's one for each of them, you see."

Of course, I thought. The masts have to be folded down onto the deck before you can slide the ship through the neck of the bottle.

I stood up but my head was swimming and I lost my balance. I fell forward, instinctively throwing out my hands. There was a feeling of shock as my right forearm hit the nearest of the two rails with all of my weight behind it.

Grundy helped me to my feet. Something was amiss with my right arm and I bent it close to me, cradled in my left hand. Grundy frowned. "You've cut yourself, mate. We'll have to bandage that up proper."

I glanced down and saw that he was right. There was a ragged gash in my right forearm. Smooth, pale sand poured out and fell to the deck.

# THE UNHAUNTED HOUSE

"You're not going to chicken out on me now, are you?" Karen's expression was an odd blend of irritation and disappointment.

Brian glanced quickly at Talbot House and took a deep breath. "No, I said I'd come with you and I meant it. I'm just afraid that we're going to get into trouble."

Karen tossed her head and Brian remembered why he'd agreed to this clandestine outing in the first place. If she wasn't the sexiest girl he'd met since transferring to Wilbur Whately High School, she was at least a close contender. He'd never had much luck with the opposite sex even though he was presentable enough and he was determined not to blow his chances now. "How do we get in?"

Reassured, Karen gestured vaguely toward the house, which was half hidden by the spruce trees that crowded in on every side. "I thought we were going to have to break a window, but I found a key. Would you believe someone put it under the front doormat?"

Brian shivered at the thought. "I still can't believe you went in there alone. If anything had happened, no one would have ever known."

"I waited until it was dark, and there was a full moon that night. I wouldn't have had the nerve otherwise. And I was careful to get out long before daylight." They had reached the white picket fence that surrounded the abandoned property and Karen paused a second, then pushed open the gate. "Anyway, the stories all say that the weird stuff only happens during the day." She glanced up at the sun and blinked. "That's why I have you along – to protect me."

Even though he knew he was being manipulated, Brian felt a brief surge of pride. Karen was the most popular girl at school. She was constantly attended by a crowd of fawning girls and an even larger contingent of boys seeking to win her affections. There was a long list of people who would have jumped at the chance to be alone with her, even here. He took a deep breath. "All right, let's do it."

They made their way quickly across the neatly trimmed lawn to the front door. Flowering shrubs had been arranged in unnaturally orderly beds to either side of the main entrance and he pressed his arms against his sides, determined not to brush against them. Technically he supposed they were trespassing, although Talbot House had stood empty for more than a generation. Brian had heard strange stories about the Talbot family, most of which he felt certain were lies or exaggerations, but there must have been a grain of truth there somewhere because even the adults in town avoided the property.

Karen stuck her hand in a pocket of her jeans and produced a key. Brian was suddenly convinced that this was not a good idea after all, but it was too late to back out without looking craven. The lock operated smoothly and the door opened without a sound. "Come on, before someone sees us." He followed Karen inside.

They were standing in a good sized vestibule from which two very large adjoining rooms were visible, one to each side. Even with the door closed behind them, their surroundings were brightly illuminated. The spruce trees shaded the windows but there was a large skylight three stories above that seemed almost to focus the sunlight. Brian could see every detail, the imperfections in the woodwork, the paintings – mostly landscapes – that covered the walls, the delicate pattern of flowers in the carpet beneath his feet. There was an ornate table to their left and a matching one to their right, each holding an elaborately sculptured lamp.

Brian shivered.

"What's wrong?" asked Karen, whose voice was tinged with excitement.

"I have the strangest feeling that nobody is watching us." It was true. The house felt completely empty, as though every lingering hint of personality had been sucked out of it.

"You noticed it too!" She touched his arm and his heart beat faster. "Not everyone is sensitive enough to pick up on that. Did you know that no one has ever died in Talbot House? Not ever."

Brian frowned. "You're kidding me. That's not possible." New houses always felt empty, of course, until their first death, but that was understandable and visitors made allowances, although usually no one was invited to visit until someone, or at least something, had died there. The death of even an elderly pet usually took the edge off, and if some people occasionally hastened their demise, it was almost always an act of kindness.

Karen shook her head. "No I'm not. I checked it out. The Talbots all died in hospitals or while they were away from home. I read the obituary columns all the way back to when the house was originally built. It's almost as if the family was cursed."

It sounded like the kind of story someone would make up just to scare people and Brian remained skeptical. "In a house this old, someone must have died. Maybe not violently. Maybe of some disease so terrible that it was all covered up."

She shook her head. "Nope. Not even a guest. And there were no serious injuries when the house was being constructed either. There was a Lawrence Talbot who was confined to his room for two years, but they took him to a hospital a month before he died."

"He was probably dangerously insane."

Karen glanced around, then leaned toward him and whispered conspiratorially. "No, it was cancer. The family tried to keep it a secret but one of the maids spilled the beans. It was quite the scandal at the time." She glanced around nervously and her voice dropped even lower. "And there was a mix up when the Talbots bought the property. They thought this area used to be an Indian burial ground, but there was an error in the map. It wasn't consecrated either and as far as anyone can tell, no one was ever lynched, scalped, or murdered anywhere on the property."

"But they built here anyway?" Brian found that very difficult to believe.

"Well, they didn't know the truth until after the house was already finished and by then it was too late."

The more Brian learned about Talbot House, the less he liked standing within its walls. He kept glancing toward Karen, who was wearing a filmy halter top and tight jeans, and decided that it was after all worth the risk. "So what do we do now?"

"Explore, of course. I walked through most of the house the night I came by myself but I couldn't find anything, not even a warm spot."

"They usually don't show up except in the daytime."

"Let's explore!" Brian reluctantly followed Karen's lead as she took him on a tour of the ground floor. She pointed out several objects she'd noticed during her first clandestine visit. The furniture in the formal dining room was uncovered and the thin patina of dust that coated everything was only mildly comforting. The chairs and couch in the sitting room were draped with sheets, which Brian found reassuring, but the paintings on the walls were so relentlessly cheerful that he felt a touch of dread and hurried onward.

There was a grandfather clock in the library.

"I wound it to find out if it would work when I was here that night. Want to see something weird?" Karen didn't wait for an answer. She stood on her tiptoes and opened the glass door to expose the face of the clock. Brian was so captivated by the sight of her straining body that he didn't notice what she was doing until she settled back down. "Just wait a minute."

He glanced up then and noticed that she'd set the clock to one minute before twelve. He'd been subliminally aware of the creepy, regular ticking but now it seemed to have become impossibly loud. Brian caught his breath and felt his heart quicken in his chest as the seconds passed and then it chimed.

The echoing bongs of the clock were heartening and he was almost relaxed when the clock fell silent, leaving him hovering in anticipation. "What happened?" he wondered aloud.

"That's it!" Karen clapped her hands together. "I tried it half a dozen times. Not once did it strike thirteen. Isn't that the creepiest thing you've ever seen?"

It was the creepiest thing he'd ever heard, actually, or more accurately not heard. "I suppose it could just be broken." His explanation sounded weak even to Brian.

Karen shook her head. "It's not just the clock. Did you notice how quiet it was when we closed the door?"

"Well, it didn't creak, but this is an old, empty house and hasn't been kept up."

"None of the doors creak, Brian. I tried every one. It's almost as if the hinges had been oiled."

"Who would do that? And why?" He didn't expect an answer, and didn't get one.

The library was the most comfortable room they'd visited. The only windows here were set high above and were too narrow to admit much light so the entire room was filled with flickering shadows. There was a large fireplace at one end whose mantle had been carved into a row of miniature gargoyles. Brian gravitated in that direction then recoiled suddenly.

"What's wrong?" Karen had been scanning the titles of the books but had noticed his flinch.

"I thought I heard a sound. Music." It was gone now but he turned his head, trying to decide where it had originated.

"Maybe someone nearby is playing the organ."

Brian shook his head. "No, it sounded like an accordion. I think it was some kind of polka." His face was pale when he turned in her direction, but fortunately the light was comfortably dim. A nice somber fugue would have cheered him up and he tried to recreate one in his head, but the eerie sound of the accordion filled his thoughts. "Find anything over there?"

"The Talbots had bizarre tastes in reading matter. No best sellers, no copies of the *Necronomicon*, not a single elder scroll." She raised a hand and pointed, but hesitated before actually touching anything on the shelf. "*Anne of Green Gables*," she read aloud. "*Little Women. Sense and Sensibility. Heidi. Pippi Longstocking*. I've heard of some of these books, but I didn't think I'd ever see copies. My uncle had *Heidi*, but he kept it locked up in a safe so that us kids couldn't read it. "

Brian glanced up and noticed the painting over the fireplace. A large dog was standing alertly in a field while an indistinct man in a checkered jacket aimed a gun at the sky. Brian moved back and forth, watching carefully, but no matter where he stood in the room, it never seemed as though either the man or the dog was looking at him. He shivered despite the warm air. "I don't think we're going to find anything," he said quietly, trying to disguise the fact that he hoped he was right.

"We just got here. We have to give it a chance." Karen turned away from the bookshelves. "You're not going to wimp out on me now, are you?"

"No, I just think we're wasting our time. Why don't we go have a picnic in the cemetery or something? This place depresses me. You said you searched it before and you didn't find anything. Why should it be any different now?" But he knew why it might be different. Karen had visited during the night, when it was safer. Anything might happen in such a bizarre place during the day.

"I just looked into some of the rooms. I didn't really explore. And I never found the attic or the basement."

The thought of a basement cheered him up considerably and he suggested that they search for a way down. The two of them spent several minutes lifting rugs in various rooms, but they were unable to find a single trapdoor, and even though Brian checked all the usual places, he couldn't locate a release for a secret passage anywhere. It was Karen who finally solved the problem.

"Brian! Come here! I think I've found it."

She had wandered into the kitchen at the back of the house, a refreshingly gloomy room with cobwebs in the corners. Brian had been examining the floor in the back hall and had just recovered from a fright. Something dark and furry had been watching him through one of the windows and for a brief moment he had thought it might be a cat or a squirrel. Fortunately he was able to recognize it as a rat before it turned and scampered out of his line of sight.

"Where are you?" He listened for her voice because she was not immediately visible.

"Over here!"

Brian walked around the oversized refrigerator and found Karen standing in an open doorway that he hadn't previously noticed. "What is it?"

"It's a stairway."

"What use is that? We want to go down, not up."

Karen shook her head, exasperated. "Not a regular stairway, silly. This one goes down to the basement."

Brian found that concept difficult to accept, but when he joined her and glanced down the dark passageway, he was forced to admit that she was right. It was certainly the most unusual way of accessing an underground room that he'd ever heard of, but he already knew that the Talbots had been eccentric.

The basement was the most pleasant and welcoming part of the house. There were spiders in the rafters, and so much debris – old furniture, cardboard boxes, gardening tools, etc. – that it felt as if everything might collapse and bury them at any moment. Brian felt a great weight lift from his shoulders. "At least they weren't completely nuts," he said lightly.

Just as he spoke, they turned a corner and gasped simultaneously at what lay before them. Fully one third of the basement had been paneled and carpeted. There was a pool table in the center of the carpet and a dartboard had been mounted on one wall. Brian was as shocked by the near obscenity as he would have been if he had found someone praying in a church.

"I think we should go back upstairs," Karen suggested in a low, tight voice.

"I think you're right."

Neither spoke of their experience even after they had reached the relative normality of the kitchen, but when Karen closed the door to the stairway, Brian positioned a chair under the doorknob as a safety precaution. He would not have been surprised if the unnatural atmosphere that pervaded the house had originated and spread from the malignancy in the basement. No wonder none of the Talbots had ever died here. If Brian had feared imminent death, he would have crawled to the door and outside rather than perish within those foul walls.

"Seen enough?" His voice was husky and he was sweating.

For a few seconds, he thought that Karen would agree to leave now, but she had visibly gathered her courage. "We still haven't found the attic." More reluctantly than ever, with a sense of foreboding that left his mouth dry and head aching, he followed her up two flights of stairs to the third floor.

By this point, Brian had become fairly inured to the general peculiarities of the house. He didn't show any visible reaction when they peered into several bedrooms, despite the tasteless bright colors and frilly trims on the quilts and curtains. He was unable to contain his disgust when they found the nursery, however. One wall was filled with shelves that held toys in the shapes of cuddly bears, delicate ballet dancers, and floppy eared dogs. "How could anyone do this to their own children?" he wondered aloud, and Karen bobbed her head in agreement, apparently too shocked to speak. She reached out and tentatively touched one of the dolls, a clown with an exaggerated face, the closest thing to a normal toy that they could see.

It didn't take long to find the attic, accessible by means of a pull down staircase. They ascended cautiously, Brian leading the way, and he was relieved to find himself in a large, gloomy space indirectly lit from two heavily curtained dormer windows, one at each end. For a brief moment Brian thought he saw a welcoming apparition lurking in one corner, but it was just a dressmaker's dummy. His gaze moved from one shadow to the next, seeking some semblance of normality, a familiar shapelessness, but he was repeatedly disappointed. A large blocky object turned out to be a steamer trunk rather than a coffin, a dark stain on the floorboards was paint rather than blood, and even most of the spiderwebs were frayed and obviously long abandoned.

Karen fearlessly explored on her own despite Brian's admonition that she should stay close. She was clearly less disturbed than Brian and as they had probed deeper into the house, he had sensed a quality to her actions that worried him. Karen was not just curious; she acted as though nothing in the house was influencing her. He would have felt much better if she had spoken in tongues or fallen into a trance, but neither happened. It became increasingly obvious that whatever strange attraction held Karen originated within her own mind, not from some external source. He told himself that once they were outside again, subject to the normal discorporate influences of the world, she'd be all right.

"There's nothing here," he said at last. "I think we should go. The atmosphere in this place can't be healthy."

Karen turned to him, her expression troubled, and he thought she might argue. But after completing some brief inner dialogue, she nodded and followed him down the staircase. They descended to the ground floor and Brian headed directly to the front door, but when he glanced back, Karen was nowhere in sight.

He found her in the library, staring up at the painting above the fireplace.

"What's wrong?"

At first she didn't appear to have heard him, but she answered at last, without looking around. "Have you ever been really popular, Brian?"

"As much as anyone, I suppose. Everyone is popular at one time or another. It's a part of life that we have to learn to accept." He felt uncomfortable talking about such intimacies with a girl he hardly knew.

"I think I've always been popular. I was such a beautiful baby and my family took me everywhere. They had lots of friends. And when I started school, it was even worse. I could never go anywhere on my own."

Brian didn't know what to say, so he said nothing. Karen sighed and slowly turned around. Her face looked sad for a moment, but she shook herself and set her jaw as though she'd just made a difficult decision. "Okay. Let's go."

He led the way back to the front door, checking a couple of times to make sure she was following. It opened as silently as it had before, but it didn't bother him this time because he knew he would be outside in a moment or two and would never return to Talbot House again, not even to be with Karen. He started to turn and then there was pressure against his back and he stumbled forward over the threshold and nearly lost his footing. She had pushed him out!

The door slammed behind him.

Brian tugged at the doorknob frantically but it was obvious that the lock had been thrown. "Karen! Karen! Can you hear me?"

Her voice came faintly through the door. "I can hear you, Brian."

"Unlock the door, Karen."

"I can't do that."

Brian bit his lip, not understanding. "I'll break one of the windows then and you can climb through."

"There are bars on all of the windows, Brian." Her voice seemed unnaturally calm.

"Then I'll go get help."

There was a long pause before she answered. "I'd rather you didn't do that. I want you to just go away and pretend we never came here."

"But if I do that, you might be trapped in there forever!"

"That's right. That's what I want, Brian. I want to stay here forever."

He shook his head, refusing to accept what she was saying. "But why? You'll be alone in all that emptiness."

"That's what I'm hoping. I'm tired of being popular, Brian. I'm tired of being welcome everywhere I go. I could pick a house at random and knock on the door and I'd be drinking hot vinegar and eating frog legs with someone's Mom and Dad or listening to music with kids our own age within minutes. Sometimes I feel so popular that I want to kill myself."

Brian started to argue some more, but she cut him off. "No. I've made up my mind, Brian. I'm staying here. For the first time in my life, I'm someplace where I feel I don't belong. That's worth more than anything to me, Brian, even life. Goodbye."

And then she fell silent.

Brian never entered Talbot House again. Every once in a while he stopped just outside the white picket fence – but only when it was quite dark. Sometimes there was a light in one of the windows, and he sensed somehow that Karen was still there. His only consolation was that when she finally died within those walls, as she must certainly do if she remained, that the house would finally be at peace.

# THE BLACK ROSE

Some pretty desperate characters had passed through the town of Hopeless over the years, but none more dangerous than the Black Rose and the Silverfish Kid. They rode in one hot summer morning, without fanfare, all covered with trail dust, inside and out. There was no mistaking Rose even from a distance; her thick black hair fell almost to her waist and the distinctive ebony flower bud was displayed on her saddle, her boots, and on each of the holsters that rested against her hips. If she hadn't been with him, the Silverfish Kid might have cut an impressive figure with his silver handled pistols and the fancy rhinestone studded shirt, at least from a distance. Close up, he was just another punk kid with a fancy wrapper. Rose had pale white skin that never tanned or burned, and rumor had it that something scary had happened to her once that scared all the pigment out of her skin and into her hair, which was as black as the darkest of nights.

Hopeless sprang up after a false rumor of a gold strike in a forgotten corner of the Arizona territory. There was a saloon and a general store and a hotel and a blacksmith. The barber did a little doctoring and a lot of dentistry. The whorehouse was directly opposite the hotel, and it was better maintained, and more frequently patronized. There was no church, no sheriff's office, and the town hall hadn't been used in years; in fact, the faded sign over the front door still said "Hopeful", the town's original name. A handful of crumbling shacks were scattered around, mostly tenanted by broken down gunfighters and retired outlaws who'd tucked away just enough to live on. Hopeless survived because it was in the middle of nowhere, and lawmen usually found excuses not to ride out that way. Retired outlaws weren't going to bother anybody, and the active ones wouldn't stay in Hopeless for longer than a drink or two.

Old Ben Walters was the first to spot them. Ben's bladder had been bothering him and he was up early, relieving himself against the back wall of Oates General Goods. Something moved on the horizon and he raised one hand to shade his eyes, squinting because a brisk morning breeze was blowing the dust around a bit livelier than usual.

Most people in Hopeless knew Rose only by reputation, but Old Ben had been visiting his sister in Shawnee when she killed Deadpan Dooley right in front of the Baptist Church, and blew off Deke Wilson's cock when he tried to backshoot her. Deke later cut his own throat when the town doctor left him alone for a few minutes.

Ben hastily tied up his pants and headed for the saloon, figuring it was worth a free whiskey to be the one to announce the newcomers. Sam Grimm, the barkeep, would just be opening up, and his wife would be serving corn meal muffins and eggs to anyone willing to pay a dime for a plateful. As he made his way down the alley to Main Street, Ben wondered who the second rider might be. He couldn't remember ever hearing that Rose kept company with anyone longer than a single night.

As he'd expected, the saloon was open for business. Tom Grogan and Dewey Martin were sitting at a table, playing cards and drinking coffee that was almost certainly laced with whiskey. One of the whores from across the street was wolfing down eggs in a corner. Sam was behind the counter, polishing the frame around the mirror. He glanced back over his shoulder when he heard the doors swing open, nodded without changing expression, and turned back to his work.

"Got visitors coming!" Ben nearly fell over a stray chair in his haste to get to the bar. "It's the Black Rose and some feller."

Sam Grimm turned around and his face showed just the slightest hint of interest. "Black Rose, you say? Haven't heard that name in a while."

"She keeps to herself. Never heard tell of her partnering with anyone."

"Sounds like she's not riding alone today."

"Something's changed, that's for certain."

Mary Grimm was pouring a cup of coffee for Ben when the hoof beats became audible. He left it sitting on the bar and walked over to the swinging doors. They were coming slowly down Main Street, the unidentified man in front. Sam Grimm joined him, nodded to himself and turned away. "That's the Silverfish Kid. Saw him over in Winslow when I went for supplies beginning of spring. Just starting to grow fuzz on his chin and already killed four men."

Old Ben's brow wrinkled. "Heard tell of him from one of those Comancheros came through here a couple of months back. Said the men he killed weren't real gunfighters, just farmers that he picked a fight with."

"Well, they're dead farmers now." Sam turned and was about to return to his polishing when Tom Grogan joined them.

"He's bad business, the Kid is. Figured he wouldn't last long; he's never been that fast." Grogan took off his hat and scratched the bald patch in the middle of his filthy mat of hair. "Saw him take down Dermot Cross a month back. Queerest thing you ever saw. Cross should have shot him dead before the Kid even had his gun out, but his pistol got tangled up in the holster and wouldn't come free. Three shots in the chest and down he went."

"Dame Luck is fickle," said Sam.

"Maybe. Jack and Curly Blackburn tried to bushwhack him when he left town the next day. Didn't see it myself, but they had their younger brother along to hold the horses, and young Jeb says Curly's feet went out from under him just in time to spoil the ambush. Slid down from behind his cover and took a bullet right in the face. Jack comes up behind the Kid with a dead bead on his back, but he's got a bad shell in his shotgun and it doesn't fire. He gets gutshot and dies in little brother's arms."

"Sounds like the kid got himself a good luck charm."

The twosome pulled up in front of the saloon and tied off their horses. Ben retreated to the bar and pretended to be interested in his coffee, but Sam stayed at the door and swung it open to admit the newcomers. "Welcome to Hopeless, folks. What can I get you?"

"Whiskey." Rose had a deep, gravelly voice that seemed to echo inside her throat. She brushed past Sam and headed straight for the bar. Her eyes swiftly catalogued everything and everyone in sight. She was a striking woman, if not conventionally attractive, not yet thirty but with eyes infinitely older.

The Kid stuck his thumbs inside his gun belt and sauntered in without speaking, his face lit by an exaggerated grin that emphasized all of his worst features. A pencil thin, lopsided mustache hung over a comically weak chin. His eyes were narrow and a little bit glazed as if he'd been buying peyote from the Indians or drinking a mite too much and too often. There was a curly white scar on his temple, and one of his ears was missing its lobe. He looked to be around eighteen.

Sam sighed and followed, poured Rose a whiskey. He poured another for the Kid, who picked it up and sipped, then grimaced and set the glass down hard enough that some of the liquid splashed out. "That's pretty raw, barkeep. Why don't you bring out the good stuff?"

Sam refilled Rose's empty glass. "Folks around here don't take much interest in high priced drinks. This is as good as it gets."

"Shit! I've had better served as medicine." He smiled, revealing a pair of wooden teeth, and leaned forward. Something that sparkled even in the dim light glittered against his none too clean chest. "C'mon now, barkeep. I bet you've got at least one bottle of the good stuff tucked away for yourself."

Sam's voice remained flat but he carefully avoiding meeting the gunman's eyes. "We don't do much drinking ourselves. You might try Miss Gordon across the way. I hear she keeps some fine brandy around for special occasions."

The Kid's face twitched. "Who the hell is Miss Gordon?"

"Runs the bordello." Rose answered without looking up from her drink, which was already half gone.

"What the hell's a bordello?" There was a dangerous whine in the Kid's voice now.

"It's a whorehouse," Sam explained quietly. "Right across from the hotel next door."

The Kid laughed, an ugly, high pitched sound. "Oh, well, we'll be paying her a visit soon enough, won't we, doll?" He put his arm around Rose and gave her a squeeze. She didn't react in any way, just continued to sip at her whiskey. The Kid glanced around the room. "I'll bet y'all wonder why anyone keeping company with a fine looking woman like this would be interested in visiting a whorehouse."

No one was, but that didn't stop him from explaining.

"I got me some powerful needs. Rose here gets plumb tuckered out sometimes trying to keep up so whenever we get the chance, I like to spread myself around a bit." He leered at Sam, who carefully pretended not to notice. Rose abruptly tossed down the rest of her drink and extended her arm. Sam made the bottle reappear and poured her another.

The Kid's eyes grew hard for a second and Sam casually reached down to where he kept his shotgun. But the moment of tension passed and the kid finished off his whiskey and tossed a coin down so hard that it bounced and fell behind the counter.

"C'mon, Rose. Let's find ourselves something decent to drink." He was off toward the door without looking back. Rose removed some coins from her pocket and placed them carefully on the polished bar before following, her face as expressionless as ever.

Dewey Martin stood up and came over to the bar, his voice low. "That there's trouble," he said quietly. "No sense at all and a bad temper to boot. She must've been pretty desperate to fall for that one."

Mary Grimm stepped out from the shadows where she'd been standing. "That's not the way it is. She hates him, pure and simple. He's got a rope on her though, one she can't slip. He'd better hope she never does."

It took less than a minute for Emma Gordon to take the Kid's measure. Not very bright, a brittle personality caught between the image of himself he was trying to create and the one he actually was. The Black Rose was more of a mystery. Her reputation said she was an introspective loner who only broke the law when it was necessary, but who never seemed to hesitate when the need arose. Rumor had it she'd killed more than twenty men, and none of them had been pokes with roving hands or sloppy mouths. That type she treated roughly, but broken bones and broken pride both healed eventually. The ones she killed were a different breed, living by their guns. Even the one lawman on her tally had been a corrupt bully who used his office to legitimize his crimes.

"We heard tell you had soft women and hard liquor, and we're of a mind to enjoy them both."

Emma gestured toward the overstuffed couch, but neither the Kid nor Rose made a move in that direction. "It's a little early," she said quietly. "The girls have to rest some time."

The Kid pulled a handful of coins from his pocket and tossed them down on a mahogany tabletop. "They can sleep once we're done. Rose and me have been riding all night. We need some relaxing and we need it right now."

Emma drew a deep breath. "All right, have a seat and I'll call them down."

Apparently soothed by her quick surrender, the Kid visibly calmed. "And don't forget the liquor. The good stuff, not the crap they serve over in the saloon."

"I'll bring some brandy."

Ten minutes later, three younger women descended from the second floor, two of them yawning and rubbing their eyes. Emma brought a fancy silver tray with a bottle of brandy and two glasses, set it on the mahogany table and made the silver coins disappear. "This is Lily and Milly and Carlotta. Mandy's got a fever and Marybeth's out, probably eating breakfast over at the saloon." She poured the brandy.

The Kid emptied his glass with one toss and smacked his lips. "That's smooth, right enough. Ain't you got any bigger glasses than this?"

Emma ignored him, let her eyes flicker over to where Rose stood. She hadn't made a move toward her drink, was staring flatly out the front window toward the street. "I charge two dollars per visit. The girls keep all their tips so if you're pleased, you don't have to worry about the money going to me. Drinks are extra. My girls are clean and they're good at their job and I don't tolerate any violence."

At some unseen signal, two men stepped into the room, one black, one at least half Apache. They didn't say anything, but the message was clear. The Kid glanced in their direction, then laughed nervously. "I don't treat my women badly, do I, Rose?"

She didn't answer, and he repeated the question, a bit more sharply.

"No, Kid, you treat your women just fine." Her voice was completely neutral, but Emma gave her a quick glance, and a small frown.

The Kid glanced over at the three women and his finger pointed at Milly. "We'll take that one."

Looking neither pleased nor unhappy, Milly stepped forward and took the Kid's hand in hers. "Right this way, lover."

She started to lead him toward the stairs but he stopped and turned back. "C'mon, Rose. Don't let's keep the lady waiting."

For just a split second there was a flicker of expression on Rose's face, but it passed too quickly to be recognized. Then she turned and followed. Emma watched them climb the stairs, troubled in her thoughts, then shook her head and shot a look at the two men that warned them to stay on their toes.

Milly led them to a surprisingly large room with an unsurprisingly large bed and started to remove her clothing. The Kid plopped himself down in a caneback chair and watched while the Rose stood motionlessly just inside the door. Milly was down to her underwear when she paused.

"What's the story? Is she going to watch or what?"

The Kid laughed unpleasantly. "No, love. I'm the one who's gonna do the watching."

Milly glanced back and forth between the two, not understanding until Rose sighed audibly and began removing her own clothing.

Marybeth returned while Emma was still standing at the foot of the stairs, wondering what was going on above her head. "They here?"

Emma glanced at the younger woman, nodded. "They're upstairs with Milly."

"Poor Milly. She always gets the queer ones, don't she?" Marybeth spotted the untouched glass of brandy and took it without asking. It felt wonderful burning its way down her throat. "Anything wrong?"

"I don't know, Marybeth. Something just doesn't feel right."

Milly recovered from her surprise and gave a little shrug. "Long as you're paying, I got no problem with that." It took only a few seconds to remove the rest of her clothing, and when she was completely naked, she turned to size up her prospective lover. Rose had just shucked off her shirt and vest and was crouched over, working on her jeans. She straightened up just about then and Milly got her first good look, and that's when she started screaming.

The Kid was amused at first, but he heard heavy feet rushing up the stairs and he sighed. "I wish you'd just shut up and get down to the loving," he said angrily, and Milly closed her mouth and stretched out her arms for Rose, and then someone was knocking on the door and the Kid pulled his gun and eased it just far enough open that those outside could see the muzzle. The two roughnecks were standing in the hall, and Emma Gordon was right behind them.

"No call to get excited folks. Everything's fine. The lady just saw a mouse run across the floor. Now if we'll all just get back to minding our own business, I'll be taking care of mine." No one moved for a handful of long seconds, and finally the Kid let the door slide a bit further open, almost as if by accident, and let those who were outside see the two women locked in a squirming, passionate embrace on the bed. "C'mon folks, I'm not getting my money's worth standing here jawing with you all."

Another beat and Emma nodded. "Just remember what I told you about not hurting my girls."

"I won't hurt a hair on the pretty thing's head, ma'am." And he closed the door.

The Kid and the Black Rose left about an hour later, crossed to the hotel and got themselves a room for the night. Emma Gordon went upstairs right after they left to check on Milly, found the girl naked, huddled under her blankets, apparently unharmed but in a state of mild shock. Emma asked her repeatedly what had caused her to scream, but Milly never said a thing.

More strangers showed up in Hopeless later that day, and this time it was Crazy Ed Kane who brought the news. Crazy Ed was well into his fifties, a respectable age for a broken down gunfighter who had at least five enemies somewhere for each of the fifteen notches on his belt. Ed got lucky late in life, doublecrossed his partners after robbing a train, and retired to Hopeless with enough gold to last more than a lifetime. But he also picked up a disease from a whore down in Juarez, and his brain was so addled that no one knew when he was talking straight and when he was getting times and places confused.

So Dewey Martin went out to check and sure enough, there was a big cloud of dust heading their way. "At least eight or ten riders," he told the group assembled in the saloon. About two dozen regulars had drifted in during the afternoon, more than usual, thirsting after information about the Black Rose as much as for the liquor.

"Posse?" Sam leaned forward on the bar, thinking hard.

"Might be."

Sam tapped his fingers. "All right, someone better go warn our visitors." He didn't much care what happened to the Kid, but Hopeless only existed because it protected those who claimed refuge there. They wouldn't draw their guns to drive off the law because that would bring them the wrong kind of attention, might even goad someone in authority into doing something about the rogue settlement, but there were places where fugitives could hide safely right under the noses of the law.

Old Ben hobbled up the stairs, one hand pressed against his sore kidney. He knocked on the door of number six, and it opened so quickly that it was obvious Rose had been standing right there. Beyond, he could see the Kid roll over in the bed.

"What the hell is it now?"

"Company coming. Could be the law. We've got a place you can hide, down in the basement. Behind a false wall. Someone's already taken your horses out for a stroll so they won't be spotted."

The Kid rolled out of bed with surprising grace. "Ain't hiding from nobody. Won't be necessary."

Half an hour later, an even dozen hard looking men dismounted in front of the saloon. Tom Grogan identified one of them as Sheriff Bartlett from Parker's Passing, a good sized town about a hundred miles to the west. "He's a tough man. Beat a drifter to death once."

Sam Grimm sighed and walked outside to greet the newcomers.

"Afternoon, gentlemen. Welcome to Hopeless. First drink is on the house."

Bartlett adjusted his jacket so his badge showed. "We're not here to drink. We're looking for someone. Tall thin man with a bad laugh, short woman with black hair and a white face."

"And what makes you think they're hereabouts, Sheriff?"

But Bartlett never had a chance to answer. The Kid and the Black Rose appeared as if by magic, standing in the middle of the street. The Kid looked confident, Rose indifferent. The sheriff's men slowly moved apart, some checking to make sure they had a clear reach for their holsters, others moving rifles to a more convenient position.

"Don't you know when to quit, Sheriff?" The Kid seemed both peeved and pleased. "How many of your deputies do we have to kill before you get the message?"

Sam stepped back and away, and the handful of onlookers who had emerged from the other buildings in town began to retreat as well.

"One of those you cut down was my kid brother. You didn't really think I'd just let you ride away after that, did you?"

"Would've been better for you if you had." The Kid sighed dramatically. "Well, I suppose we ought to get this over with."

Afterwards, no two people ever agreed on just exactly what happened, but Sam Grimm stood straight and watched and what he saw was that Rose got off three shots before any other gun spoke, and three men fell in the street and never got up again. Then there was lead flying every which way, and Sam hastily found himself some cover, but not before he watched Sheriff Bartlett fumble his revolver and drop it in the dirt, and a horse shied and knocked over two of the deputies, and another took a bad step and lost his balance, and still another had his gun jam. A minute later, not one member of the posse was moving, and impossible as it seemed, both the Kid and Rose were still standing.

The kid raised the back of his hand to his mouth and stifled a yawn. "You see to things here, Rose. I'm going back to bed." And he turned and walked back toward the hotel as though nothing at all had happened.

The townspeople were already crowding around to see if any of the deputies had survived, and to help themselves to their belongings. Sam grimaced and looked at Rose and she looked at him. "C'mon inside. I'll get you a drink."

The saloon was deserted. Sam poured her a whiskey, and another for himself, and they sat at a table and looked at one another. "Been a long time, Rose."

She glanced around uneasily and he shook his head. "Mary's gone back to the house." He swallowed some of the whiskey. "I told you I was married, Rose."

"Yes, but it's different, seeing her like that. You always said you were the settling down type, but I never really believed it."

"And you weren't. Aren't."

"Do you love her?"

He hesitated before answering. "She's a good person and a good friend. She's loyal to me and supports me in every way. I can't imagine living without her. Yes, I love her, Rose. Not the way you and I loved each other, but more comfortable like."

She let a ghost of a smile tickle the corners of her mouth, but it was gone almost as soon as it arrived. "Do you ever miss what we had?"

He hesitated again. "Yes, I do. I wouldn't trade what I've got for it, but I don't have any regrets either."

"Then you're a lucky man, and she's a lucky woman." She finished her drink and turned to look toward the swinging doors, and when she did, her vest flapped open revealing what lay beneath.

"You've been hit!" Sam was on his feet, alarmed.

Rose glanced down at the hole in her silk shirt and shrugged. "Just a scratch. I'm not even bleeding." And she laughed, but it was thin and humorless. "Don't fret."

He eased back down into the chair. "What happened, Rose? Why are you with him? He's trash."

"I've got my reasons."

"Reason enough to get on the wrong side of the law? Someone's gonna come looking when twelve men disappear, and sooner or later word will get out how they died."

"Don't push it, Sam. I don't want to talk about it."

She started to get up but he reached out and caught her arm. "Do you remember the promise we made that night?"

Her face was still a mask but her eyes reflected a terrible sadness. "Don't make me do this, Sam. You're better off not knowing."

"We promised each other the truth, Rose. I've kept my side of the bargain. Are you going to renege now?"

She met his eyes, held them, waited for him to waver. He never faltered. He was the only man who'd ever matched her stare. "Pour me another drink."

He did, she drank it, and he waited some more. "Rose?" he prompted.

"All right, damn it!" She stood up. "You want the truth? Here it is!" She opened her vest and then she unbuttoned the black silk shirt beneath it and Sam saw the neat little bullet hole in her shoulder, the flesh torn, but no blood, not a drop. That wasn't the worst part though. There were three other three bullet holes in her abdomen. They weren't bleeding either, but they were filled with a churning mass of maggots.

She gave him an eyeful, then buttoned her blouse and sat down. He sat stunned while she poured out two more drinks.

"How?" It was the only thing he could think to say.

"The Kid did it. He took some kind of talisman off an Indian about a year ago. Wore it around his neck, eventually figured out that it granted wishes. Apparently he wished that he would win every gunfight without getting a scratch. We crossed paths shortly after that and he, well, he killed me. Damned bird flew between us and took my first two shots, the third was a misfire."

Sam was visibly shaken, but his voice was calm. "What did you mean, he killed you?"

"Just what I said. I'm dead, Sam. Then he wished that I was alive to do his bidding or something like that, and so I am, more or less, and I have to do exactly what he tells me. Frankly, I liked it better dead. Only good part is the Kid can't get it up, so he doesn't bother me that way." She sighed. "But he does like watching me do it with others. Men, women, animals, doesn't matter to him."

"I'll kill him." Sam started to rise and Rose pulled him back down.

"He'd kill you, Sam. Even if you snuck up on him from behind. Even if you had four men holding him down. He's immune, you understand. He can't be shot."

Sam shook his head. "I don't get it. If he can wish for anything he wants, what the hell is he doing in a rathole like this?" He spread his arms to encompass the entire town.

"The boy's not too bright for one thing. For another, the charm doesn't always work. Takes a couple of months between wishes. He just wasted one last night in fact. Wished his whore would stop screaming and be quiet. She's quiet now, and always will be. He just wasn't thinking what he was doing."

Sam's eyes narrowed. "Screaming? He didn't hurt one of Emma's girls, did he?"

She glanced away so he couldn't see her eyes. "Didn't hurt her exactly. Scared her a lot. She's never gonna be the same again though."

"Oh my God!" Sam was up and running before Rose could stop him, and when she followed him outside, he was already at Emma Gordon's door. He disappeared inside.

Puzzled, Rose started to walk that way, noticing that all of the bodies had been removed from the street. She was standing in front of the hotel when Sam reappeared, running in her direction.

"Emma's gone after him," he said hoarsely. "She's already killed two men for roughing up her girls. I've gotta stop her."

Rose stepped aside to let him pass, not interfering, but not caring. She followed more for lack of anything better to do than for any other reason.

Sam reached the landing at the top of the stairs and paused for breath. All of the doors were closed and there was no one in sight. There was nothing but silence. He had a presentiment that something terrible had happened, and wanted to turn away, but he couldn't abandon Emma. So he walked to the door and raised his hand to knock.

The door was ajar.

He pushed it open slowly, ready to bolt if he saw a gun pointing in his direction. Instead he saw the Kid, lying in his underwear on top of the blankets. The Kid was smiling, but not with his mouth. His mouth was twisted into an expression of surprise and shock, and his smile was a bright red crescent under his chin.

Emma Gordon sat on a chair beside the bed with a straight razor in her lap. She looked up at Sam with her face set resolutely. "He hurt one of my girls," she said quietly. "No one hurts my girls."

Rose entered the room, looked down at the mess on the bed, and for the first time since coming to Hopeless, she smiled.

The Black Rose left Hopeless around dusk that evening. She had a final drink at the saloon, then saddled up and headed out of town without saying where she was going. The last rays of the failing sun touched her as she went, and reflected brilliantly from the shiny bauble she wore around her neck. She wondered how long it would be before she could use it.

.

# A CUP OF COCOA

Even as undergraduates, Peter Moncrieff and Jason Oliver never saw eye to eye. Peter had a mechanistic view of the universe that drove him into the sciences as surely as if he'd been a plaything of the gods. He was convinced that reality was a puzzle constructed from identifiable components, and that if we didn't understand how some aspect of that reality functioned, then it was simply that we had yet to solve that piece of the puzzle. Jason was just as firmly committed to the scientific method, but he believed that it was a tool to help us observe the forces that surrounded us. The fact that we could describe them did not, in his view, mean that we understood them. Peter never doubted that his future lay in physics. Jason drifted from one branch of science to another and ended up in archaeology.

Despite their fundamental differences, Peter and Jason remained close friends. Their work took them all over the world, but they corresponded regularly by letter and later by email. When happenstance brought them together, they invariably engaged in brief reminiscences followed by intense but never heated arguments.

Peter's relationships with women never lasted long enough to end in marriage. Jason's marriages never lasted long enough for him to develop a relationship. Peter was a fiscal conservative; Jason was only concerned with economics and politics when they impacted his funding. Peter attended church regularly, but did not believe in God; Jason believed that there was a mechanism powering the universe that might be called a god, but he didn't attend church.

I've worked for Peter since finishing college. Although he has an orderly, one might even say rigidly organized mind, he has no patience for anything he considers minutiae. Left to his own devices, he would not pay his bills until he received an eviction notice or the power went off. He likes to eat well and can afford to, but he abhors cooking, shopping for groceries – or any domestic activity for that matter. Peter learned to drive when he was fourteen, and hasn't renewed his driving license since he was twenty four. He keeps impeccable notes of his work, but cannot be bothered to organize or file them.

That's where I come in. I was originally hired as a research assistant to take care of his correspondence and remind him of his schedule of classes, lectures, and meetings. Over the course of time, my responsibilities expanded to include those of personal secretary, valet, chauffeur, chef, and general factotum.  It was three years before he could consistently remember my name, but my annual salary increases suggested that he was more appreciative than he let on. I am nearly ten years younger than Peter, and reasonably attractive, but he has never so much as hinted at a flirtation.

We were in Minneapolis for a conference when I received the call from Jason, who was currently working on something called the McKinstry Mounds up north of us. "I rented a cabin just outside the city and there's a really nice restaurant just a few miles away."

I flipped through my mental appointment calendar.  "I don't know, Jay. Peter's pretty tightly booked."

"Come on, Sandy. We haven't seen each other in almost a year. And I've got something to show the two of you that'll really knock your socks off."

"Peter and I prefer to keep our clothing where it belongs." But I knew that Peter wanted an excuse to avoid dining with the local Congresswoman, whose appalling idiocy was difficult to ignore. "What about tomorrow evening? I think I can move things around a little."

"Great." He gave me quite unnecessary directions; we have a GPS in the van.

It was February and the ground was covered with snow, although the roads were clear. I don't mind snow but I hate the cold and it was down into single digits during the warm part of the day. We found the restaurant without any difficulty. Jason was late, but not very late, and that was not unexpected either. He looked much as he had the last time we'd gotten together, perhaps a bit more gray hair.

The meal was surprisingly good given the rundown décor. I didn't talk much; I never did. The two of them exchanged recent histories, although I doubt that the flow of information was entirely understood in either direction. Jason complained about the lack of funding sources; Peter complained about the time he wasted buttering up contributors. I had a credit card to cover travel expenses so I picked up the check. By then my attention had drifted away from the conversation so I was a bit startled when I realized Peter had committed us to following Jason back to the cabin he'd rented.

I glanced at my watch. "We have a really early start tomorrow, Peter."

Peter dismissed my concern with a wave. "I know. You'll manage, Sandy. You always do. And Jason here insists that he has something really important to show us."

So we followed his rusting jeep through a series of winding roads to what literally was a cabin, though an elaborate one. There was a gas powered generator to run the lights and heat, and it did a good job with the former but only an inadequate one with the latter. A couple of degrees cooler inside and we could have seen our breath.

"Can I offer you something to drink?" Peter never touches alcohol and I never drink when I'm driving. "Something hot, I mean. Coffee? Tea? Cocoa?"

It was a foregone conclusion than we'd be having a hot chocolate drink. One of the few things that Peter and Jason agreed on was their abhorrence of coffee and tea. Myself, I prefer coffee, strong and black. But I'm adaptable.

Jason and I had matching mugs – courtesy of some chain fast food restaurant he patronized. Peter drank from a somewhat larger, elaborately designed one that looked as though it might have been handmade. We sipped at our drinks while Jason recapitulated his earlier summary of his present project in more detail. As much as I enjoyed his company, I was impatient to be on our way. I hadn't been kidding about how much we needed to get done in the morning and I wanted to be in bed before midnight.

The hot drink was welcome and I accepted a refill with enthusiasm. Jason did the same but Peter indicated he still had a nearly full cup, which was surprising since I'd seen him drink from it several times. Once or twice Peter tried to focus the conversation on the marvelous revelation that had been promised, but Jason always managed to skitter away and I began to wonder if that had just been a fabrication to entice us here. But why?

I was still chilly so I got up and wandered around while the two of them talked. I noticed that there was a thermostat, set at fifty degrees. There was a pause in the conversation and I jumped in. "Why do you keep it so cold in here, Jay?"

"Saves fuel. I'm on a tight budget." He resumed his description of some sort of burial mound quickly and I frowned. This was, by his own admission, one of the few times he had been adequately funded. There was no reason why he couldn't afford a little extra heat.

I almost refused another refill, but I was shivering a little so I acquiesced. Jason topped up his own cup and offered to do the same for Peter. "No, I'm fine." But this time Peter frowned and looked down at his drink.

"Is something wrong, Peter?" Jason's voice was thick with suppressed mirth, or excitement, or both.

"Is there a false bottom in this or something?" Peter lifted the cup to eye level and examined it thoughtfully.

"What is it?" I walked back over to join them. Jason was grinning from ear to ear and Peter was looking increasingly puzzled.

"Do me a favor, Sandy." He handed me his drink. "Take this out to the kitchen and empty it into another container." I looked at Jason, who could barely sit still. He nodded.

I found a relatively clean sauce pan and emptied the hot cocoa into it. There was just about a full cup. Apparently Peter had drunk a good deal less than I had thought. I carried pan and cup, the latter now empty, back into the room and showed them to Peter.

"That's odd." He took the pan and sloshed it around, then took the empty cup and examined it again.

"Is something wrong?" Jason's amusement was so apparent that I was certain we had finally reached the point of this get together.

"Are you into magic tricks now, Jay?" Peter set the empty cup down on an end table and handed the sauce pan to our host.

"Not at all. This is, in a manner of speaking, a scientific experiment."

Both of us stared at him. "What kind of experiment?" asked Peter.

"I'll explain in just a minute. Aren't you going to drink your cocoa?" He glanced toward the end table and, automatically, Peter and I followed his gaze.

The cup looked just as it had before, but there was steam rising from the top. Peter reached down and picked it up and from where I stood I could tell it was full again.

You've probably heard the story of the never ending penny, a magical coin that reappears in the protagonist's pocket no matter how many times he spends it. Well, Jason insisted that he had found the never empty cup. "I bought it at a yard sale. It was empty then, of course."

Naturally Peter and I thought he was joking. Jason insisted that we pour the contents into the sauce pan again, which Peter did. This time the cup remained empty. "It doesn't work if you're looking at it," explained Jason.

Peter laughed. "Of course not. Okay, what's the trick? I admit it's a clever one."

"No trick. Just set it down over there and look toward me for a second."

The cup was full again when we glanced back. I'll skip over the next few minutes and summarize. If we kept our eyes on it, nothing out of the ordinary took place, but given a couple of seconds unobserved, the cup replenished itself. The only way we could forestall this was by turning it upside down.

There was no longer any question of returning to our hotel any time soon. Fortunately Jason turned up the thermostat; our chilly surroundings had been contrived to make certain we accepted the offer of hot cocoa. Peter was like a child with a new toy. Here was a novel element of the universal puzzle for him to solve. He began talking about loops in time and possible weak spots between dimensions and other abstractions I couldn't begin to understand.

And he had to experiment, of course. We covered the cup with an opaque cloth, and it refilled itself, and a translucent one that we could just see through, and it remained empty. We filled it with various other liquids – water, milk, prune juice – and the contents remained unchanged until we emptied it out again, after which it once again contained hot cocoa.

"It was the first thing I put in it when I bought the damned thing," said Jason. "I wonder what would have happened if I had used it to hold my loose change."

Peter tried mixing half cocoa and half of various adulterants. He placed the cup in the refrigerator and tried heating it in the microwave. Various solids – flour, salt, household cleaner – rendered the contents undrinkable until the cup was emptied, after which it refilled itself with unadulterated cocoa. The cocoa also remained at the same temperature, whatever the exterior circumstances. It came out of the freezer still steaming and dropped not a single degree no matter how long left to itself. After ten minutes in the microwave, it still refused to boil. Jason had already conducted all of these experiments and more, of course, so he just looked on with amusement.

"This is amazing, Jay. You've stumbled onto the manifestation of a new natural law."

Jason's expression suddenly became more serious. "No, I don't think so."

"What do you mean?" Peter looked acutely distressed. "You're not going to tell me this is some kind of trick after all."

"No, it's not a trick. But I don't think it's a natural law either. I think it's an exception."

Now I'm not a scientist by any stretch of the imagination. I was trained as a laboratory assistant and I hadn't even worked in that capacity for a decade or more. But I was savvy enough to have followed the arguments between Jason and Peter in the past and I knew that Jason's concept of "exceptions" was as close as there was to a genuine bone of contention between them. Jason insisted that there were anomalies in the universe, that these were exceptions to natural laws. He was pretty hazy about how they had come about and what their ultimate purpose – if any - was, but in the short run, he insisted, they proved that no matter how long and hard we tried, we would never understand everything about reality.

"Authentic Persian rugs always incorporate at least one misweave," he would say. "Because the weavers believed that only God was perfect. The exceptions are misweaves in the fabric of the universe."

Peter would inevitably counter that Jason was proposing the existence of an anthropomorphic god and Jason would riposte that he was positing a creative force, not necessarily a conscious one. I usually tuned them out when they switched to this channel of debate.

Eventually I borrowed a blanket and napped on a ratty couch while the two of them argued and theorized and experimented and, presumably, drank lots of hot chocolate. The sun was up when I opened my eyes, and after stumbling to the bathroom and washing my face, I retrieved my cell phone from my bag and started calling to make excuses for our absence. "Car trouble," I muttered. "Peter's not feeling well." Other excuses sufficed in other instances.

Peter and Jason were sitting in the den, looking exhausted at last. The cup of hot cocoa stood on a coffee table between them, steaming merrily away. Peter stared at it accusingly, Jason thoughtfully. He seemed less pleased with himself than he had when I'd given up the night before, as though he now regretted having shared his secret with anyone, even us.

"I don't suppose you have any coffee?" I couldn't face the prospect of hot cocoa right then.

Jason blinked, then nodded. "The cabinet to the right of the sink, way in back. I think there's some instant there."

Peter stirred himself. "We have to take this to the Institute, Jay, no matter how you feel about it. This could open up an entirely new branch of physics. If we can replicate the effect, it could change the world. Water for the deserts, food in the midst of famine. I can't even begin to imagine the possibilities."

I walked past them to the kitchen, found the instant. The seal had never been broken so I microwaved myself a cup.

They were still arguing, Peter with increasing fervor, Jason more defensively. I didn't entirely understand his objection, and I'm not sure he did either. Sometimes he suggested that this was knowledge for which we were not yet ready, but at other times he insisted that one could not extrapolate from an exception to a scientific principle, that the cup would never be analyzed because it could not be analyzed. "It's outside the limits of science."

"Nothing lies beyond the grasp of science, Jay. We constantly extend our reach."

The coffee felt wonderful even if it was instant and I drained it quickly even though it was hot. I had just put a refill in the microwave – this cup did not replenish itself automatically – when I heard raised voices from the other room. I had been present when Peter became actively angry more than once but I'd never heard Jason shouting before. Then there was a startling sound of shattered glass and sudden silence.

I walked quickly back to the den. Both men were standing, no longer angry. Each wore an expression of terrible loss, and when I saw the broken fragments of the magical mug lying on the floor, I understood why.

"What a terrible accident."

Peter looked at me. "It wasn't an accident," he said quietly, his voice devoid of emotion. "He broke it on purpose."

I looked at Jason, who nodded, then dropped back down into his chair. "I had to. I couldn't let you take it, Peter. You must understand that."

"No, I don't understand it at all." Peter also sat down. He looked as though he'd aged a decade and his voice was drained of color. "Do you realize what you've done?"

"No I don't. But that's the point, don't you see?" Jason looked back and forth between us. "If we understand everything, then we've reached the end of our story. There's nothing new to look forward to." He took a deep breath. "I could have let you take it, Peter, and I believe that no matter how many tests you ran, no matter how sophisticated your equipment, no matter how brilliant you and your colleagues might be, you would never figure out the underlying principle, because there is no underlying principle. I think the cup was a self contained phenomenon that could not have been explained or replicated. It would not advance science because it was not of science."

"Are you trying to tell me it was magic?"

"What's magic? If magic is any process that acts external to science, then I suppose you're right. But if you're asking me if I think someone muttered some mumbo jumbo while it was baking in its kiln, then no, I don't think it was magic. It was    just…an exception."

"If you were convinced that I would fail, then why not let me take it away? What could it have hurt?"

Jason rubbed his face with his hands. "There's a chance that I was wrong. You might somehow have found a way to reduce the process to some arcane blend of mathematics and physical properties and some vagary of quantum physics." He sighed heavily. "I wasn't worried that you'd fail, Peter. I was horribly afraid that you might succeed."

I found a broom and swept up the shards.

# CHOOSING SIDES

Even as an infant, Alex Cadelman was chronically indecisive. When his doting parents arranged two mobiles above his cradle, his eyes darted back and forth from one to the other, never focusing on either for more than a second or two. If his mother tucked him into bed with a stuffed animal, he wrapped both arms around it and was content. If his father added a second, he rolled back and forth between them for a few seconds, then curled up in a ball hugging only himself.

When his mother fed him, he cleaned the spoon promptly when it was proffered, but when he grew older, he dawdled over his meals, utensil in hand, unable to decide where to start until a soft command of "eat your peas, Alex" or "finish your chicken" nudged him into action. His mother unconsciously catered to this indecisiveness by choosing his clothing for him every morning until third grade, and he only managed on his own thereafter through the expedient of selecting the leftmost shirt in his closet, the first pair of socks his hands found in the sock drawer, and so on. Sometimes this resulted in wildly inappropriate ensembles, the worst of which he repaired when his mother impatiently told him to "change your shirt" or provided similar direction.

Alex was in most ways an exceptional student. His talent for language and mathematics were coupled with curiosity and creativity. He always did his homework, but stopped immediately when he was done, never choosing to anticipate his teachers. His grades were almost always at or near the top of his class. The "almost" was a consequence of multiple choice tests, the bane of his young existence. More than one teacher was convinced that he filled them in virtually at random despite his clear grasp of the subject matter. At essays, fill-in-the-blanks, and oral presentations, he was unrivalled by his classmates.

In due course, Alex became interested in girls, but there were so many of them to choose from that he never quite decided to ask one of them out. He had casual friends of his own sex, but not many of them and no one who was really close. Although tall, broad shouldered, and well coordinated, he could never quite decide which school sport to try out for and therefore tried for none. His first semi-romantic experience came during his senior year when one of his not-so-close friends asked him to double date because his new girlfriend's parents didn't trust them to go out alone. Since the other couple chose the movie, everything was fine until they stopped at a restaurant afterwards. Alex took so long contemplating the alternatives that he ended up having a cold drink while the rest of them ate, and all three became convinced that Alex was "weird".

Fortunately Mrs. Gibbons, the guidance counselor, was a take-charge kind of person. She insisted that Alex apply to a variety of colleges, justly confident that his excellent grades would make him appealing to all. The acceptances arrived in due course, Cornell, the University of Michigan, Harvard, Duke, Yale and Colgate. It is quite possible that Alex would have let the deadlines for acceptance pass if Mrs. Gibbons, whose son had attended Yale, hadn't remarked one afternoon that he should "send an acceptance to Yale today." Relieved by the semblance of a decision, Alex did so and subsequently found himself in New Haven.

He was second in his class as a freshman, and first as a sophomore. Once again he was blessed with a counselor who perfectly suited his needs. Calvin Wright was an unhappy man who despised the students he was supposed to guide. When Alex was due to choose courses for the next semester, Calvin made a selection almost at random and Alex never quibbled. As a consequence, he studied everything from political science to poultry science, and excelled at everything.

When Alex arrived to start his junior year, he discovered that Calvin Wright had not been reappointed and due to an oversight he was for the moment without an assigned guidance counselor. Temporarily rudderless, he drifted around campus asking teachers, acquaintances, and even strangers for advice about course selections. Their competing and often contradictory opinions only made matters worse and finally, on the eve of registration day, he found himself walking the streets at random. In a rare moment of decisiveness, he turned into the first bar he encountered and ordered a drink.

"What kind of drink?" asked the unshaven, heavily muscled bartender who sported a flaming sword tattoo on his right arm..

Alex, who had just turned twenty-one and was not much inclined toward alcohol in any case, blurted out the first thing that came to mind. "A glass of wine, please."

"Red or white?"

Panic threatened to overwhelm him and he almost bolted toward the door. The bartender's eyes pinned him to the stool and he shrugged noncommittally. "Whatever is easiest."

Time passed. He nodded without listening to the bartender, lost in his own thoughts, and his empty wine glass was replaced with a new one. Alex was a bit surprised when he noticed that the Merlot had somehow renewed itself, but astonished when a hand closed on his elbow.

"Buy a lady a drink, young man."

The words were phrased as a statement rather than a question, so Alex was spared the necessity of deciding either way. "Sure," he said, and a glass appeared in front of her as if by magic.

It was only then that he turned to fully appraise his companion. She was older than him, quite a bit older, though dressed well short of her years. Alex had no experience of prostitutes, but her body language, garish clothing, excessive makeup, and forwardness left little doubt in his mind that this, indeed, was a street walker, a whore, a tart, a lady of pleasure. He wondered if he should ignore her or rebuff her, was unable to decide, and turned back to his drink.

If it had been up to him, the conversation would have been stillborn, but his companion was more persistent. "Are you a Republican or a Democrat?"

Alex didn't realize he was being addressed until she repeated the question. "I don't know, independent I guess." In fact, he had only voted once in his life. He had spent so much time in the voting booth that the poll workers had thought he was ill. Ultimately he had pushed levers at random and fled.

"Which do you like better, baseball or football?"

He had never been able to decide which team to support and had given up watching sports. "I don't have much time for either."

"What did you think of yesterday's Supreme Court ruling?"

"I thought both sides made good arguments."

He was trying to decide, unsuccessfully, whether to leave the bar or just ignore the woman's persistent questions, when her latest finally registered. "What did you say?" He turned to face her directly, noticing the slightly smeared mascara, the too wide, too crimson slash of her lipstick.

"I asked if you wanted help making decisions from now on. You obviously can't make your own."

He almost nodded, tried to turn it into a shake, ended up with something in between. "I'm sorry, lady, but you don't know anything about me."

She sat back on the stool, rocking precariously, and put both hands on her hips. "Why, of course I do. What kind of a fairy godmother would I be if I didn't know my mundane godchildren?"

"You're my fairy godmother?" The corners of his mouth twitched upward into a smile.

"That I am, youngster. Recently appointed. Somehow you got overlooked for a few years, but I'm here to fix everything." She smiled at him and he realized just how unattractive she really was.

"Great! I feel so relieved."

"You don't believe me?"

"How could you tell? Look, lady, just leave me alone would you?" He started to turn away but she reached out and caught his elbow.

"If I'm not your fairy godmother, then how do I know about your friend Leigh?"

Alex blinked. Leigh had been his imaginary childhood companion, sometimes a boy his own age, sometimes a girl. "What are you talking about?"

"Leigh went away when you were seven, right?" His father had told him that he was too old for an imaginary companion and that it was time to give Leigh up, so he had done so.

"How do you know about Leigh?"

But she ignored his question. "And what about those magazines you kept wrapped in plastic and hidden out behind the barn on Blackwood's farm?"

"Hey!" Alex looked around guilty, feeling like an adolescent again. "Who are you anyway?"

She crossed her arms and smirked. "I told you, I'm your fairy godmother and I'm here to help."

"Who says I need help?"

Her head tilted from side to side. "I'll leave it up to you then. Do you need help or don't you? Just tell me that you don't and I'll go away."

The truth was that Alex felt on the one hand that he should be able to choose his next term's courses on his own, but on the other hand, if he chose poorly he would be wasting time as well as his parents' money. "Maybe I do. Maybe I don't."

The woman sighed and shifted her body so that she could reach into her bright purple, sequin encrusted shoulderbag. "I brought this for you. It should do the trick." She extended her hand toward Alex, palm up, displaying a tarnished silver coin.

"I don't need your money," he said, mildly offended.

"It's not money I'm offering," she answered curtly.

Alex dithered, torn between revulsion and curiosity, because now that he actually looked at the coin, he could see that it was no currency familiar to him. "Take it," she said firmly, and he hesitantly but obediently reached forward, took the coin from her, and examined it more closely. It was larger than a quarter but smaller than a half dollar, and there were no words or numbers on either side. One face displayed the head of a lion, the other a rear view of a peacock with its tail feathers in full display.

"What is this?"

"What does it look like? It's a coin."

"Yeah, right." He turned it back and forth, fascinated despite his skepticism. "How is this supposed to help me?"

"Surely that's obvious. Whenever you find yourself caught between two choices, you simply toss it into the air and abide by its decision."

Alex laughed. "You're out of your mind. You're telling me to make important decisions about my life at random."

The woman tilted her head to one side and held it there, examining him thoughtfully. "As opposed to letting other people make these decisions for you, or not making them at all?"

He shifted uncomfortably and his eyes moved away from hers. "Sometimes there are people who know more than I do, and sometimes it's best not to act until it's absolutely necessary."

"Ah," she said triumphantly. "But doing nothing is a decision in itself. So there's nothing to be lost by letting the coin choose for you. Trust me, Alex, it always knows what's best for you."

That didn't sound right to him. She reached out and took his arm again, and her grip was surprisingly strong. "Just try it then. What have you got to lose?"

"Nothing, I suppose." He couldn't meet her eyes and turned away, discovered that he'd finished his wine and looked around for the bartender.

"Just be sure to give it back to me when you don't need it any more," she said quietly.

"Right." The bartender noticed him and reached for the half empty bottle of Merlot. Alex glanced back toward the woman but the bar stool was empty, and when he turned around and surveyed the mostly empty room, there was no sign of her. The bartender was refilling his wine glass. "Excuse me, that woman I was talking to. Do you know who she is?"

A disinterested shake of the head. "Never saw her before. That's another four bucks."

Alex half expected to find that the coin had disappeared as well, but it was still in his hand. Shaking his head, he tucked it into a pocket and forgot about it. Until the next morning.

He had risen before dawn, sat half dressed in his apartment reading course descriptions, drinking coffee, and pacing the floor. After three hours he had constructed forty-four tentative schedules for the next semester, all of which seemed to him equally appealing. And he was still only two thirds of the way through the list of course offerings. Clearly something had to be done, something radical, something decisive.

That's when he remembered the coin. He checked his pockets, didn't find it, realized that he was wearing different clothing and went to his closet. There was no difficulty then, as he had continued his habit of dressing from the left hand side, hanging up fresh or still wearable clothing on the right. It was in his pants pocket.

The entire incident seemed dreamlike now, but the coin was undeniably real, solid, and exactly as he remembered it. He carried it back to the table where he'd spread out his forms and booklets and a notebook and set it down. Then he turned to the stack of potential course arrays, took the topmost in one hand and the coin in the other, glanced through the list and closed his eyes.

"All right. Heads I make this my schedule, tails I try another." And he flipped the coin. It was tails, and he turned the sheet face down and selected the next. "Same thing again." The coin flew through the air. He snatched it and slammed it down on the table. Tails again. Another sheet discarded.

Alex continued in this manner, growing increasingly uneasy after twenty-eight consecutive displays of the peacock's nether regions. He was beginning to think there was something peculiar about the coin, some oddity of weight and balance that made it always land in the same orientation, when the twenty-ninth throw came up heads. He stared at it stupidly for several seconds, then looked at the course list in his other hand. It looked completely reasonable to him, but of course so had all the others.

"What the hell?" He folded the sheet, placed both it and the coin in his pocket, and went off to register.

That marked a turning point in Alex's life. He used the coin with increasing frequency thereafter, at first telling himself that he didn't really believe that it was more than simple chance. He began to date, deciding whom to ask out by flipping the coin, and his proposals were invariably accepted. Within months he lost his virginity, declared himself destined to practice law, moved to a more sumptuous apartment, and acquired a steady girlfriend. He proposed to Grace during the first term of his senior year, and was completely unsurprised by her acceptance. Sometimes the results of the coin toss puzzled him, leading to less than entirely satisfactory results, but he told himself that only meant that the other alternatives would have been worse, or that this seemingly errant choice was actually more welcome in a larger, imperceptible web of consequences.

Law school passed with surprising ease. Grace graduated and started her career as a library assistant, and they were married a year later. Alex hovered on the cusp of criminal vs business law, but the coin relieved his anxiety by choosing the latter, for which he was temperamentally more suited in any case. Several law firms competed for his attention, and he spent an hour flipping his coin before typing his letter of acceptance. He and Grace looked at homes in the suburbs of New Haven and when she had narrowed the decision to two equally appealing houses, he made the final decision by consulting his magic coin.

No one knew the coin's provenance, of course, not even Grace, although she must have suspected what most of their other acquaintances didn't, that Alex's frequent use of the coin was not just an amusing affectation but something very serious to him. When she began to crave children, she broached the subject to Alex, who asked for a day or two to think the matter over. He was particularly careful not to let her see him use the coin that time and apparently she convinced herself that he hadn't, but deep down she must have known the truth. Fortunately, the coin's decision had coincided exactly with her own, and three years later she gave birth to their second child, a girl to complement Alex Junior.

It was the children, however, who unwittingly drove the first wedge between them. Alex unwisely made no secret of the fact that he had used the coin to decide which preschool their son should attend, which resulted in a rare period of discord in their marriage. The incident sharpened her awareness of the situation, however, and she began to regard her husband's obsession with increasing alarm. On more than one occasion she considered stealing the coin and throwing it away, but in each case she realized that not only would she be avoiding rather than dealing with the issue but that she would be violating the trust that had been established between them.

The conflict, once ignited, burned hotter as the years passed. Grace no longer simply sulked when Alex reached into his pocket to choose a restaurant or when he approached a voting booth. Heated arguments became more frequent, and by the time it was Melody's turn to toddle off to pre-school, they were sleeping in separate bedrooms. Neither of them found separate-but-equal tolerable, however, and both were aware that their increasingly acrimonious relationship was affecting the children.

"Do you want a divorce?" She asked at last. When Alex instinctively reached for his pocket, she stood up and tearfully stormed off to her room.

Distraught, Alex drove the Mercedes into New Haven, parked near Yale, and walked the well lit campus for two hours, contemplating his future. More than once he recalled Grace's last words to him and his hand crept toward his pocket, but on each occasion he arrested the movement. If the coin should tell him to answer in the affirmative, he thought his heart might break.

His mental turmoil fulminated until he thought his head would burst, and he turned away from the campus, toward the downtown. He wanted a Bloody Mary, or perhaps several. It was only a matter of minutes before he spotted the flashing red sign of a not very fashionable bar and stepped inside. There were a handful of customers scattered among the booths and tables, but Alex went straight to the bar and mounted a stool.

The bartender approached and Alex blinked. There was something familiar about him, but his mind didn't make the connection until he noticed the flaming sword tattoo. The man's hair had turned grey and much of the muscle was now fat, but he seemed as formidable and taciturn as ever. "What'll you have?"

He wanted a Bloody Mary. "I'll have a glass of wine, please."

"Red or white?"

"Whatever is easiest." The bartender brought him Merlot.

Alex took the coin out of his pocket now and placed it on the bar. The lion looked up at him, perhaps reproachfully. He tried to contemplate life apart from Grace and despite the recent unpleasantness and uncertainty, he couldn't conceive of such a thing. If he made that choice, if he let the coin make that choice for him, then possibly it would lead to some abstract "better" life in the future. Could that future reward in any way compensate for the end of his marriage?

For the first time in years, Alex was at a loss. He could not decide whether or not to flip the coin. But if he didn't, he would never know whether or not he had chosen correctly. The coin would always stand in mute reproach and its very existence would add a note of uncertainty to whatever future he selected for himself.

Alex shook his head and drank some Merlot, licked his lips, and spoke in a stage whisper. "If you're listening, fairy godmother, come take this thing away."

And a hand touched his elbow.

"How are they hanging, Alex?"

It was the aging prostitute who, unlike the bartender, looked exactly as she had more than a decade earlier. She even wore the same clothing, right down to the sequined handbag. Despite having carried a miracle in his pocket for all those years, Alex was still struck dumb.

"I don't suppose you'll be needing this anymore." She reached out to the bar and made the coin disappear. "Thanks for bringing it back."

Alex waited for the shock of loss to hit him, but instead felt a wave or relief so profound that he almost fell off the stool. "No, I should thank you for coming. I don't think I could ever have found the courage to just throw it away."

"Throw it away!" Her face twisted in mock outrage. "Throw away my magic coin? I should say not." She folded her arms and beamed at him. "So tell me all about your life, my boy. I've not had time to keep a close eye on you."

Alex smiled back, reached into his pocket and left a more than generous tip on the bar. "Sorry," he said. "Maybe some other time. I have to go." He slid off the stool.

"And where would you be off to in such a hurry?" Now she pretended to be offended.

Alex raised his chin, looked her squarely in the eyes, and replied firmly. "I've decided to go home to my family. Good night, madam, and thanks again." And he was gone.

This time it was the woman who was sitting alone when the bartender returned. His expression was mildly curious. "Hey lady, what was that business about a magic coin?"

She raised her arm and tossed him a coin. He caught it in mid-air and held it close to his face, squinting at it and turning it back and forth, forward and reverse. "What's this, some kind of optical trick?"

"Why, whatever do you mean, young man?"

"Well, both sides are the same, but depending on how you hold it to the light, it either looks like a lion's head with a furry collar, or some kind of bird showing its ass." He placed it down on the counter top. "How can you tell which side is up and which is down?"

The woman smiled. "I guess you just have to make that decision for yourself."

# HOUSEBOUND

I believe that ten days have now passed since I became trapped in my own house, but it might be as few as eight or as many as eleven. I am uncertain because there are periods during which none of the rooms I enter have outside windows and all the clocks have disappeared. I sleep when I'm weary without knowing if it is day or night, perhaps in a bed, perhaps in a chair. The rooms are not always recognizable. I chanced to enter my study the other day, but it wasn't my study, not exactly, although it had some of my things in it.

I found this spiral notebook today so I have decided to keep a record of my experiences, before I completely lose the gift of language. Where to start is a problem. Perhaps with my name, while I still remember it. I was christened Arthur Wade Wellstone. I attended an assortment of colleges, my curricula designed by my father to prepare me to succeed him at the helm of Wellstone, Inc. It is entirely possible that I loved my parents, but during these past few days my memories of them have faded. I remember remembering them, but I can no longer actually visualize what they looked like.

The first time I noticed a change in the house was on the second anniversary of their death, which may or may not be coincidental.

I had just returned from a two week business trip to Europe. I'd been away from the house before, but this was the first prolonged trip since I'd moved back home. I was tired and irritable and somewhat preoccupied when I arrived. Jonas let me in and offered his services, but I dismissed him rather brusquely, intending to go directly to bed. I had chosen not to move to the master bedroom, and my feet knew the way to my own quarters so well that there was no need for me to think about where I was going.

Not, that is, until I realized that I didn't know where I was.

My house is very large. There are a total of twenty rooms arranged on two levels with the servants' quarters in a separate building. There were perhaps twelve rooms that I used regularly but the rest - guest bedrooms, my father's office, and others - were locked up. My first reaction was to assume that I'd made a wrong turn.

It would have been a reasonable explanation except that none of the rooms had a red door as did this one. It was locked or perhaps the door was just stuck in the jamb. In any case, my impulse to look inside came to nothing.

I turned back the way I had come, or at least the way I thought I had come. Nothing looked familiar here either and it seemed to take much longer than usual to reach the staircase. I was halfway down, intending to interrogate Jonas about the altered door, but decided to wait until morning. This time I arrived in my room without incident.

The following morning I went looking for the red door, but without success. I concluded that either I'd been so fatigued that my senses had played tricks on me, or that I'd dreamed the entire incident.

For the next several days I was unusually busy. Situations change rapidly within such a diversified entity as Wellstone, Inc. My father had been an excellent negotiator and had impressed on me the importance of personally involving myself with every aspect of the company's operation. There were dossiers in my office containing the personnel files on all of my key people, as well as expensive but occasionally revealing reports prepared by a private investigator.

During this period I experienced brief periods of disorientation, both at home and elsewhere, which I attributed to fatigue. Father had always been impatient and irritable when I failed to match his seemingly limitless energy, and I could almost feel his disapproval of my weakness. These episodes always passed quickly and I simply told myself that I needed to make time for a brief vacation. .

The accident at the Verona plant came at the worst possible time. News of the explosion dominated CNN. The horrible loss of life and associated bad publicity was particularly humiliating because this scenario had been raised by one of my subordinates. The plant was situated in a densely populated residential area, maximizing the potential loss of life in the event of a catastrophic failure.

After spending more than two weeks dealing with the press, local officials, and the survivors, I returned exhausted and depressed.

My nerves were scraped raw and I dismissed Jonas rather curtly, preferring seclusion to servile attendance. My mind was numb and I drank two brandies for supper and went to bed early.

Some time later I found myself awake, mouth dry and stomach rumbling. I drank a glass of water, then decided to find something to eat. The house was dark and silent, a scattering of nightlights providing adequate but not abundant illumination. At the foot of the main staircase, I turned left, or at least I believed I had, but I was distracted and moved more from habit than conscious effort.

I flicked the light switch in what I supposed was the kitchen but found myself instead in my mother's sitting room. That meant that I had turned right instead of left, so I reversed direction and crossed through the spacious foyer into what should have been the kitchen. But somehow I ended up in the greenhouse, and the door that would have allowed me to go back inside was secured. Clad in only a bathrobe and slippers, I was compelled to suffer the ignominy of rousing Jonas from his bed in the guest cottage. Jonas retrieved his key without so much as a reproachful look.

Wellstone stock, already anemic, plunged even further. I took a disastrous personal loss. To add insult to injury, the Board had clearly lost confidence in me. My father's admonition never to reveal a wound, however painful, prevented me from resigning.

Three nights later, I woke from a sound sleep in an unfamiliar room. It was arranged roughly in the same fashion as my bed chamber, but it was much larger and the furniture cruder. The closets were bare, and the only clothing I could find consisted of a flannel shirt, a pair of well worn jeans, and some inexpensive loafers. I stepped outside the door with considerable trepidation, convinced that I had been drugged and kidnapped, but to my consternation I found myself completely alone. My explorations were similarly disquieting. Many of the rooms bore a strong resemblance to those with which I was familiar, as did many of the furnishings, the books on the library shelves, the oriental rugs, the vivid tapestries. But they were arranged in unexpected combinations within the rooms, and even more unsettling, the rooms themselves had apparently been shuffled, so that the greenhouse was now appended to the bathroom, and the kitchen opened off the library rather than the foyer.

The foyer itself bore a strong resemblance to my own, with one exception. There was no front door, just an unbroken wall where it had stood.

I soon discovered that all other means of egress were similarly missing. Exhausted, nerves on edge, I returned to the second floor where the library had been located, and where I kept the liquor cabinet. To my utter amazement, the library was no longer there. I was quite certain that it had opened off the hall directly opposite the master bedroom, at least in this version of the house, but when I stepped through the door this time, I found myself in the pantry.

The library, as it happened, was back on the first floor. I tracked it down eventually, found the liquor cabinet and drank myself into oblivion.

There's little else of these past ten days that I can recall clearly. There was food in the kitchen but no electricity so I was reduced to eating raw vegetables and canned tuna. Lacking power, I could make no use of any of the appliances and the telephones are all missing. Only the lights function normally, although I have noticed that if I leave them on when I leave a room, they have been extinguished when I return.

It finally occurred to me that I might break a window and escape in that fashion. I was thwarted in this as well, because as soon as the thought entered my head, steps were taken – I have no idea by what agency – to prevent any such deliverance. All of the external windows are now shuttered, and I no longer have access to the greenhouse.

I am writing this at the kitchen table. The mess I left behind has been cleared away and the cupboards have been restocked, but I have little appetite. I am clearly imprisoned but I have no idea what crime it is that I have committed.

Another day has passed, or so I believe. Although there seems no point to further exploration, I am restless and have carried this notebook through a succession of rooms. I dare not leave it behind because I might not find it again.. It is the only unchanging thing in my environment, or more properly, it is the only item whose changes I control.

A short while ago I happened upon the room with the red door again. This time I was able to force it open and enter. At first I was puzzled, because it was clearly a child's room, a nursery in fact, and there was no such place in my house. It was only as I was about to leave that I saw a familiar stuffed animal propped against a rocking horse, and it was like a key that opened a lock. Memories flooded over me and I slowly turned, re-examining everything with a sense of profound wonder. It was my own nursery, the furnishings long since cleared away at my father's insistence. The shock was so intense that I finally left, consumed by memories, and when I recollected myself, I was in one of the guest rooms. Subsequent efforts to find the red door again have so far proven unsuccessful.

I have a new anxiety today, one which alternately alarms me and gives me hope. I have heard sounds from elsewhere in the house, purposeful sounds, some of which I think might be human voices. At first I shied away but once it was clear that I was in no imminent danger, I discovered that my curiosity and need for human company was stronger than my fear. I have since attempted to find my unseen companions, but no matter how promptly I respond, I have yet to see any physical evidence that I am no longer alone.

Later. Still no success, but during my last visit to the kitchen, which was at the time attached to the guest bathroom, I found the remains of a meal, a meal which I had not eaten.

Later still. I have torn several pages from this notebook and written messages, which I have then placed in prominent places, suggesting that we congregate in the foyer. In at least two instances, those messages have been removed, but I have been waiting on the staircase now for what must be at least several hours. Twice I have heard the sounds of movement, but no one has appeared. I am tired and discouraged, but will try again tomorrow.

I grow to understand my situation even less with each passing day. I woke this morning with some enthusiasm, convinced that the enigma in which I am trapped has a solution, if only I have the wits to find it. But just when I think I am beginning to understand the rules, they change.

I found the kitchen clean and orderly and was making myself a sandwich for breakfast, devilled ham smeared on a hard roll, when I was startled by an ambiguous sound from near at hand. Before I had time to investigate, something burst in through the open doorway, ran past me, and exited into what should have been the pantry but probably was not, all before I could react in any useful fashion. I didn't get a good look at it, but it had four legs and fur.

Breakfast forgotten, I spent what must have been hours searching. There were hints of its presence – a clatter of tiny footsteps from over my head, a brief series of bumps and once a crash, as if something glass had been overturned and shattered, but I never caught sight of it again. By nightfall, or what I judged to be nightfall, I had abandoned the hunt and I sit at present in the library, dispirited.

I must remember to confine my sleeping to a bed. This morning I woke in a chair with a stiff neck and a back ache. My mood was somber as I prepared for the usual morning search for the kitchen. It was nowhere on the ground floor so I climbed the staircase and had barely reached the landing when a commotion broke out below me. I turned and leaned over the rail, just in time to see my four footed visitor, which appeared to be a small doe, bolt across the carpet from left to right. The sight of it was still registering when a second figure burst upon the scene, a human figure this time, although an ungainly looking creature. It ran hunched forward, it wore some rough, colorless fabric wrapped around its loins, and it carried a crudely fashioned spear!

I must have called out because it paused suddenly, glanced up in my direction, and then hurried on in pursuit of its quarry. I should have followed. I would have, except that something about the creature's face struck me as oddly familiar. And in any case, I doubt very much that I could have caught up before the shifting realities of the house shunted him to some new location.

It was a considerable while later, while passing through my mother's sewing room, that I happened to glance at the wedding photos she had arranged in an elaborate triptych on one wall. The face of the savage hunter was that of my father.

My predicament grows less comprehensible with each passing hour.

I have not written here for the past three days, or for my last three periods of wakefulness, however long that might be. This is not because nothing of note has happened but rather because, paradoxically, so much has.

A low murmuring roused me from sleep, an almost subliminal sound which drew me out of my room and into the hall, where the disturbance resembled human speech more clearly. Barefoot and bare-chested, I walked slowly to the landing and looked down into the foyer. It seemed larger than usual and was certainly more crowded. Three rough structures stood in one corner, a kind of hybrid, half tent and half hut. Two adults were crouched a few meters away, building what appeared to be a fire in the middle of the floor. At the far end, a much smaller individual – a child – was attempting to climb the drapes.

I suppose I should have descended immediately, but my sense of propriety overruled my enthusiasm. Father had always stressed the importance of first impressions, so I went back to my room to dress, a wasted effort as all of the clothes I had been wearing the previous day had mysteriously vanished and the closet and bureaus were empty. By the time this fact had registered, the foyer had been restored to its usual pristine state.

The disappointment was not as great as it might have been. Although I had yet to make contact with my housemates, there had been a clear progression. Sooner or later our worlds would intersect more determinedly. I was certain of it. But the remainder of that day passed uneventfully and I fell asleep once more consumed by doubts and apprehensions.

Something touched my cheek and I opened my eyes. A child, a female, stood at my bedside, a rather disheveled looking waif with round, sad eyes and delicate features. She was quite pretty, but there was a furtive look about her and she recoiled when she saw that I was awake, then bolted through the door.

"No! Wait!" I called and followed, but it was probably just as well that I failed to find her as I was now completely unclothed. I mended that by fashioning a towel into a kind of kilt, then conducted another fruitless search of the house, calling out occasionally, trying to speak in a calm, reassuring tone. No one answered, no one appeared.

I made several fruitless circuits of the house, and during my fifth visit to the library I turned to the liquor cabinet, but instead of the beveled glass containers I found two bulging, leatherlike pouches, both filled with liquid. The first appeared to be plain water but the second, though bitter and sour, was clearly alcoholic, and I drained more than half of it before setting it aside.

On the small end table beside my chair was a lamp, an ashtray, and a small cameo portrait of my mother. I sank down into the seat and stared at it in wonder, for her face, though altered by age, was discernibly the same as that of my young visitor.

I have no idea how much time has passed since my last entry. I have been too preoccupied to add to this history. No, that's not entirely true. On several occasions, I have attempted to record what has been happening, but in every instance I have been unable to do so. The ability to fashion words into these abstract symbols seems to have become as transient as everything else in my environment. That may be just as well, as there are only a few blank pages left.

But at the moment, the old skill has returned, although it takes me much longer to form each word than it did in the past, and when I glance back at what I have already written, it seems an incomprehensible jumble.

It was a tedious process, but I have made contact with the tribe. There are six adults and four children, two of each sex. The three adult males vary in age from late adolescence to elderly, the three women are tiered similarly although each is noticeably younger than their respective mate. The oldest couple has a son who is nearly grown, the middle pair have a son and daughter, both in their mid-teens, and the youngest have a daughter, the one who visited my bedside. They speak, but no language that I recognize, nor do they respond to mine. Some of their clothing has been fashioned from towels or draperies, the rest consists of animal skins. The women forage for food in the kitchen and pantry, the men hunt the occasional doe. I have seen no evidence of any other animal life, although berry bearing vines have sprung up in the pantry.

The males all bear my father's face, altered only to reflect their apparent age. The females are variations of my mother. I cannot explain this. They are not close relatives, they are the same.

Although they have a spoken language, it is nothing I can comprehend and they don't understand my words any better than I do theirs. At first they were wary. The women ran off when I approached, the men warned me off by brandishing their weapons and shouting. Eventually I managed to win a measure of their trust. They will not share their food with me, but if I bring my own, I am allowed to sit by their fire and eat with them. There is considerably less furniture in the house now, and a permanent burn mark in the center of the foyer, but they have not touched anything in my bedroom and none of them seem to have entered it since my first encounter with the child.

Until today I was merely tolerated, but my patience has finally borne fruit. The oldest of the three males approached and I stood before him, eyes respectfully downcast. He muttered another incomprehensible speech, then thrust his spear forward, offering it to me. Tentatively I accepted it, raising my eyes to try to determine what else was wanted.

He nodded toward the cooking fire, then rubbed his bare, protruding belly with slow, exaggerated motions. His meaning was self evident. He wanted me to find food for the tribe. Instinctively I knew that this was a test, that if I succeeded, I would have proven myself one of them. I smiled and nodded, indicating that I understood, then turned and left them.

There is no apparent pattern to the appearance, or disappearance, of the does. Sometimes I see several in one day, or perhaps the same one several times, sometimes I see none at all. I prowled the upper floors at first, reasoning that the presence of the tribe below would scare them off. Room after room proved empty, emptier than ever before. I wonder what will happen once all the flammable materials in the house have been exhausted. Will we be reduced to eating everything uncooked? Will the house grow cold when winter comes, if it hasn't already? I have no idea what the date might be.

A familiar fear assails me. What happens if I fail this test? Will I have another opportunity to prove myself or will I be forever disenfranchised? As this possibility grows more prominent in my thoughts, I find my early confidence giving way to nearly paralytic anxiety. What if I cannot measure up to the tribe's standards? What if I am not man enough?

It is much later now. I have failed. It would have been bitterly disappointing to have tried and fallen short; it is immeasurably more devastating to have faltered even before making the attempt.

I had nearly despaired of finding my prey before fatigue forced me to sleep. A dozen or more visits to every room had been unproductive. Exhausted, I sank into one of the few remaining armchairs, in what used to be one of the guest bedrooms. I must have dozed off, because I woke with a start, having slipped partway down, banging my elbow painfully against the carved wooden arm.

Eyes stared into mine from only a meter away. It was a doe, head raised from where she had y been grazing on one of mother's rugs. She watched me closely but without evident alarm. My spear was resting against the wall, near my right hand, and I reached for it very slowly, not wanting to frighten the animal off. She seemed oblivious to her danger, and my heart raced with the prospect of making the kill, winning my admission into the tribe. I closed my fingers around the shaft and slowly raised it over one shoulder. My legs were stiff and sore, but I couldn't strike while sitting, so I pushed up, ever so slowly, until I was fully erect, the spear poised for the strike.

At the last moment, as the muscles in my arm tightened for the final blow, the doe raised its head and looked at me and there was something familiar and almost human about its face. In that moment I hesitated and lowered my arm. The doe took one last bite of the carpet, then wandered off, unconcerned. I never saw her again.

The tribe was no longer camped in the foyer, even the burn mark was gone, although the missing furniture has not been restored. I don't understand, but I know that I will never be one of them.

Later. I am more confused than ever. I found the nursery again, although this time my childhood toys and furnishings were mixed with more recent items, the desk from my study, the mirror I brought back from Paris. I have gotten into the habit of avoiding my reflection in the bathroom mirrors and the haggard and unshaven reflection which looked at me with panic in his eyes seemed like a stranger. But I paused this time and took stock of myself. True, my hair was long and my beard full, but neither was as disreputable as I had imagined. In fact, the longer I regarded my image the more content it appeared. There was something familiar about the eyes and the expression, something that I finally recognized.

There was a touch of the doe in my face, or a touch of my face in the doe. I don't pretend to understand that either, but I think I am beginning to comprehend what has happened to me.

I glanced down into the foyer a few moments ago, and something seemed out of place. It took a few seconds to register, but then I realized what it was. The front door was back. Stunned, I turned away, wondering what it meant, excited by its presence but worried as well, worried about what it might mean, what might lurk beyond the door. Whatever it was would be the unknown; I was certain of that.

Suppressing my anxiety, I descended, but by the time I arrived, the wall was back in place. I expected to feel shattered by the discovery, but that wasn't the case. I know now that when I am ready to face what lies beyond, a world in which the rules aren't known in advance and in which I have to find my own way and decide for myself what paths are worth following and which are not, the door will be there and I will open it and walk through and never look back.

But first I have to get my house in order.

# THE KNIGHT OF GREENWICH VILLAGE

The dragon soared with outstretched wings above the Empire State Building and disappeared behind the rising tier of skyscrapers just beyond. It wasn't really a dragon, of course, any more than the spires and pinnacles of Manhattan were the abutments of a gigantic, sprawling castle. But to Albert Lance, the airliner was a mythical beast and the entire city a land filled with enchantment and wonder, the source of endless heroic adventures perceptible to Albert alone, his personal Camelot.

A few minutes earlier, he'd dealt with the ogre that lived in his building, its den strategically placed across from the main entrance. To everyone else, Rocco appeared human, but Albert saw his true soul, a small convoluted knot of self interest and pointless cruelty.

"Lance! I've been trying to catch you all week. That goddamned mess of yours downstairs has got to go. Either you take care of it, or I'll hire someone and add the cost to your rent. You hear me?" Rocco was short and squat but his shoulders were so broad that Lance marveled he was able to get in and out of his apartment without turning sideways.

"But no one else is using that space." He'd been Sir Albert on the elevator ride down from the eleventh floor, but now he felt the persona slipping away. "There's plenty of room left."

"Maybe so, but it's not your room. The other tenants have the same rights as you do, you know. They're just goddamned books, Lance. You must've read 'em all by now. What do you want to keep 'em around for? Throw 'em in the incinerator, why doncha?"

If there'd been any doubt about Rocco's ogrish nature, it was banished by that unholy suggestion. "I couldn't do that! I mean they're...they're books."

Rocco shrugged. "Whatever they are, they go tomorrow or else."

"Give me a break, Rocco. I'm really busy this week. I'll take care of things Saturday, I promise."

"All right, Saturday then. But this is the last time I'm gonna talk to you about it. You hear what I'm saying to you?"

With the ogre outmaneuvered for the moment, Albert had left the building. The crisis remained unresolved; there was just no possible way to fit the overflow from his library back into the three small rooms he occupied. But at least he could delay dealing with the situation for a few days. Some solution would offer itself, as had always happened in the past. Sir Albert had never been defeated by a challenge, large or small.

On the way to the subway, he helped an elderly woman cross the street/rescued Lady Guenevere from a crumbling cliff by carrying her across a tightrope stretched above a bottomless abyss. Two blocks further on, he evaded Cerberus himself, a foul tempered terrier fortunately restrained by a short leash. Harpy pigeons fluttered around his head as he broke into a jog, realizing that he was in danger of being late to work again. Pedestrians called out in anger as he brushed past during his descent below street level, but he ignored their crude remarks. Peasants never understood the requirements of chivalry, the weight of obligation pressing down on those selfless defenders of civilization.

A giant serpent rushed out of the mouth of a subterranean passage and obediently came to a stop. After a great struggle, Sir Albert had managed to bend the king of these creatures to his will, exacting as its life price the promise of safe passage within their bellies to wherever in Camelot he wished to travel. He stepped inside, and the serpent flowed forward into its lair.

Albert reached the front entrance to Bidwell and Carter only a minute after he was supposed to be sitting at his desk, and briefly entertained the hope that he might reach that sanctuary undetected. But Mrs. Criswell had been watching for him, and even as he took his seat and typed his sign-on, she moved swiftly down the row of data stations to stand directly behind him.

"Late again, Lance? That's the third time in two weeks."

Sir Albert gritted his teeth, knowing that capture by the slaveholders was a necessary test of his courage, and that by the end of the day, he would have inspired his fellow captives with the will to revolt. But for the moment, he must bend his neck to the lash of the chief overseer's cruel tongue.

"I'm sorry, Mrs. Criswell, but an elderly man collapsed in the street and I had to find someone to help him." He had no compunctions about lying to the overseer; even noble slaves were entitled to mislead their captors.

She had moved to one side, so that she could watch his profile. Albert carefully kept his eyes on the screen, which had already changed to the data entry program he fed every day. "I see," she said quietly. "And last Thursday, you witnessed an automobile accident, and Monday it was a purse snatching. What will it be next week, I wonder? Armed robbery? A volcano in Central Park? Or perhaps Martian invaders immobilizing the subways with their death rays?" Albert knew it had been a mistake to let her see him reading a science fiction novel at lunch that time; she'd been making sarcastic references ever since.

"I'm really very sorry, Mrs. Criswell, but you know that my performance is above average. I'll work through the morning break if you'd like, to make up for being late."

Criswell smacked her tongue against the roof of her mouth, a coarse, impatient sound. "That's not the point, Mr. Lance. Everyone else here manages to get to work on time, every day, and without being diverted by petty disasters, real or imaginary. I expect you to do the same. Do you know what the job market is like out there today?" She gestured toward the row of windows at the far end of the room. "I could have six data processing managers begging for this job in an hour, if I wanted. So either straighten out or get out."

"Yes, Mrs. Criswell." But he was speaking to her rapidly receding back.

Despite the morning's upset, Albert was able to drop into input mode with practiced ease, converting hard copy of the previous day's polling information into electronic statistical data. At first, he'd found the work interesting in itself, trying to imagine the personality of an interviewee from the pattern of answers displayed on each survey. But the randomness of it all bothered him after a while. There was no correlation between educational level and philosophical orientation, income and political stance, and little consistency even within the same sample. Faced with the growing possibility that it was all just random after all, he disengaged his mind and began processing the data mechanically, allowing himself to concentrate on his secret life.

The morning passed quickly after that. After a meager meal of bread and water/tunafish salad and lemonade, Albert left the company cafeteria where, as always, he had remained alone in an isolated corner. He consulted the water cooler oracle on the way back to his station, deftly changed routes when he spied overseer Criswell ahead, and spent the rest of the day dreaming of dragons and beautiful princesses and assorted derring do.

The slaves revolted right on schedule, streaming out of the ravaged gates of Bidwell and Carter into the freedom of early evening. Rather than brave the crush on the subway, Albert walked two blocks downtown and bought himself a simple supper from a street cart/itinerant farmer, ate it quickly while window shopping at a series of novelty shops. He ignored the efforts of an older man in disreputable clothing to extort his extra change, briefly fingering the broadsword he carried disguised as a ballpoint pen in his jacket pocket. When he finally returned to his apartment building in lower Manhattan, he was carrying a small plastic bag that contained three new paperback novels, even though his unread backlog had already grown to well over two hundred.

There was a message from his mother on the answering machine.

"Albert, this is your mother calling. God, I hate these things! Listen, Albert, I want you to call me back tonight. No excuses this time. Your father and I deserve better than this. We didn't mortgage the house to put you through college just so you could fritter your life away playing with computers for minimum wage. Dad's been asking around, and Mr. Stoughton at the bank is looking for someone to help out with the new system they're putting in, and your father put himself out to mention that you had a real talent for things like that and Mr. Stoughton has agreed to talk to you about it if..." And that's where the tape had run out, long before his mother's breath did the same.

He hastily rewound and reset the machine. His parents had long since fallen under the influence of the evil sorceress Morgan Le Fay, and he had yet to devise a method of freeing them from this vile bondage. After scribbling "Call Mom" on a post-it note, Albert stuck it on his message board, where it joined a dozen others with similar messages.

Albert remained restless and upset despite several futile attempts to lose himself in the book he'd been reading, so he decided to go for a walk. Ignoring the siren calls of disturbed automobile alarms, avoiding the ever present wild boars with their characteristic bright yellow coat and checkered crests, Sir Albert strode courageously out into the growing darkness.

Washington Square Park was a place of great enchantment for Sir Albert, and he drew strength with each breath as he stood leaning against the boulder from which he had once wrested an enchanted sword. Bands of elves and gnomes were scattered about the park, carrying boom boxes and dressed in garishly designed clothing. As a knight of the realm, Sir Albert's primary responsibility was to human beings, but he had extended his zone of tolerance to the little people as well, even if their mischievous nature often disturbed him.

But tonight, there were too many unsettling thoughts running through Albert's head to allow him to sit passively and watch. It was only a matter of time until he lost his job at Bidwell and Carter; it was well known that Mrs. Criswell never let up on anyone she disliked until she'd driven them out. Nor could he continue to avoid dealing with his parents forever. They had already threatened to drive into the city to visit, and he'd only put them off by promising to be better about keeping in touch. Nor had he admitted to them that Gwen, the girl he'd supposedly been dating for the past year, was no more than a product of his imagination.

Albert rose and started off toward the Village, with no specific goal in mind, knowing that he would find adventure no matter where his feet led him, that there was danger and challenge on every block.

But for once his imagination seemed to fail him. College students and panhandlers remained exactly that, and try as he might, the grills of passing taxis refused to curl into tusked mouths. When he passed the Black Goat Tavern, the facade remained neon and glass, and the sign continued to flash "HERLIHY'S PUB", flickering and buzzing.

Impatiently, Albert turned left, walked down a dimly lit alley and continued toward the east side. This wasn't a route he'd travelled often, and the nature of the businesses behind the individual store fronts changed so often, each trip had been a journey of discovery.

A few minutes later, Albert knew that fate had directed his footsteps this evening, that the trials of the day had been designed to lead him to the greatest challenge he had ever faced. He was standing in front of a Greek restaurant whose specialties appeared, paradoxically, to be beef stroganoff and veal parmigiana, when he glanced across the street and picked out the nondescript sign identifying a dimly lit bar.

It was called La Sangreal, and Sir Albert turned the head of his tall white charger toward his destiny.

If anything, it was darker inside than on the street; the decor was hardwood with slick, synthetic coverings, browns and blacks and brass studs that glittered weirdly in the light cast by scattered, red bulbs. Albert needed little of his imagination to superimpose an infernal overlay, peopling the shadows with imps and goblins and diminutive demons. Narrow booths divided the left wall, and far in the back, a small, cavelike room was dimly visible through half opened sliding doors. A lair of trolls, no doubt.

The only conventional illumination was behind the bar, an oval of small bulbs flashing in sequence to counterfeit a constant clockwise flow. The oval was set around a narrow shelf on which a single object sat, perfectly centered, positively glowing. It was a wide rimmed cup with two delicately sculpted handles set directly across from one another. The design was simple, the lines clear and clean, and Albert knew what it was from the outset.

The Chalice, the Holy Grail, the cup from which Jesus drank at the Last Supper, spirited away by Joseph of Aramathea along with the spear that drew Christ's blood, protected through the ages by sinless guardians until one of them suffered a lapse and the holy objects were lost forever.

Or perhaps not forever after all.

He stepped through the door, his eyes sweeping from side to side. The bartender didn't even look in his direction, a tall, spindly man wearing a turtleneck, with unruly black hair that fell down to his shoulderblades. There were few customers in view, only three of the eight booths were occupied and the small, sexless figure slumped at the far end of the bar seemed to have fallen asleep.

Sir Arthur entered, his sword concealed within the folds of his purple cloak, and approached the tavern keeper.

"What can I getcha?"

He sat at the bar, waiting for the head to settle on his mead, trying to act casual as his eyes hungrily caressed the shape of the Grail. Despite its simplicity, it was the most beautiful object he had ever beheld, and Sir Albert knew that he would not be able to rest until he had liberated it from this den of thieves and infidels.

By the time Albert accepted a second drink, the bar was considerably more crowded and noisy. The sleeper had stirred and shuffled out into the street, still not betraying his or her gender. He rarely touched alcohol and sipped diffidently, so intent upon his veneration of the sacred object suspended before him that he almost failed to notice when a familiar face entered.          It was the Black Knight, his deeply scarred cheek unmistakable even in the garish light. Although Albert didn't know the Black Knight's real name, he had from time to time noticed Rocco speaking to him in the lobby, and a short while later bored looking young women paid his landlord short visits. Albert had also seen him passing small packages to other unsavory looking individuals on the street. He was a large man, with hard eyes but a soft body, flesh that hung loosely from jowls and clutched him tightly around the waist.

His presence here only served to confirm Sir Albert's conviction that he had been drawn to this den of evil for a purpose, to rescue the Grail. He shifted slightly in order to study his presumed opponent, and only then realized the Black Knight was not alone. A young woman stood at his side, long blonde hair, lightly freckled face, relatively plain features neither pretty nor unattractive, quite obviously not old enough to be legally served. She stood awkwardly, clearly uneasy, fingers clenched tightly around the straps of her shoulderbag, blinking in the uncertain light. There was a lack of focus in her eyes which made Sir Albert believe she'd been drugged.

A fair damsel to rescue as well as the Holy Grail. It seemed too good to be true. In fact, Albert's innate caution began to stir under his knightly persona, a silent plea for discretion that Sir Albert decided to heed. For the moment.

The bartender and the Black Knight spoke in hushed tones, and the few words Albert was able to overhear did not convey any real sense of what they were talking about, although the young woman was clearly part of it. A wooden cutting board with a small loaf of bread and a bar of pale cheese appeared and the Black Knight accepted it, then led his companion by the arm into the dark room in the rear. The bartender deserted his station long enough to slide the fanfold door shut, and Albert hastily turned his head to avoid being caught staring.

After a reasonable interval had passed to avert suspicion, he asked about a restroom and was directed to a small archway just this side of the partition. Although he lingered there for a few seconds, the rumbling conversation from the booths was loud enough to prevent him from hearing any sound from beyond the barrier, and the discovery that he really did need to relieve his bladder turned his attention elsewhere.

Sir Albert descended into the lower levels of Hades, avoiding a mop and bucket sitting on the landing, ignoring the magical incantations scribbled all over the walls, reached the foot of the staircase. There were four doors here, all closed, and he used the one marked "Hombres". It was a filthy hole, obviously used to imprison recalcitrant slaves or perhaps some monstrous ghoul or other inhuman beast.

He hesitated at the foot of the stairs. Two of the other doors were unmarked, and the first was locked as well. But when he tried the second, he found that it opened immediately. It was a closet, with a single bare lightbulb set in the ceiling, filled almost to overflowing with cartons of toilet tissue, paper towels, mops and brooms and other cleaning supplies, a complete porcelain sink with a large crack in the side, and a jumble of unrecognizable boxes, bags, and miscellany.

The sliding door was still in place when he returned to his seat at the bar, and it remained that way for the next two hours. Albert was working on his sixth beer, didn't realize how lightheaded he was getting until he slid off the stool and almost lost his footing. This earned him a pointed look from the bartender, but he smiled and pulled enough cash from his pocket to cover the tab and a generous tip, dropped it on the bar.

"Guess I'm done for the night. One last visit before I go." He nodded toward the stairway.

The bartender shrugged, made the money disappear, and turned to another customer.

Albert had to brace himself with one hand against the wall on the way down, moving his feet slowly and methodically. His lack of experience with alcohol was taking its toll, and he felt incredibly sleepy. In Hombre territory, he stood with his forehead pressed against the wall while he used the urinal, then spent an unnecessarily long time washing his hands so that two other patrons had returned upstairs before moving as quickly as possible to the storage closet and slipping inside.

The light went off as soon as the door closed, but Albert managed to reach the rear of the small room without making too big a racket, then sat down on the floor behind a block of crumbling cardboard boxes. Although he intended only to remain there quietly until after the bar was closed and everyone had left, he drifted off to sleep instead.

What woke him up was the clatter and bang when the mop and bucket were thrust inside the door. The wash of illumination barely registered before it was gone, the door slammed shut, and Albert sat in the renewed darkness, trying to remember where he was and why. Then Sir Arthur reasserted himself.

There was no sound from outside, and the door opened easily. After a moment's thought, Albert paused to unscrew the mop handle, testing its balance. A crude staff at best, but it would have to do.

Although he'd planned to wait until the bartender was gone for the night, it occurred to him now that the bar must have a security system and he might well find himself locked in if he waited that long. So he crept cautiously up the stairs.

The sliding door was partly open, and there were voices from beyond, low, indistinct. The bar seemed otherwise deserted; only a single short fluorescent mounted above the front door was still lit. He moved silently across the floor, slipped behind the bar, and lifted the Grail down from its resting place with swift, smooth motions. It was cool and hard in his fingers, which tingled electrically, although that might have been his imagination.

The outside door was tantalizingly close, but Albert was cautious. He grabbed a towel from its hook behind the bar and gently wrapped the Chalice, tucking the ends in so that it made a tight bundle, then carried it around to the front of the bar, still listening for any sign that the voices from the rear might be coming closer.

And that's when he heard the young woman's voice.

It wasn't a scream, more a cry of protest, but the sound stirred Sir Albert's memory of the fair maiden he'd seen languishing in the clutches of the Black Knight. Without making a conscious decision to act, he set his prize down on the bartop and approached the sliding door.

"C'mon, kid. You can't back out of this now." It was a deep, gravelly voice. The Black Knight.

An inarticulate response, low and intense, then louder. "Let go of my arm!"

Laughter, two men. Albert reached the edge of the door, slowly turned to look inside.

There were four round tables more or less evenly spaced around the room. The chairs were upside down on top of three of them, legs pointing toward the ceiling; the floor glittered wetly where it had been freshly mopped. Three figures sat at the fourth table, the Black Knight, the bartender, and the fair maiden. She appeared to be attempting to rise, but her forearm was held pinned by the Black Knight.

Sir Albert ignored the thin voice of panic and stepped around the door, the mop handle concealed behind his back.

"Let her go!" It would have been more effective if his voice hadn't wavered, but their reaction was immediate, three sets of eyes turning in his direction.

"What the...?" The Black Knight was surprised, perhaps even amused, the woman confused, but the bartender was actively angry. He rose and stepped around the table, both hands clenched into fists.

"This little asshole was here earlier," he said hoarsely. "I wondered why I never saw him go out."

He kept coming, moving quickly, and Albert fought an automatic impulse to step back, or even better, turn and run. But Sir Albert overruled him and, just before the other man could strike, he pivoted, swung the mop handle in a short, vicious arc. Although the bartender attempted to duck away, he wasn't quick enough, and the shaft landed across forehead and cheek with a satisfyingly loud crack.

Albert moved forward as his opponent staggered back against one of the tables, and jammed one end of the stick into the unprotected midsection. The table tilted to one side and the bartender crashed to the floor, groaning.

All traces of amusement were gone as the Black Knight swore softly and rose to join the battle. Albert noticed that his staff had split with the second impact, but he raised it anyway, wondering if Sir Albert had finally gotten in over his head. The heavier man approached cautiously, removed something from his pocket that clicked and then glittered in the dim light, the smooth edge of a highly sharpened blade.

"I'm gonna open you up, boy."

Albert was prepared to meet his own fate, when someone else took a hand. The young woman had quietly gotten to her feet, lifted a chair above her head, and now she brought it crashing down against the Black Knight's back. It wasn't a disabling blow; she lacked the strength to do much overt damage. But it caused him to lose his footing on the slick floor, and he stumbled forward awkwardly.

Albert slammed the mop handle down across the crown of his head, and followed up with a foot driven directly into the villain's groin. A foul blow, perhaps, but there were so few vulnerable spots in a knight's armor, one took advantage of whichever offered itself. The Black Knight was down, groaning, experiencing unfamiliar pain and defeat.

"Let's get out of here!" It was the woman, her eyes filled with concern, one hand on his arm. Conflicting emotions whirled through Albert's mind, triumph, surprise, fear, wonder, confusion, and he made no effort to resist as she pulled him out of the room.

But he did retain the presence of mind to grab the Grail before allowing himself to be led out into the street.

It was cooler outside, and windy, and the change brought him back to himself. "Where are we going?"

She shook her head, long blonde hair brushing her shoulders. "I don't know. Away from here."

Albert nodded, to himself not the woman. "Where do you live?"

"Nowhere. Not yet, I mean. I just got here a couple of days ago."

"Got any money?"

"Some." Not enough, he guessed. Desperate, or a runaway, or perhaps just a dreamer, Albert realized. He knew about dreamers. Available prey for a fast talking pimp, a dose of some come hither drug slipped into a free and badly needed meal.

"I've got a place," he offered. "Not far from here."

She stopped, turned to face him, and he felt the touch of her eyes searching his face, suspicion written broadly across her own.

"There's a couch you could use," he added, though it would need to be cleared off. "Until you find something better, I mean."

The wariness didn't disappear, but it softened. "All right. Thanks. What's your name?"

Sir Albert began weaving a new script, trying to decide what happened <u>after</u> the damsel was no longer in distress, but unbidden memories interfered, his inability to function at work, to deal with his bullying landlord, and for the first time, Albert resisted and the knight shrank back into oblivion.

"Albert. Albert Lance. Come on; it's this way."

But they made one brief stop first. As they were passing a row of trash cans set out for the morning pickup, Albert paused, weighed the Grail in one hand. Except it's not the Grail, he told himself, it's just a fancy glass cup used to decorate a lowlife bar. "No more fantasy," he said aloud, then smashed the bundle against the side of one of the trashcans. The glass shattered noisily and made a brittle sound when he dropped it in with the garbage.

Two hours later, a homeless drug addict named Bohort was searching the garbage for anything he could salvage for use or sale when he found a fancy cup wrapped in a heavily stained towel. It was a real find, since the glassware seemed to be in perfect condition, without so much as a chip out of its many faceted surface.

Bohort placed it carefully inside his grocery cart and walked off, taking the first steps on his own personal path to redemption.

# FOODWORLD

When Toni Huston decided that she couldn't possibly make it through the evening without a bag of potato chips, that decision altered her life forever.

It had been an upsetting, frustrating day, dominated by a single argument that had started at breakfast and lasted into the evening. Her parents hadn't actually forbidden her to apply for a summer job at the State Park; they considered themselves far too enlightened to make arbitrary rules for a twenty year old. But they nibbled around the edges of her resolve, raising doubts, fanning small embers of insecurity, until she was genuinely worried that she might be making a mistake.

Toni was supposed to think things through overnight and come to a decision in the morning, but she was already resigned to giving in. Just as she always did.

"I'm going out, Mom." She moved quickly through the living room, hoping to escape before her words registered.

"Out? Where?" Her mother glanced up from the magazine she'd been reading. "It's almost ten o'clock."

"Just to the store. I won't be long." Her hand was on the doorknob.

"But everything is closed by now..."

The door was open. "I'll find something. See you." And she was outside, beyond the reach of whatever else her mother might have wished to say. Then down the walk to her car, the subcompact her parents had picked out for her, just as they had made every other major decision about her lifestyle.

By ten o'clock, even the convenience stores are closed in Managansett, but just over the town line in Scituate, a giant discount food warehouse advertised that it was open 24 hours a day. Toni backed the car out of the driveway, already wondering if she was being foolish. For a moment, she considered abandoning the trip, but the image of her mother's habitual self satisfied nod of triumph stiffened her resolve.

"I'm old enough to make my own decisions. Why can't they understand that?"

It was a short drive, barely ten minutes on the empty roads, but she felt a fresh wave of anxiety in the nearly deserted parking lot. For long seconds, she sat in the car, ignition off but the key still in place. A tension headache was starting to tighten the muscles at the back of her neck and she considered starting the engine and going home empty handed.

"No! Stop being such a baby!" They were the same words her mother had spoken fifteen years ago when she'd finally reclaimed Toni from the customer service desk at the local Stop & Shop.

"Where were you?" She'd asked/demanded tearfully when her mother appeared.

"I told you not to get out of sight, didn't I? Maybe this time you'll learn to do as you're told."  She'd learned, all right.

"But I was scared!"

"Stop being such a baby."

Toni got out and slammed the door harder than necessary.

Foodworld was more than just a grocery store. In addition to food, their buyers purchased carloads of special merchandise - lawn furniture, automotive supplies, videotapes, remaindered books, games, small appliances, flower arrangements, all scattered through the store in tiny islands of commercialism. The aisles were arranged in a variety of patterns, different sizes and shapes, like some gigantic jigsaw puzzle, and it was common for people to get confused about where they were, or wander into dead ends.

As she stepped inside, Toni heard voices and the chatter of cash registers in the distance, but the building was so huge and cluttered, she couldn't actually see anyone. Ignoring the flutter in her stomach, she entered the maze.

At the first intersection, Toni noticed an elderly woman picking through a bin of apples. Her pockmarked face and twisted body suggested a vaguely menacing air. Toni deliberately turned her head away as she walked past, so she was startled when something touched her arm.

"Missy, help an old lady, would you?"

Toni stopped, tried to keep her face neutral. "Pardon me?"

"Be a dear and tell me which of these I should choose." Toni involuntarily took a step back as the woman thrust both hands forward, each cupping a shiny red apple.

Boy, did you ever pick the wrong person to ask, Toni thought to herself. I can't even make my own decisions, let alone someone else's. "They both look about the same to me, ma'am. Your guess is as good as mine."

The woman frowned, creating even more wrinkles. "Nonsense! There's always one choice that's better than the next. You just don't want to tell me."

How did I get into this? Toni suppressed an urge to snap at the woman, hastily pointed to her left hand. "This one then."

The woman's eyes never left her face. "Are you sure? You're not lying to me, are you?"

"What difference does it make?" Toni's voice broke a little and she felt on the verge of tears. Why was this happening to her? "They're so close it doesn't matter."

"Every decision matters, missy." The woman still held her arms forward, cupping the apples. "Sometimes just in the manner of the choosing."

Toni wanted to turn and run, down the aisle, out of the store, into her car and home to hide in her room. But instead she leaned forward, examining first one apple, then the other. "There's a small bruise on that one, near the stem, so the other one's better."

The woman nodded and let her arms drop. "Thank you, missy. I'll take them both." And she dropped the apples carefully inside a clear transparent bag and set them in her cart.

Toni walked away as quickly as she could manage without actually running.

She found the chips eventually, but it took considerably longer than she had expected, since they'd been moved to an oversized, irregularly shaped island facing a wall of cereal boxes. If any store employees had been around, she would have asked, but in the past they hadn't proven to be of much help and in any case she hadn't seen anyone. Not even another shopper since the apple lady.

Toni struggled with the choice of sour cream and onion versus barbecue for several seconds before realizing she was being indecisive again, finally grabbed one at random. Maybe they're right after all, she thought to herself. I can't even buy junk food without having a crisis.

Her thoughts still unsettled, Toni headed toward the cash registers. Or at least, that's what she thought she was doing.

Although she turned into what she thought should have been a direct route to the front, Toni reached a cross aisle which forced her to turn either left or right.

"Wonderful floor plan," she whispered aloud, then turned left, planning to resume her original course at the next intersection.

She reached a corner, canned goods on every side, but had no choice except to turn left, which forced her in exactly the wrong direction. At the next crossing, she turned right, then right again, making her way through international foods, enormous bags of polished rice, and pet supplies. This last was in an island by itself, and when she made her way around its curve, she discovered the only other exit route ran diagonally away from the flea collars and pet toys.

"It can't be," she told herself. "I just wasn't paying attention."

A few steps further, she was forced to turn left. "This is ridiculous," she said aloud, starting to get angry. "What kind of idiots are running this place?"

Five minutes and a bewildering number of turns later, Toni's anger had been replaced by nervous frustration. She had no idea where she was now, or which direction might lead to the exit. What's more, she hadn't seen or heard anyone since the woman with the apples, although once or twice she thought someone might have been speaking in a low voice a few aisles away. And the shelves seemed taller somehow, or perhaps she was growing shorter like Alice in Wonderland.

Toni didn't want to make a scene, but when she passed the same powdered milk display for the third time, she couldn't stand it anymore.

"Hello!" she called, careful to keep her voice cool and controlled. "Is anyone there?" No one answered; perhaps no one had heard her.

After another ten minutes, she dropped the chips in front of a tier of applesauce, now frightened as well as angry. She moved quickly, almost at a run, head turning from left to right as she passed between cliffs of groceries. At each junction she paused, trying to decide which direction was more promising. Her palms were moist and she began nervously rubbing them against her jeans. Despite the air conditioning, perspiration beaded her forehead. The absurdity of the situation might almost have been funny, but Toni was in no mood to laugh.

"You are going to feel really stupid when this is all over," she told herself. Nervously she glanced at her wrist, but she'd left her watch on the dresser in her room. There was no real way to tell how long she had been searching for an exit, but she suspected it must have been over an hour by now.

A few minutes later, she climbed one of the enormous racks, trying to figure out where she was. Off in the distance she could see the row of banners which hung

over the checkout registers, advertising sales, insisting that
Foodworld was the best choice for Rhode Island shoppers.
For a second or two, she considered walking along the top
of the shelf rather than descending back into the cavernous
aisles, but since she'd have to climb down from one in
order to get to the next, she'd just be wasting time.

After another fifteen minutes of random turns and
twists, she scaled a wall of baby foods, accidentally
knocking several to the floor where they smashed messily.
Ignoring the damage, Toni reached the top, then descended
carefully on the far side.

Despite a lingering fear that someone would see her
and call the police, Toni kept going in the same fashion. At
this point, she'd almost be willing to get arrested, just to get
out of this place. Her arms and legs were sore; she wasn't
used to this much exercise. "Some park ranger you'd
make." Her voice was hoarse with exhaustion and tension.
Hand over hand, one step at a time, she climbed over each
metal framed shelving unit, abandoning her dignity but at
least headed in the right direction.

Or so she believed until she put one foot down in a
puddle of spilled baby food.

Toni froze when she identified the mess beneath her
feet. "It has to be a coincidence," she whispered, retreating
so that her back was pressed against the shelves. "I couldn't
have gotten turned around, could I?"

But maybe she had. Everything looked the same
from up on top, a sea of prepared foods and toilet paper and
bottled beverages spreading away in every direction. It
would only have taken a moment of inattention. She might
easily have gotten turned around without noticing.

Toni collapsed, sitting beside the spill of creamed
fruit and meat paste, legs crossed, blinking back tears. Her

arms and legs hurt; she rarely exercised this much in a week, and she was tired, frightened, and suddenly hungry.

"Well at least I can do something about that!" There was a display of tinned meats just a few meters away. Ignoring a tiny voice that insisted she was stealing, Toni stood up and walked purposefully forward.

A short time later, she was licking the oil off her lips and fingers, three empty sardine tins piled neatly on the shelf beside her. She would rather have eaten tuna, but there was no way to open the cans.

With her stomach satisfied, Toni felt better, but when she tried to resume her trek, she was so exhausted she decided to rest first. She crossed to a display of disposable diapers, sat with her back against the yielding bundles. "Just for a couple of minutes," she whispered, already half asleep.  What was intended as a nap became much more, and when Toni next opened her eyes, her back was sore, limbs stiff. She climbed unsteadily to her feet, wondering if she'd actually slept through the night without having been discovered.

"I don't believe this!" She felt a twinge of panic. Her parents would absolutely murder her, she just knew it. "Hello! Is anyone there?" Maybe this was all just a dream. She couldn't possibly have become lost in a grocery store. That was just too absurd.

But twenty minutes later, Toni was no better off than she'd been the night before.

She breakfasted on melba rounds and fruit punch, and later found some cinnamon donuts. "You may be going crazy, girl, but at least you'll be well fed."

Somewhat more clearheaded, she forced herself to remain calm and began marking each intersection by placing a small pile of boxed groceries in the center of the floor. Toni assumed that no one was around to pick things up, since she still hadn't seen or heard another human being, and if she kept this up long enough, she figured she'd eventually find her way out through the process of elimination.

At least to some extent, she succeeded. No longer was she passing the same displays of tissue paper, packaged dinners, and canned sauerkraut. But in another sense, the situation grew even more disturbing. Toni noticed an increasing number of unfamiliar items, brands she'd never heard of before, in simple paper packages and cans. Some of the boxes were dried and cracked open, spilling their contents, as though they'd been sitting around for months. Or maybe even years.

There were large gaps on some of the shelves, crushed and broken containers scattered on the floor, and some of the spilled food had been there long enough to dry into unrecognizable piles of sludge.

It was hours later when she saw the feral cat.

For some time she had been moving as directly as possible toward a faint hum, drawn to the one element in her environment which seemed to indicate a specific reference point. The air grew progressively cooler as she advanced, almost chilly. Toni was still pausing at each intersection, but by now there were so many items spilled from the shelves, she often had to clear an area in which to place her marker. A faintly unpleasant odor grew steadily stronger, and by the time she finally reached the source, she already had a pretty good idea what to expect.

One of the neon lights over a section of frozen French fries was flickering noisily, threatening to die, humming and crackling with electrical fury. Just beyond, packages of vegetables, ice cream, and meats lay on the floor, most of them ripped open, the remains of their original contents moldy and unpleasant looking. A few meters away, a very large tabby cat raised its head from a package of half thawed hamburger patties and hissed warningly.

Ignoring the challenge, Toni advanced, happy to have found another living creature, however unfriendly. The cat rose to its feet, protecting its meal, back arched, tail thrashing angrily back and forth, and this time the hiss was a snarl.

Toni froze. She and the cat stared at one another, gazes locked, and when the contact was finally broken, it was Toni who retreated, close to panic, turning to half run down a side aisle. She was so upset by the encounter that it was several minutes before she realized she had forgotten to mark her trail for at least a dozen turns.

Toni collapsed beside a cardboard display of the Jolly Green Giant. She was crying, her shoulders shaking, scared and confused. "Why is this happening to me?"

The Giant didn't answer.

She had no idea how much time passed, how long she sat there before realizing she was no longer alone.

Something had moved, just out of her line of sight, at the far end of the aisle. Toni turned her head, watching carefully, and finally spotted a dark form behind the stacked rolls of paper towels. At first she thought the cat had followed, but this was a much bigger animal, and the way it advanced so quietly and cautiously made her nervous. She got up quickly and started off in the opposite direction.

A box of crackers fell from a shelf to the right. Toni caught a glimpse of tawny fur as something moved silently from one hiding place to another. Two of them then, whatever they were.

She started to run, turning at random whenever she reached an intersection, afraid to look back. The panic fed on itself and the faster she went, the faster she wanted to go. If debris cluttered an aisle, she jumped over it without hesitation, sometimes risking a dangerous fall.

When she stumbled into the encampment, the man standing there was almost as frightening as the mysterious creatures pursuing her. The litter was thick enough that she couldn't possibly keep running, but her momentum was so great that she couldn't entirely stop either. One foot became tangled in a box filled with empty soda bottles and she fell headlong into a pile of empty cans, boxes, and plastic wrappers.

"Are you all right?"

The fall had driven the wind from her lungs and Toni was too breathless to speak for several seconds. She did get a clearer look at the man, whose face was covered by an unruly beard that made it impossible to guess his age. His hair was long and matted, and there was something odd about his clothing. It was several seconds before she realized he was wearing what appeared to be a robe made up completely of dish towels sewn inexpertly together.

"Who are you?"

"Who? Me? I'm..." He hesitated and his eyes seemed to be looking at something distant and invisible. "Dan, I'm Dan. Yes, that's it. And who are you?"

"I'm Toni." She tried to get up, but it was difficult getting her footing because the floor was slippery with smears of spilled food. "Something was chasing me."

Dan glanced back the way she'd come, then back. "They won't come here. They know better." He nodded at the shelves just past the rubbish heap. Toni followed his eyes and saw a row of dark brown shapes. Animal heads, like cats but bigger, fiercer. "We got an arrangement, me and them. Our own hunting grounds."

Standing, Toni could see that Dan had settled in for a long stay. He'd cleared off one of the produce islands and covered it with a thick mattress of dishtowels, mop heads, and other soft materials. This was obviously a major intersection, with six wide aisles veering off in different directions, but all of the shelves within sight were picked clean of edibles.

"What is this place?"

Dan shrugged. "This is where I live."

Toni shook her head. "You live here? Why?"

He looked genuinely puzzled. "Why not? It's as good as any other. Everyone's got to live somewhere. There's lots of room if you're looking for a place to stay."

"Oh, no." She backed away, even though he'd made no attempt to approach. "I just want to find my way out of here."

Dan lowered his head and his voice was suddenly lower. "Ain't no way out of here."

She didn't want to believe him at first, but when she climbed atop the shelves, she could no longer see the front row banners and the walls were all lost in the distance. There was neither sound nor movement other than the ceiling fans; no one shopped or restocked the shelves or swept the filthy floors.

Maybe there really was no way out.

In the days that followed, Dan taught her how to forage for food without being stalked by the cat creatures, but otherwise he seemed very shy, rarely spoke, and kept to his own side of the produce island. Toni tried to talk him into exploring further, but he just blinked and changed the subject whenever she brought it up.

Days passed, weeks.

She started to lose track of time, spent her waking hours alternately searching for favored foods or reading the stock of movie magazines she'd found two rows down. They talked about teenaged stars she'd barely heard of, Bobby Darin and Sandra Dee and Tuesday Weld, but at least they helped pass the time.

Then, early one morning, she found an apple sitting on the floor in one of the side aisles.

"I'm going to look for the way out," she announced a few minutes later. "Will you come with me?"

Dan wouldn't raise his eyes from the box of cereal he'd been eating. "Told you. There's no way out of here. You're wasting your time."

"But I have to do something. I have to try!"

"Why?" He sounded genuine curious, but he still didn't look up, and Toni suddenly realized he was frightened, terrified, not by the cats but by the possibility of giving up everything he knew, everything that was safe and familiar.

"Because I don't want to stay here anymore."

"I think we should talk about it. It's safe here."

She hesitated only for a second. "I've already decided. I'm leaving, with you or without you." It felt good, just saying the words.

He glanced up then, only for a second, then dropped his eyes. "You'll be back."

She almost did turn around, when she heard rustling from above and saw something dark and threatening jump silently from one shelf to another. But instead of retreating, she took a can of soup in either hand, and the next time she spotted one of the cats, she tossed one overhand, missing the mark but scattering a display of aquarium supplies.

They closed in again moments later and she tossed two more Campbell's Soup missiles, after which, the stealthy noises stopped.

An hour or two later, she found another apple. It was sitting all by itself in the middle of an intersection, close to the left hand turn. She picked it up and continued in that direction.

There were too many apples to carry, but she ate one or two as she followed the trail, left then right then right again. As time passed, the floors were cleaner, the shelves more fully stocked, even the lights a bit brighter.

Despite everything, she was still surprised when she rounded a display of snack food and saw the row of cash registers. A large banner overhead read: "FOODWORLD: WHERE SMART PEOPLE SHOP TO CHOOSE."

Toni felt only half awake, as though emerging from a vague, already fading dream. She picked up a bag of potato chips and moved forward.

Only one register was open, a single customer patiently waiting while her purchases were rung up. Toni was not surprised to see that it was the same old woman she'd encountered when she first arrived, however long ago that might have been.

"I'll be out of your way in just a minute, missy." The cashier was almost finished filling a single paper bag. "Did you find what you were looking for?"

"Yes. Yes, I think I did." Toni placed the bag of chips on the belt, but she knew that wasn't what they were talking about.

"I thought you would. You have a good night now." And then she was gone.

When the cashier handed Toni her change, she asked the date. "May 24," was the curt reply. "At least, for another hour or so." Toni followed her eyes to the opposite wall, where an oversized clock read 10:32. She'd been in Foodworld for less than half an hour.

Her parents were both sitting in the front room when she arrived home.

"Did you find what you wanted, dear?" Her mother was apparently still reading the same magazine.

"Yes, I think I did."

Her father was sitting on the couch, touched the mute button to silence the television. "Your mother and I were a bit concerned. It's kind of late to be gallivanting around, you know."

"I needed to get out for a while. It did me a lot of good, helped me decide some things."

Her parents exchanged looks that she couldn't quite decipher, but it didn't matter. "I'm going to take that park service job. It's about time I took some responsibility for my own life."

Her mother shifted uneasily and her father cleared his throat. "Your mother and I agreed to respect your choice, Toni, but I thought we'd already decided you needed time to think about this."

Toni resisted the urge to laugh. "I've thought about it long enough. I'm sorry if you're disappointed, but if it's a mistake, at least it should be my mistake. And I'll have no one to blame for it but myself."

There was an uncomfortable pause, but her father nodded. "All right, so long as you realize that, I withdraw my objection. I suppose it's time you took a few risks." And after a moment, her mother smiled and nodded as well.

"Thanks. See you in the morning."

Upstairs, Toni was suddenly so tired that she flopped down onto the bed without opening the bag of chips, didn't even undress before falling sound asleep. And in the morning, it all seemed like a distant magical dream, one that she might have forgotten forever until she turned to the plastic Foodworld bag and found within it not the bag of chips she'd purchased the night before, but two apples, both almost perfect, except that one had a small bruise near the stem.

# PRISONERS

The prisoner woke in darkness. There was nothing remarkable in this because he always woke in darkness. He lived in an absence of light so absolute that he might as well not have eyes at all, although he had half formed memories of a world that was brightly lit and full of colors. Sometimes he could sense movement, a shimmering of the opaqueness in front of him that never quite resolved itself into actual forms, so there was undoubtedly some light in his cell, barely perceptible.

His hearing was perfectly fine although it provided little information. He was alone in the cell and always had been and although he had pounded on the walls from time to time in hope of eliciting a response from some other inmate, he had never been successful. The only time his hearing was of use was when they delivered the meals. Not once had he ever heard any of the guards approach, nor had he ever seen them. There was a narrow cutout in the door of his cell with a small iron gate at each end. His captors would place food there three times a day, their advent announced by the metallic shifting of the grate, and at some unpredictable time afterward they would take the empty tray away.

The prisoner had tried speaking to the guards, but no one had ever answered. He had tried propping his gate open so that he could at least see their hands as they placed the tray within the chamber, but when he did so his meal never arrived, would not arrive until he had resignedly closed the gate. And almost immediately there would be the clash of metal against metal as the other side was thrown open and he would be fed again.

The prisoner did not know who he was or what he had done that merited such harsh punishment. He had fragmentary memories of the outer world, trees, sky, rolling fields, lofty buildings, even people, although none of the images he dredged from the inner recesses of his mind ever struck a particularly sharp chord. It was as though he had known them all, but only casually, or perhaps a long time ago.

He knew the cell intimately and found that comforting. There was his bunk, fastened to one wall with a thin mattress and a single blanket that somehow never seemed to need washing. Someone had carved a hole in one corner of the rock floor where he could relieve himself. At one point he had contemplated the possibility of enlarging this as an escape route, but the stone was hard and smooth and he had only his fingers. Since there was no smell at the rim, he concluded it was probably far too long a drop to be of use to him even had he been able to pry away bits and pieces from time to time. The prisoner wasn't sure how long ago he had reached that conclusion. There was no way to measure the passage of time except perhaps by counting the meals he had eaten and even then he wasn't sure if they adhered to a regular schedule. At times he had been half starved when the food arrived; at other times he had difficulty forcing it down.

The only other objects in the cell were the clothes he wore, beltless pants that clung to his hips, a rough shirt that sometimes chafed. Like his blanket, these also seemed to clean themselves somehow, or perhaps he had just become oblivious to the dirt. And then there was his talisman, an oddly shaped piece of metal that depended from a thong – leather he thought – around his neck. The prisoner had no idea what the talisman stood for – something religious no doubt – and while he had no religion he cherished the talisman nevertheless and took comfort from it.

At some point he had resolved to escape. He had held back the metal cup from which he had drunk a sour but not unpleasant liquid that was his most frequent beverage. There had been no reprisals and a fresh, identical cup had appeared at the next meal. With this cup he had begun to scrape away at the wall opposite his bunk. He made no effort to conceal his activity; no one ever entered his cell, and if they could see him without doing so, then no subterfuge was possible. The rough scraping of metal against stone had been comforting, until it became so commonplace that he could no longer consciously hear it.

The prisoner had no idea how long he had been working – months certainly, perhaps years. When he was able to reach through with his hand, he felt both elation that there had been an actual event in his life and depression that no other hand had reached out to grasp his. But he had continued to work, widening the hole, throwing the fragments of stone down the waste hole, until one day – and only after considerable effort – he managed to squirm through the hole.

He was, of course, in another cell, almost identical to his own. There were three major differences, however. First, this cell was untenanted. Second, he was able to determine this immediately because there was enough light, though just barely, to illuminate his surroundings. Third, and perhaps most important, the cell door was not secured.

The prisoner stepped out into a shadowy corridor, half expecting to be set upon by guards, beaten soundly, and thrown into another cell like his own. None of these things happened.

He walked to the door of his own cell and for the first time in his life saw the outline of the lock, two vertical cuts crossed by one diagonal. It looked familiar nevertheless and vaguely unsettling; he found himself fingering his talisman as he walked further along the corridor.

The dungeons were enormous, literally hundreds of cells, but whenever he tried one of the doors he found it unlocked and no one within. Could it be possible that this enormous facility was maintained just to ensure his confinement? It seemed grossly out of proportion to his crimes, no matter what they might have been.

The prisoner found no indication of his guards either. There was a small room fitted with four bunks at the foot of a broad staircase that led up into the shadows. The only light here came from windows slit into the walls a hundred feet above his head. For all their remoteness, they provided the brightest images he had glimpsed in years and he found himself blinking and looking away whenever his eyes strayed toward them.

The bunkhouse was empty. The beds were made up but obviously had not been in use for a long time. There was a layer of dust on the blankets as well as on all of the other surfaces in the room. He felt uncomfortable all the time that he was inside and breathed a sigh of relief when he emerged.

There were no doorways anywhere on the floor of the dungeon. The only egress seemed to be the staircase. Although he had expected to find himself experiencing elation at the prospect of freedom, there was caution in his mind as well. Escape could not be this easy. This was all part of some elaborate plot to raise his spirits and then dash them down. He became so convinced of this that he went back the way he had come, located his own cell with some difficulty. The door was locked and he had almost decided to slip back through the hole in the adjacent cell when his hand brushed against his talisman and he glanced down.

The talisman consisted of two parallel lines, crossed diagonally by a third. Tentatively he lifted it to the lock. It lined up perfectly. He pushed it in and turned and, with a barely perceptible click, the lock engaged. The prisoner opened the door thoughtfully and glanced at the inner surface. The same three lined indentation was there. Had he known, he might have simply unlocked the door and stepped out at any time.

He went inside and stretched out on his bed. A few seconds later he rose, closed and locked the door, then returned to the bunk, and closed his eyes.

When he woke, there was a tray of food waiting for him. He ate just as he had done so many times in the past and returned it to the chamber, then sat on his bed for a long time, thinking. When he rose again, the chamber was empty. The door opened easily when he inserted his talisman and turned it.

The dungeon was quiet and empty. He explored for a while and discovered that his talisman opened every cell where he tried it, presumably every cell in the dungeon. But had he simply traded one very small cell for another larger but just as restrictive?

The staircase was higher and steeper than he had expected. When he reached the landing at the top, he was shaking with weariness. It had been a long time since he'd gotten regular exercise, if there had ever been such a time, and his body protested. He sat on the top step for a long time, catching his breath, staring down into the shadows that washed through the dungeon like the gentle waves of a receding tide.

Eventually he stood up and looked around. There was not much to see, just a bare stone platform and a door set into one wall. A very large door. The prisoner came closer and saw that there was a locking mechanism and that the pattern was identical to that of the cells below. Tentatively he inserted his talisman and turned it. There was a click but no other sign that anything had happened. He placed one hand on the rough surface of the door and gently pushed. It gave way before him.

The prisoner's movements became furtive for the first time as he emerged into a dusky passageway lit indirectly by light entering through stained glass windows overhead. If there had been tapestries or other furnishings, he might have skulked timidly along, but there was no such concealment and he finally shrugged his shoulders and marched straightforwardly down a much wider corridor, almost a room, certainly so by the standards to which he was accustomed. On his way he passed several open chests – great wooden boxes with polished brass staves – each filled to overflowing with jewels, golden ornaments, and other material riches. He was tempted to slip a few of these into his pockets, until he remembered that he didn't have pockets.

This passageway debouched into a much larger enclosed space with arched ceilings that towered so high above him that he could not make out the details of the paintings and engravings that adorned them. There was a raised platform at one end and what might have been an altar, although there were no recognizable icons or other objects with the exception of occasional caricatures of people posed with hands clapped over their ears or eyes. He felt immediately out of place, as though he had stepped into some sacred place which might be profaned by his presence. But then he noticed dead leaves gathering in the corners, and the offal of rodents scattered here and there and he decided that whoever was responsible for this magnificent place had already allowed it to become defiled far past his poor ability to add or subtract.

He found another door and passed through into another room just as large and just as magnificent, but clearly with another purpose. The elaborately caparisoned, elevated chair at the far end was almost certainly a throne, though no one at present occupied it. The ravages of time and nature were not as obvious here because the dead leaves and offal had been gathered up and placed in obscure corners, behind draperies, and in other locations not immediately visible, as though they were treasures of some sort hidden away for later retrieval.

It took longer to find the next exit, and when he brushed aside the curtain that concealed the archway, he took a hasty step backward. There was no doorway here, just an opening leading to a courtyard open to the sky. The prisoner had no idea what might have happened to his captors, but he was certain that he would find somebody once he left the building.

But he did not. The courtyard was deserted. It was wide and flat and the wind raised dust that swirled in odd patterns that dashed themselves into oblivion when they met the featureless wall that lay beyond the courtyard stretching as far as he could see in either direction. The prisoner began moving roughly parallel to the wall, which gradually curved to his right, and in due course he reached the market place.

It occurred to him that he had not eaten yet that day, and he was overwhelmed by hunger the moment he saw the displays of foods – piles of fruit, boxes of nuts, chunks of cooked meat skewered on sticks, trays of confections, pitchers of fluid, a variety of raw and cooked vegetables so varied that he could not begin to put names to them all. But there were no people.

He wandered among the carts and stands for several minutes, searching for the proprietors. The foods were fresh, the meat and bread warm to the touch, the drinks still cool, but no one appeared to be watching over them. At last he shouted aloud, surprised by the harsh croak that was his voice, an inarticulate cry of inquiry, but there was no reply except a wavering echo.

He took a skewer of meat casually, as though considering whether or not it was worth his time. When no one cried out in protest, he took a step away, and then another, and then hastened to a shadowed corner where he devoured the meat almost without chewing. There was no outcry. No change at all. Emboldened, he sallied forth again, acquired another two skewers and a pitcher of some sweetish, fruity liquid. The meat disappeared quickly, the fluid following soon after.

He ate three pieces of fruit, picking the best looking and avoiding the second layer, which was spotted with bad spots and decay. No one protested.

Although he was beginning to feel nervous about his foray and was entertaining reassuring thoughts about returning to his cell, he decided to press forward a bit further, and thus it was that he came to the stairway, a narrow construction that zigzagged up the side of the ever present wall. The prisoner decided that this would be his last experiment of the day, a climb to the top from which point he might learn something about his location.

The stairway was longer and steeper than he had thought and more than once he considered turning and going back the way he had come. But his awakening sense of freedom was not so easily bridled and he pressed forward, reaching the summit on legs that shook with strain. He was so exhausted that he sat down immediately and began massaging his calves, deferring the moment when he would look about him.

What finally stirred him to move was the thought that night might fall before he could return to the familiar, although he had no sense of what time it was and indeed had never noticed any change in the light, or lack of light, entering through the dungeon windows. Nevertheless he hoisted himself to his feet, took a deep breath, and crossed the parapet to the outer edge of the wall.

The landscape spread out as far as he could see, rolling fields and meadows, scattered copses of what appeared to be carefully tended trees, even dark lines that might have been tracks for horse carts. There was a good sized pond off to his right, and a smaller one to his left. It looked to him like spring or early summer, although he could not have said why, but at times he saw one or another tree slowly shedding its multicolored leaves. There were no villages, no animals in the fields, no traffic on the horse tracks, no people anywhere. But there were signs of people.

From his vantage point, he could see five other castles, widely scattered, each configured in a different shape but wrapped around the same purpose. It was then that he realized that he must be in a castle as well, probably one very much like and unlike those around him. In vain he watched for any indication that he was not alone, smoke from a fire, a distant figure plowing a field, even a bird gathering twigs for a nest. But nothing moved that was not motivated by the gentlest of breezes and after a while he turned away.

By the time he reached his cell, he was too tired to think.

It took the prisoner two more days to find the great gate, set into the wall, held closed by a system of counterweights which he could not begin to understand. He had just decided to search for rope with which he might lower himself down from the parapet when he noticed a familiar icon, one slash across two parallel lines. It was a locking mechanism of some kind and when he inserted the talisman, the gates slowly opened with a great rumbling and creaking that he found distressing. He had just stepped through when he felt a rush of panic, wondering if once outside he could ever gain re-entry. His cell was not perhaps the ideal habitation, but there was food and security here. Outside there might be privation, hunger, even death.

He stood just beyond the wall's outer edge, watching the raised gate warily, prepared to rush forward if it started to descend, and only turned away when he noticed another receptacle for his talisman, this one mounted on the outer wall. Presumably the gate could be raised from this side as well. Reassured, he turned and walked through the fields and that night he slept under a tree that was covered with pinkish white blossoms.

The other castles were farther away than he expected. The prisoner had improvised a pack from some sturdy drapes and had gathered enough food to last five days comfortably, confident that he could drink from the several streams that threaded through the landscape. But it took eight days to reach the nearest castle, and when he arrived he discovered that he could not gain entry as easily as he'd hoped. There was an iconic receptacle, but this one consisted of two lines crossed at right angles by two much shorter ones. He could not insert his icon.

Fortunately he had chosen a castle with low walls. There was a towering tree that leaned close enough and grew tall enough that he could, with some difficulty, leap onto its narrow parapet. Except for inconsequential details, it was much like what he thought of as "his" castle, including a deserted but heavily provisioned market place.

It took him four days to find the entrance to the dungeon, and another two days to break down the door with a pair of ceremonial axes he found in a throne room surprisingly similar to the one he'd first entered. The dungeon itself so closely resembled his own that he wondered briefly if he had hallucinated everything that had happened since he'd first left his cell.

He spent an hour searching the dungeons. All of the cell doors were open except for one, which was locked. The prisoner pounded on the door and shouted but there was no response from inside. There was no way to know if the cell was occupied or empty. Or was there?

Crouching, he lifted the outer gate of the food chamber, hearing the all too familiar slide of metal on metal, then slowly lowered it again, although not all the way. For a few seconds, he thought that nothing would happen, but then the inner gate opened and he caught the briefest glimpse of a hairy forearm in the gloom, and a hand that probed around the food chamber. Then there was a grunt of exasperated dismay and the hand withdrew.

"Hello!" He called, noting the way the syllables spilled over his tongue and lips, as though he had never spoken, or at least not that particular word, before now. "I'm a friend. Can you hear me?"

The inner gate came down with a crash.

Refusing to be discouraged, the prisoner stood up and fumbled for his talisman, but the locking mechanism on this cell was modeled on the two crossed sets of lines, not his pattern, and he could not unlock it. He crouched again.

"Do you have a talisman? It's the key to the cell. You can be free whenever you want to be."
There was no reply. There was no reply the rest of that day. There was no reply when the prisoner carried fresh fruits and broiled fish down from the market place and placed it in the food chamber, although the food itself disappeared promptly, although only when the outer gate was once again in the closed position. He tried cajolery, then reason, then lost his temper and ranted at the man in the cell, but nothing had any discernible effect. Nevertheless, he kept at it for ten days before refashioning his pack and setting off for the next castle.

He could not find a way into the second castle, or the third. The fourth had a yawning gap in its wall, as though some siege engine had pounded away at it, and once again he found a single occupied cell in the castle's dungeon. He was able to ascertain that this prisoner was a female because she spoke to him, although only once. And what she said was "Please go away." And so he did.

The fifth castle wall was also impenetrable, and he never reached the sixth.

For some time he had been aware of a dark line on the distant horizon, and as he traveled he grew closer to it and was able to distinguish its nature. It was another wall, as formidable as those that surrounded the castle, and on a much greater scale. It disappeared in both directions without any hint of a break and only the slightest suggestion of a curve, as though all the castles he could see were enclosed within it, as they might well have been. After the fifth castle, discouraged by his failures, he decided to take a diversionary trip to the base of the wall.

A day later he saw faint lines marring the smooth surface ahead of him. On the day following that he was able to determine that they were staircases, some quite direct, some meandering for great distances before finally reaching the top. He chose one of the most direct routes and altered his course. The following day he slept at the foot of the wall and the day after that he began to climb.

It was an arduous trip because the stairs were not in good repair, apparently not in frequent use, and also because he was forced to carry water as well as food. He stopped frequently to catch his breath, occasionally taking a mouthful of water, but despite the fatigue in his muscles he felt a growing sense of elation, as though perhaps he was about to make a great discovery.

He reached the top in the middle of the afternoon. The land beyond the wall looked something like that within, but it was wilder, with long stretches of dark looking woods interspersed with tilled fields and flowing meadows. There were no castles outside the wall, at least none that he could see, but there was something else. There were people.

The prisoner could see a small village, if half a dozen low huts could be called a village. Several four legged creatures grazed nearby and a handful of people moved in the streets. It took him a few seconds to recognize that these were really people like himself because they wore colorful clothing, no two dressed alike, and they moved with obvious ease and enthusiasm rather than being weighed down with doubt and fear.

He stood up and waved and, after a second, they waved back. Then they began talking among themselves and after a few moments, three of them started toward the base of the wall far below the prisoner. They were obviously coming to talk.

But talking proved to be impossible. He could tell that they were shouting to him, and no doubt his own hoarse croaks were equally unintelligible. The distance was just too great. The prisoner explored along the parapet in one direction and then the other, but as far as he could tell there were no staircases on this side of the wall, no way down at all. And then a fourth person arrived from the village, a heavy set man who labored under the weight of a long, straight object that looked to the prisoner like an impossibly large animal horn.

Two of the other men helped to lift the object and point the wide end up toward the prisoner, who briefly wondered if it was some kind of weapon. But then the last man stood at the narrow end and when he spoke, the prisoner could hear him, not easily but quite clearly.

"Come down. Join us."

The prisoner raised his hands to show his frustration. "How?" he called back, knowing they could never hear him.

"You have to find your own way. It's different for every person."

This made no sense to the prisoner, but they repeated the same words several more times. And then, to his dismay, they turned and carried the horn, or speaking tube, back to the village and never looked back at him.

The prisoner spent two weeks exploring the wall but never found anything that might allow him to descend the outer side. There were no gates or breaks, no staircases or ladders, nothing but endless expanses of polished stone. He considering digging his way through the base of the wall, but it was thirty feet thick and the stones so hard that no makeshift tool he employed did more than scratch their surface.

He thought about gathering ropes and plaiting them together, but there was no place on the top of the wall to secure one end. He considered carrying large chunks of rock up the staircase and using them to anchor it, but his early experimentation on the ground disheartened him. The rope always slithered free.

It was the bird that gave him the idea. He was standing on the parapet one morning, wistfully watching the villagers out in their fields, when a bird alighted beside him. "Can I borrow your wings, little friend?" he asked playfully, but his face turned serious. He had no illusion that he could fashion any kind of artificial wing that would allow him to fly to the ground, but that might not be necessary. His idea was risky but he could think of no better, and a future in which he sat within sight of others of his kind but was forever separated from them was even worse than the privations of his cell. He set to work.

Like all human endeavors, it took longer than expected. He built four wings in all, one for each arm and each leg. The first he constructed on the ground, but the ascent to the parapet thus laden was so arduous that he simply ferried up his materials and built the remaining three on site. About two miles from where he had first climbed to the top a good sized pond lay only a few feet from its base. A free fall dive from this height would undoubtedly have broken every bone in his body, and the spread wings he had constructed would not slow him enough to make a direct descent to the ground possible, but if he combined the two he just might have a chance.

The villagers must have been watching him because when he finally completed all of his preparations, they gathered in strength at the side of the pond, at least twenty of them, a larger number than he had ever seen before. They made no attempt to hail him, but their purpose was obvious. They would either greet him when he arrived successfully, or bury his dead body.

The prisoner strapped on his wings and climbed awkwardly onto the outer wall. Just as he was about to jump, he remembered something. He grasped his talisman and lifted the thong over his head. "Whatever happens, I won't need this anymore." And he threw it behind him and jumped.

Oddly enough he felt no fear. There had been too much of that in the past and he'd exhausted his capacity for it. The drop was exhilarating and he almost forgot to extend his arms and legs. But then he did and for a second there seemed to be no change. The wind crowded into the cloth pockets of his wings and he jerked in the air once, twice, his plummet slowed but not stopped.

He looked down and the surface seemed to be coming up very quickly, but it was water and that made it difficult to judge distances. In any case, it was too late to make any adjustments. He closed his eyes briefly, then snapped them open. Whatever happened next, he wanted to see it clearly.

The prisoner hit the water with a loud splash.

He had a bad moment when one of the wing straps refused to release, but he wrenched it off and reached for the surface, surprised to discover that he could swim. The shock hit him then and he floundered in the water, might have sunk back down if several of the villagers hadn't jumped in and pulled him safely to the bank.

When he could breathe easily again, he raised his head and found himself facing a handsome looking man with a heavy beard.

"What's your name?" asked the man.

The prisoner hesitated, then realized that he did indeed have a name. And so he told it to them and they all went off together.

# NATURAL LAW

"I do so enjoy a picnic," said Miss Harrington. "I feel that it's quite important not to lose touch with the natural world. Don't you agree with me, Mr. Shaw?"

Artemus Shaw disguised his incredulity with a pretended cough, bobbed his head vaguely. They were seated on cushioned chairs in a screen house almost within view of Harrington Hall. The servants had brought china place settings, sterling silver flatware, and crystal wineglasses from the house, arranging them on the marble topped table that the groundskeepers had carried out earlier in the day. Their meal had been carefully trundled from the kitchen on wheeled carts, kept warm by chafing dishes whose oil fueled heaters were efficiently sheltered from any stray breeze that might blow them out. They were dining on stuffed Cornish hens and drinking wine freshly imported from France, while the servants kept watch for any stray insect that might have penetrated the fine mesh of the fabric stretched over the ornate framework that surrounded them. Artemus was dressed plainly but practically while Miss Winifred Harrington was fully coifed and corseted, her only concession to their "natural" surroundings having been the choice of relatively sensible footwear. Even her parasol was more decorative than functional.

"So tell me about your adventures, Mr. Shaw. You promised to do so. Father says you've been quite reticent but I assured him that I'd draw you out."

Artemus sighed. There was no way escaping this. Her father had been one of the major underwriters for his recently concluded expedition and was a potential benefactor for the next. Winifred was his only daughter and her infatuation with the dashing but untitled young Artemus, though unrequited, may have seemed serious enough to warrant financing the removal of the young man from England for a year or so, surely long enough for her affection to fade. If that had been the elder Harrington's motive, it had been ill fated as well as misguided because it had endowed Artemus with an air of mystery and sophistication that, if anything, had increased his desirability in her eyes. Winifred had written to him at regular intervals during his absence, repetitious, vacuous missives that had reached him in batches whenever a river trader ventured far enough into the interior of Africa to deliver them.

"There's not a great deal of interest to speak of," he replied, not entirely truthfully.

"Oh come, Mr. Shaw. Fourteen months in the unexplored jungle among savages and fierce animals. I'm quite jealous really. The greatest excitement I've experienced during your absence was a trivial mishap with the carriage during a visit to London. Surely you can top that."

Artemus sighed but surrendered to the inevitable. "Well, I did encounter one remarkable fellow down there. He was a native, but an educated man, though quite obviously mad."

"Educated, you say? And a native. Do you mean he could read and do his sums?"

"Oh, that and more. He spoke in a most refined manner although his accent was atrocious, of course."

"I hardly think his manner of speech could be remarkable. One can, after all, teach a parrot to speak or dress a servant in fineries, but in neither case do we alter their essential nature." She seemed blissfully unaware that one of those servants was within earshot, or more likely she simply didn't care. "I find madness quite fascinating, however. One of father's cousins is not quite right in his mind and there are times when it is even necessary to lock him in his room. He is never allowed to go about unattended. It would be scandalous. But I must say that his ramblings are at times quite bizarrely entertaining. Father says it is a great tragedy because Cousin William was brilliant as a young man." Winifred seemed poised to continue at length but she stopped suddenly. "But it is your story that I want to hear, Mr. Shaw."

"Yes, well, I met Blackwell about a week after I arrived in Matamba. I'd settled in by then and knew my way around well enough to venture out of the camp unescorted."

"And who is this Blackwell?"

Artemus blinked. "He's the native chap. I imagine he had a local name at some point, but I only knew him as Blackwell. Whether he chose that name for himself or received it from whoever was responsible for his education remains a mystery. I had gone to dicker with a local chieftain named Ndinga about employing some bearers for a brief foray into an uninhabited area nearby. Ndinga spoke no English and I had only been able to pick up a few simple phrases in the local dialect, so we were forced to resort to a kind of pidgin Portuguese. This also proved unsatisfactory and I was about to give over the project as lost when Ndinga addressed one of his people who vanished briefly, then returned with this fellow who called himself Blackwell. Blackwell spoke fluent English, as I've mentioned, and apparently was also reasonably conversant in the local tongue. With his assistance, I was able to complete negotiations on quite favorable terms."

"Beads and other flashy trinkets, I imagine."

Artemus shook his head. "Not at all. Ndinga is no fool. He was particularly interested in tools and fabrics. Be that as it may, I was about to depart when Blackwell hailed me and introduced himself formally. I can hardly hope to convey a sense of the man in his absence, but I was immediately convinced that I was dealing with a shrewd, sophisticated intelligence. He was clearly of different stock than the Matambans, taller and with a different cast to his features, but it was his carriage that marked him as an outsider. The Matambans are either surly or suppliant or a little of both, but Blackwell was neither. Ndinga made a show of the fact that he considered the two of us equals; Blackwell's manner told me that he took this for granted."

"Rather impertinent of him, I would think."

Artemus didn't quite frown. "It is their country, after all, Miss Harrington. But Blackwell was neither insolent nor sycophantic. He called me by name and asked if I had a moment to talk to him. Since I planned to rest for a while before trekking back to the camp, I acceded to his request. We found a shaded spot and Blackwell talked a passing woman into trading us a small basket of fruit for a handful of beads he produced from a little pouch attached to his belt.

"It was extraordinarily hot and damp that day and the fruit was quite refreshing. We ate two or three each before I remarked upon his mastery of English and asked where he'd learned to speak so eloquently. He hesitated briefly, then told me that most of the people where he'd grown up spoke English, an evident implausibility. I asked where that might have been and he was somewhat evasive at first, but later indicated that he was from some place called America, which I initially assumed must be deep in the interior since it is listed by no geographers of the region. He did not have the manner of a primitive tribesman, however, nor did his accent seem to me congruent to that state, but I let him believe that I had accepted his story."

"Perhaps he was a fugitive and feared you would return him to his enemies. He might have been a runaway indentured servant."

Artemus inclined his head to indicate acknowledgment of that possibility. "It seems unlikely, however, given that our government has so strongly prevailed upon the Portuguese to crack down on that practice in their territories. He quickly changed the subject, however, and proceeded to inquire about a range of subjects from the state of the railroads in England to our colonial policy in India. I must say he seemed very well informed on a variety of subjects. I was barely able to hold my own in the conversation."

"I'm sure you over estimate the man, Mr. Shaw. No doubt he chose only those subjects about which he'd learned enough to mimic a man of education."

"Not at all. Although some of his speculation was quite outrageous, his chain of reasoning was well structured and consistent, if rather fantastic at times." Artemus could see that his praise for Blackwell was not sitting well with his companion. "But despite the veneer of education, the man was at heart deeply superstitious."

"Witch doctors and magic charms and all that rot, I suppose."

Artemus shook his head. "No, his delusions were of an entirely different sort. He believed, for example, that the world was round."

"But it is round, or so they say."

"In the sense that it is circular, you are of course correct, Miss Harrington. But Blackwell insisted that it was shaped like a tennis ball rather than a dinner plate."

Her eyebrows rose and she let out an unladylike snort of disbelief. "How absurd! You are jesting with me, Mr. Shaw. Not even a primitive could entertain such a notion. Why if that were the case, what would prevent the inhabitants of the bottom half from falling off, or all the oceans spilling over into the void?"

Artemus shrugged. "Logic and reason are of little use when battling superstition, Miss Harrington, and you might recall that it was at one time widely believed even in Europe that the Earth might be a globe, until Columbus and others actually sailed to the rim and established the truth beyond question. And Blackwell had an ingenious rationale. He posited some magical force he called gravity and insisted that it held everything in place regardless of its orientation. I pointed out to him that if his theory were true, then when a ship sailed to the limits of our vision, the hull would disappear first, the topsails last, which is not the case, but he refused to credit what I said. Given that we were deep in the interior, it is possible that he was never adjacent to a body of water large enough to prove him wrong."

"Or he simply lacked the wit to interpret such evidence correctly. I can hardly believe that any reasonably intelligent person could be so unaware of the physical properties of the world."

Artemus sipped at his wine. "Oh, but that was only one of his misapprehensions. He also believed that the Earth moved around the sun rather than the reverse."

She gave him a suspicious look. "You are jesting with me, sir. Not even a savage could be unaware of the passage of the sun across the sky each day. It is an undeniable fact."

"I agree completely, Miss Harrington, that the evidence is unassailable, but according to Blackwell the night time, when the sun is moving beneath our feet to regain its position in the east, is actually created by the Earth turning to face away from the sun."

"Preposterous! We should be aware of any such motion. And do we also revolve around the moon, according to this Mr. Blackwell?"

"Ah, the moon! No, he agrees that the moon does in fact circle the Earth, but he imagines that it is a world in itself, so large that it also generates the magical force of gravity. He insisted that this was responsible for something he called the tides."

Miss Harrington frowned. "Tides? And what are those, pray tell?"

Artemus leaned forward. "A rather amusing fancy. According to Blackwell, the attractive force exerted upon the oceans causes the water level to rise and fall with the passage of the moon."

"But if that were the case, wouldn't the effects be uniform from day to day?"

"So one would think. Blackwell seemed a bit vague about this point, suggesting that the moon did not make its passage around the Earth in exactly twenty-four hours. I tried in vain to point out to him that the fluctuations in sea level corresponded with and were proportionate to the amount of rainfall in a given period, but he was not receptive to my argument."

"Most extraordinary. If nothing else, your Mr. Blackwell has an inventive mind."

"That he does, or rather did. I'm afraid Mr. Blackwell came to a rather bad end."

"And how did this come about?" Miss Harrington sat back and prepared to be entertained.

"A few days after I first made his acquaintance, I chanced to ask him how he had come to Matamba and whether or not he contemplated a return to his native land. I should mention here that while his demeanor had always been serious, he had invariably seemed in good spirits. My words had a somewhat adverse effect, however. He became pensive and insisted that he was not entirely sure of the sequence of events that brought him to that country."

"He was evading your question, no doubt."

Artemus shook his head. "No, I think not. He seemed genuinely unable to form an answer. He insisted that he had gone to sleep one night in familiar surroundings and wakened the next morning lying under a tree in Matamba. It had taken him a few weeks to learn enough of the local language to get by and he was grateful to the Matambans for their patience and charity. My companions and I were the first outsiders to appear after his arrival and he had initially believed that we would afford him the opportunity to return to this America of his. He confessed to having been badly shaken when I had informed him that I was not familiar with his homeland."

"Savages can hardly be expected to understand the scale of the world. Why, there are places here in England whose names I have never heard."

"Quite. But Blackwell seemed to think that this America was a very important place, like London, and that its name would resonate with me. I was sorry to have disappointed him so severely."

Artemus drifted off into a brief reverie from which Miss Harrington promptly roused him. "You were going to relate to me the manner of the man's demise, I believe."

"Yes. It was an unfortunate but perhaps inevitable fate that awaited him. His belief system was so incompatible with the real world that I cannot believe it was widely spread even among his own people. Such a society would not be stable. Although the man was composed, intelligent, and even rational within the bounds of his delusions, he was nevertheless quite mad."

A servant appeared as if by magic, took away the empty wine bottle, and replaced it with a fresh one. Miss Harrington made a pretense of not wanting any more, but Shaw had been through this routine before and knew that she simply wanted to appear reticent. Once they both had full glasses, he returned to his story.

"Blackwell was an ambitious sort of fellow. He was determined to return to this America place and prior to our arrival had felt constrained to rely on his own resources. The Matamban region is nearly inaccessible, you realize. Their virtual isolation from the rest of the world explains their lack of barbaric instincts; they literally have not had a human enemy for generations. In any case, Blackwell quickly determined that all conventional means of leaving were closed to him. The pass through the mountains could only be managed by a large party such as ours, and the Mokambo River ends with a waterfall of rather spectacular proportions, and the waterways beyond are riddled with treacherous rapids."

"I marvel that you were able to penetrate into such an inaccessible region. I was not wrong, I might say, in considering your courage and audacity rather out of the ordinary."

The wine was making Miss Harrington bolder and Artemus decided he must bring his story and his visit to an end before she moved from the daring to the inappropriate.

"Although Matamba is remote, there has been intermittent contact with the outside world, and in fact there was briefly a Portuguese trading post there within living memory, now deserted and fallen into ruin. The trading party all died within a single season, probably having contracted some local disease, and the Matambans avoided the area as cursed, leaving the building and its contents virtually untouched. Although most of the trade goods had been rendered worthless, Blackwell found a store of canvas and devised an escape plan so bizarre that even Mr. H.G. Wells would find it fanciful."

Miss Harrington leaned forward, her eyes gleaming with more than curiosity. One hand crept out and touched his knee and he had to exert himself to keep from flinching. "You enthrall me, sir."

"Yes," he answered awkwardly, contriving to shift position so that he was just out of reach. "It is a fascinating tale indeed. You see, Blackwell had fashioned this canvas into an enormous container, a cloth bag of extraordinary proportions. He had attached this to a kind of basket woven from local foliage, into which he had installed the small iron stove which the Portuguese used to cook their meals."

Thwarted in her effort to achieve greater intimacy, Miss Harrington was torn between the desire to look prettily wronged and her curiosity about this strange turn of events in the chronicles of Mr. Blackwell. "I confess that I find these exertions completely baffling."

"As did I, until Blackwell explained his intentions. He hoped to escape from Matamba by inflating his canvas bag with heated air generated by the stove."

"A balloon of sorts, was it not?"

"Precisely. He was convinced that he could use the balloon to lift himself from the ground and fly like some exotic bird over the ridge of mountains to the coast."

"But it is impossible for man to fly. It is against all the laws of nature."

"Well, perhaps not quite all of them. Human flight is indeed impossible, as I told Blackwell the moment he revealed his plan. He refused to take my point, insisted that this mode of travel was commonplace in his home country. It was then that I knew with absolute certainty that the man was insane and I had a presentiment of what must ultimately come to pass."

"And that was?"

"His initial attempt took place in an open field. To my great surprise, he did manage to fill his bag to such an extent that it rocked back and forth above the basket, straining to be free. Blackwell stood beside his little stove, hopeful at first, frustrated when it remained stubbornly earthbound. I felt more than a bit sorry for him, his disappointment was so acute. When he finally desisted, I hoped that the failure might have cured him of his obsession. Alas, it did not."

Miss Harrington gestured for more wine and Artemus obliged her. "The Matambans were fascinated and on the following day he convinced a party of them to help transport his apparatus to the banks of the river at the very brink of the waterfall. When I discerned his intention, I did my best to dissuade him but he would not be moved. He was convinced that he had only failed in his first attempt because of something called inertia, another magical force, and that he could overcome this obstacle by precipitating himself off the edge of the waterfall. Once in motion, he believed that he would be carried off with the wind."

"I presume he subsequently fell to his death."

"Not exactly. Once the bag was inflated, he instructed the Matambans to push the basket, and himself, off the precipice. Naturally, it immediately began to plummet into the depths. The balloon slowed his descent sufficiently that he survived the fall, although I did not learn that fact until several weeks later, when we began the trek back to the coast. Our path took us quite close to the base of the falls and then to a nearby village where we hoped to hire additional bearers. Much to my surprise, I learned that Blackwell was still alive, although both legs had been broken and his other injuries were so severe that he was confined to a pallet and was not expected to live long."

"I felt obligated to look in upon him, but I wish that I had not. He was clearly on his deathbed, feverish, disoriented, and in evident pain. He recognized me and attempted to carry on a conversation, but it was soon apparent that his mind could no longer concentrate on his immediate surroundings and that he had retreated into a fantasy world. He insisted at one point that animals changed their form over time and that elephants and such did not exist during the age of the great reptiles. We know from the fossil record that this is not true – the reptiles lived three to four thousand years ago and their bones have been found mixed with those of contemporary animals so we can be absolutely certain that they existed simultaneously. Since the Earth is only a bit more than four millennia old, there would not be time for such gradual changes as Blackwell suggested even if such transformation was possible."

"The poor man's mind was probably deranged by pain and the imminence of death."

"So I believe. As it happened, he passed on the same day. In an odd way, he struck me as quite civilized and I arranged that he be given a decent burial rather than be administered to in the usual native fashion."

"That was very thoughtful of you. I have always sensed an air of nobility in you despite your humble origins." Artemus realized that Miss Harrington had succumbed to the influence of the wine. Her words were not just inappropriate; they were perceptibly slurred.

He managed a reasonably graceful departure, pleading the press of business. Miss Harrington could make only a token protest since he was, for all practical purposes, employed by her father. Enoch Harrington remained determined to see his daughter married to someone of her own or higher station and Artemus Shaw, although a useful and not disreputable person, was simply not suitable. Artemus, for his part, agreed with the other man's aims, if not for the same reasons. He frankly considered Winifred Harrington unattractive and intellectually challenged despite her expensive education, and was much happier in her absence than in her presence.

But he was also fully cognizant of the advantages of her affection. Her father was more than willing to subsidize his explorations in order to prevent a socially compromising situation. He had already agreed to finance a new expedition and Artemus was anxious to be off on his next great adventure. The long sought entrance to the interior of the hollow Earth had finally been located and he hoped to be one of the first to penetrate into its mysterious depths.

# PERSONAL WEATHER

Nathan Melville woke up on a sultry morning with that feeling of building pressure in the air that heralded the arrival of a warm front. This was not in any way remarkable because he woke to those same sensations every morning and had done so since his birth on August 23, twenty five years earlier. It was his personal weather and he would never know another.

He showered and ate a quick breakfast, then completed one more completely unnecessary tidying up of his apartment. The impression he made tonight could shape his entire life from this point forward. Everything had to be perfect. Satisfied, or at least unable to find any further improvements to make, Nathan glanced at his watch, realized he might miss his bus if he didn't hurry, and hastily left for work.

Nathan reached the corner just as the bus was coming to a stop. The regulars were there. Old Mrs. March had her umbrella, but her intermittent showers had receded for the moment. Not so Mr. Velikowsky, whose galoshes were stained with mud. And Betty Andrews, who had rather a pretty face, was bundled up as securely as ever in her anorak, scarf, and gloves. Nathan had often wondered if her figure matched her face, but unfortunately he had never seen her unencumbered by layers of heavy clothing.

As always Nathan sat on the summer side of the bus, avoiding the rainy section at the rear. He'd barely avoided joining them because the warm front had been rising rapidly when his mother began to have contractions and if it had not been such a short labor he would have been born during the torrential downpour that followed.

He half dozed during the fifteen minute ride and almost forgot to get off at his stop. The two block walk to Webley Associates restored him somewhat and he waved a hello to Gloria, the receptionist, whom he had considered asking out on more than one occasion. Nathan had made a point of talking to her for a few moments each morning before taking the elevator to the eleventh floor and he knew a great deal about Gloria's family, hobbies, hopes and fears. They had talked about virtually everything except the weather. No one, of course, ever spoke about the weather. She'd been born during a July heat wave and wore only the minimum required and Nathan found her quite attractive.

Gloria was busy dealing with a visitor whose face was obscured by a small bank of fog. It was just as well. Nathan walked quickly to the elevator. He did not want to speak to her today, however innocently. It somehow felt like a potential disloyalty to Evelyn and today of all days he would avoid anything that might spoil the consummation of their relationship. He recognized several of the other occupants in the elevator by sight though not by name - none worked in Accounting - and he nodded courteously to the heavy set woman who was shedding melting snowflakes from her hair and shoulders.

Arriving at the eleventh floor, Nathan followed the familiar route to the Fair Weather office, relaxing as he entered its untroubled environs. There was neither formality nor seasonal segregation here and there was the usual variety of short and long sleeved shirts, sweaters and tank tops, culottes and skirts and corduroys and denim. His closest office friend, Bob Riley, greeted him briefly as he breezed by, his long hair fluttering. It was comfortable here and the weather remained fairly consistent from one end of the large room to the other.

Nathan occasionally had to visit the Foul Weather office, a task he found distinctly unpleasant. He had slipped on an ice slick on one occasion and he didn't know how anyone could concentrate amidst the sounds of rain and sleet and with constant winds stirring any papers that weren't securely fastened down. The drains in the floor siphoned off most of the runoff but there was a perpetual chill dampness in the air that he found depressing.

His in-box was half filled so Nathan spent the first hour reading, sorting, and prioritizing. He glanced at the clock every few minutes, but it seemed to move with painful slowness toward mid-morning. Conscientious as always, he would never indulge his personal whims on company time, but when his fifteen minute coffee break was due, he immediately forgot about incorrect invoices and missing purchase order numbers and his hands flew to the keyboard where he quickly sent a personal message – not a violation of company policy so long as one did not abuse the privilege.

ARE WE STILL ON FOR TONIGHT? He waited impatiently for the few seconds required before Evelyn's response appeared on his screen.

OF COURSE. I'VE BEEN LOOKING FORWARD TO THIS ALL WEEK.

ME TOO.

IS THERE ANYTHING I SHOULD BRING?

ONLY YOUR LOVELY SELF.

FLATTERY WILL GET YOU EVERYWHERE.

They had never met in the flesh, although they'd exchanged pictures and even brief videos. Their friendship had grown intellectually passionate very quickly after they'd decided that they were meteorologically compatible. Nathan was late August and Evelyn was early September, and both were born on fair weather days. June and December romances rarely worked out.

Nathan was about to respond when a priority message appeared requesting his immediate presence in Mr. Mallory's office. This was not an auspicious sign. No one ever really enjoyed a chat with Mr. Mallory, no matter how innocuous. His blustery personality perfectly matched his personal weather since he'd been born at the height of Hurricane Indira. Necessarily he had a private office and he arrived and departed from the building at odd hours and used the executive elevator to avoid scattering printouts, coffee cups, pencils, and paperclips by the wind of his passage.

Mallory was fortunate in that he had married into the Webley family, hence his initial appointment as Human Climate Relations Manager. When Ada Webley had given birth to a daughter while a line of tornadoes was passing through Wichita, it had been assumed that young Adalina would never marry, but she'd met Edwin Mallory at the Blowhard Club and it had been love at first gust. Tto be fair, he'd done a creditable job in his first position with the firm. He had brokered a compromise between the Indian Summer and First Frost factions on the Autumn level over thermostat settings and he'd eased the pressure from the Equal Employment Office by devising a containment system that allowed the company to employ those born during blizzards and hail storms, though full integration was still problematic. His promotion to junior partner was as much due to merit as to his family connections.

Although his break was not over Nathan rose and walked directly to the elevator. Mallory was on the 14$^{th}$ floor with the other executives, each of whom had a custom designed office. The Webleys, father and son, were fortunate in having drawn their first breaths during pleasant weather, but Clement Jefferson had been born while his family was in North Africa and his office had to be constantly humidified, although some semblance of equilibrium had been established by hiring a secretary born on an extremely humid afternoon.

He entered Mallory's outer office and nodded to Miss Weems. "He wants to see me." He broke out in a sweat, not his nerves but simply proximity to Miss Weems.

Miss Weems had a perfectly clear desktop and the intercom was built in so that it couldn't blow off onto the floor when Mallory came in or went out. She announced him and glanced toward the door. "Go right in."

For reasons of safety, it was a sliding door. Nathan slipped inside and grasped the handrail immediately as the wind pressed him back the way he had come. "Sorry to bother you, Melville, but I couldn't do this by messaging. Company policy. Security, and all that." Mallory was shouting to be heard and Nathan nodded to indicate he understood, while pulling himself along the rail to the nearest chair.

"Better use the seatbelt," suggested Mallory. "I think I've cycled up to Category IV again. Damned inconvenient. We're having a dinner party tonight. Adalina will be furious if we have to cancel."

Even belted in, Nathan felt better once he had grasped the armrests. Mallory had a decided updraft today. "What can I do for you, sir?"

"I need you to run a small errand for me. For the company, I mean. There's a car waiting in the motorpool. You have a driver's license, don't you?"

"Yes, sir." He'd been shouting and it sounded unnaturally loud. The wind had suddenly dropped dramatically.

"Ah, that's better. Tranquilizers help for some reason. I hope to be down to Category II by this evening."

"What is it that you want me to do, sir?" His voice was only slightly elevated now and he even raised one hand from the armrest to brush his hair out of his eyes.

"There's a bundle of financial statements waiting in the mail room. Very confidential statements. They need to be delivered to Edward Polson of Polson Associates at one o'clock precisely. I trust that you will keep this information to yourself."

Nathan nodded. So the rumors of a merger, or at least talks concerning a merger, were true. "They may have some questions. Feel free to answer them fully but don't volunteer any information. Is that clear?"

"Yes, sir. Why me, sir?"

"Because I was asked to find someone trustworthy. I like you, Melville. You mind your own business and do accurate work. You're not just a fair weather friend."

"I do my best, sir."

"Well, hop to it then. And when you're done, take the rest of the day off."

The company car was fitted with all the amenities since it was driven by multiple individuals with multiple requirements. He closed the floor drains and turned on the air conditioner, put the infrared goggles – for fogbound drivers – into the glove compartment, used the seatbelt but not the safety harness, and swiveled the hail shield out of the way. The GPS obediently brought up the location and quickest route to Polson Associates and he was on his way.

Traffic was heavy and it took Nathan longer than expected to reach his destination. He still had some time to kill and he was ravenously hungry, but his options were very limited. There were fewer restaurants in this part of the city and those that weren't part of chains targeted a specialized clientele. Hell Freezes Over catered to the winter crowd, and served mostly hot food, and the Rainforest, which seated its customers under hoods, looked dreary and uninviting. There was a Windy's and a McDowell's Golden Rainbows but he wasn't in the mood for either, nor did he care for the atmosphere in the Hard Rain Cafe. He finally settled for a burger at Chilly's, wishing he'd thought to bring a sweater.

Ten minutes before he was due, Nathan presented himself to the receptionist in the lobby, a fair weather person, and he was presently sent up to the fourth floor where an attractive woman was waiting for him. She conducted him to a meeting room where, after a very short wait, he was joined by Edward Polson. Nathan found himself involuntarily leaning away as they shook hands, and adjusted his footing. Polson had not been born in a hurricane but he was definitely brisk.

Polson began skimming the paperwork and asked a steady stream of questions, most of which Nathan was able to answer. Polson had a reputation for being longwinded but he was uncharacteristically terse. After perhaps an hour, Polson placed the paperwork in his own briefcase. "Please thank Mr. Mallory for me. My people will review these promptly." They shook hands and Nathan left.

The rest of the afternoon should have been simple. Nathan would return the company car, then take the bus home to his building. The extra time would enable him to go over his apartment one more time, just to make absolutely certain that everything was perfect for tonight. He didn't really think they'd progress to sex upon first meeting – although they'd known each other virtually for almost a year – but it was a possibility that he would not discount.

Unfortunately, he ran into difficulties on the way back. He was forced to make a wide detour around the city center because a group of radical weather integrationists had staged an unannounced but well organized demonstration in front of city hall. Gather enough person sized blizzards together and you could quickly accumulate enough snow to block thoroughfares, and a smattering of strategically placed sleeters and hailers made it difficult for police to respond effectively. Nathan listened to reports on the radio as he waited in heavy traffic, and grew annoyed at the prankish nature of the protest, which was more likely to annoy people than to gain any sympathy. From his vantage point he watched as a contingent of hot weather protestors pushed their way into an ice cream shop and began melting all of its wares. According to the news reports, a handful of miniature hurricanes had broken out of the battened down section of city hall and were running through corridors and offices, sending paperwork and other debris flying in every direction.

By the time Nathan reached Webley and finished turning in the vehicle, it was almost his normal quitting time and he sulked on the way home, feeling sorry for himself. He was in fact so preoccupied that he realized he'd forgotten to buy champagne for the evening. The only package store within walking distance was Tisdale's, and he hated going there. Tisdale had been born under heavy overcast and the gloomy interior of his store always depressed Nathan. There was no alternative, however, and when he finally entered his apartment, he'd lost a good deal of his enthusiasm for the evening.

It returned quickly as time passed. He began to feel nervous, checked his appearance in a mirror several times, and tried to gauge the stability of his current weather. There was a certain degree of variation, particularly when one was born during unsettled conditions, but most people were not conscious of these fluctuations. Determined to make as good an impression as possible, Nathan fiddled with the apartment thermostat incessantly, and was in fact doing just that when the doorbell rang.

Gathering his wits, Nathan answered the door. She looked just as good in person as in video, better in fact, and he paused a second to look at her before he remembered his manners, stepped back and invited her in.

Evelyn had brought a bottle of wine, which she held out to him. "I couldn't just come empty handed."

There was a tiny crackle as their fingers touched. Literally. Both of them jumped backward.

"It must be static electricity," said Nathan, laughing nervously. "It happens all the time."

"Of course." Evelyn smiled and looked around. "I love your apartment."

Nathan was absurdly pleased. "It's kind of small. I'm looking for one with two bedrooms." He opened the wine and poured two glasses. When he handed one to Evelyn, their fingers brushed together but this time there was no sparkle of electric current. There was, however, a faint rumble.

"Oh dear," said Nathan. "I think we may have a problem. May I take your hand a moment?"

"Why certainly." She smiled and they clasped hands. Nathan thought it one of the happiest moments of his life.

There was another rumble, louder and longer this time, and a faint flash of light.

"Oh dear," said Evelyn this time, withdrawing her hand. "That's never happened before."

Nathan sighed. "There must have been a cold front the day you were born."

Evelyn looked mildly uneasy. It was not good manners to talk about the weather. "I believe that's true," she said at last. "Does it matter?"

Nathan considered the consequences of a meeting of warm and cold fronts for only a second, then smiled with all the charm he could muster. "Not at all. Might I kiss you?"

"I believe you might." And he did. And there was a brighter flash of light and the smell of ozone and all of the apartment lights went out at once.

Theirs would be a stormy relationship.

# KONAN THE TRUCKDRIVER

The air conditioner was spitting out warm air again, so the burly, blonde headed man driving the truck pounded his fist against the underside of the dashboard repeatedly until there was a click and a sudden puff that was almost comfortably cool. Fortunately, the hottest part of the day was over and once the sun disappeared behind the distant mountains, the temperature would drop dramatically. After unloading his freight in Aquilonia, he would have to look up the thaumaturgist, Freon, and pay him for a new chilling charm.

An exit sign appeared in the distance and Konan narrowed his eyes, trying to bring it into focus as quickly as possible, easing up on the accelerator. He could read, after a fashion, but it was a laborious process and if he didn't pay attention, he'd pass the exit before he'd sounded out all of the words. Not that he really needed to. He'd driven this particular route so many times that every kilometer was engraved in his memory. The next exit was Route 13 to Kandihar. There was a fueling station and tavern at the foot of the ramp, the Black Goat Inn. He'd stopped there several times in the past. It was a hangout for evil sorcerers and he'd picked fights with so many of them that the owner had taken out a restraining order.

That was all right. There was a rest area only a few minutes further up the road. It would be an early stop for him, but he was ahead of schedule and very thirsty.

The rest area was one of the largest on the Toll Road of Eagles, with an oversized outhouse separate from the Inn and a picnic area complete with roasting spits and a sacrificial altar. He parked his rig under a willow tree and checked his load before entering the Slaughtered Smokie Diner and Tavern. Inside, he let his eyes slowly track back and forth along the row of seats lining the counter before finally choosing one of the few still unoccupied.

"Konan! Long time no see." The counterman smiled broadly, wiping greasy hands down the front of an apron that might once have been white. "What can I get for you?"

Konan shifted his upper body as he mounted one of the seats at the counter, but his shoulders were so broad that they still brushed the customer to his left. A bearded head rose from contemplation of a bowl of muskrat stew and narrow, angry eyes flashed briefly, but their owner seemed to change his mind when Konan leaned forward, placing heavily muscled forearms on the counter. A serpentine dragon was tattooed on the left, running from wrist to elbow, and an elaborately caparisoned sword adorned the right in similar fashion.

"Been doing some contract hauling down in Kush. The pay was pretty good, but it was the same route every day. Nice work for a short hauler just trying to pay the bills but not fit for a real trucker. You know how it is, Zembor." He shrugged elaborately.

"You independent truckers are all alike, Konan. Every time you find a soft berth, you decide it's time to move on. If you'd stayed with Kimmeria Trucking, you'd probably be part owner by now. A guy like you could even marry the top man's daughter, maybe rule the roost yourself some day."

The big man grunted. "More likely I'd be driving a desk. Not even a big desk. Kimmeria's a good company, but there's no future unless you marry into management or kill the owner in a duel. When I get off the road, it's going to be for something worth the effort."

"I heard a rumor you'd taken a job working for Hyrkanian Transport."

Konan made a fist. "That two dinar outfit tried to fine me for late delivery even though the problem was at their end. They overscheduled the loading docks in Iranistan and I had to sit on my ass for half a day before they could take me. But I beat them, by C.R.O.M." He reached into his hip pocket and pulled out a thin, paperback book, slammed it down on the counter. The initials "C.R.O.M." were embossed on the cover, with the full name below in smaller print, "Commercial Roadway Operations Manual".

Zembor nodded understandingly. "The big outfits can be pretty high handed unless you quote the regs. Some of the boys were in here complaining just the other day that Aquilonian Expressways expects its drivers to sleep in their cabs on long hauls now, no more motel chits. And rumor has it they're going to demand a co-payment if you hire a lady for the night."

"Typical." Konan's eyes strayed to the chalked sign posted on the wall behind the counter. "Anyway, I'll have the dragon egg special, with a double side order of sheep's ribs."

"Coming up." Zembor relayed the order to the kitchen, then placed an empty cup in front of Konan and filled it with hot mead.

"You going to be back in Shadizar for a while or just passing through?"

Konan drained the cup lustily and thrust it forward for a refill. "Looking up an old friend. Sonia Redd. Heard she was hauling lumber for Queenie Zhuvana."

For the first time, Zembor appeared mildly uneasy. "Not any more. Things haven't been at their best around here lately, my friend. The palace has had some financial setbacks. Last winter the plumbing froze in the Treasury building. Wouldn't have been so bad except the Vizier had exchanged most of the precious metals and jewels for artwork. You know, tapestries and paintings and whatnot. He said it had a higher rate of appreciation and was less subject to currency fluctuations than gold." Zembor sighed theatrically. "Too bad it wasn't water resistant."

Konan raised an eyebrow. "Tough, but what's that got to do with Sonia?"

The counterman shifted his feet nervously and lowered his voice. "Well, Queenie Zhuvana decreed a whole slew of new taxes. One of them was a mileage levy on commercial haulers and Sonia...well, you know Sonia...she never had much use for governments and rules and that sort of thing. She refused to pay the levy, so they started adding in fines and interest charges, and then she roughed up a couple of bill collectors. I tried to convince her to cooperate or move on, but she's one stubborn lady. Anyway, about a month ago, the Imperial Revenue Squad seized her rig and locked her up. Some of the guys raised bail money and she's out, but without an outfit," he shrugged, "she's out of business."

Storm clouds gathered behind Konan's eyes. "These IRS goons still have her truck then?"

Zembor shook his head. "No, they sold it for back taxes to UPS; that's United Parcels of Shadizar, a new outfit. They moved it to their terminal out west, for repainting and an overhaul before they put it into service."

"And Sonia."

"Living in a small flat downtown." Zembor refilled Konan's cup, speaking with averted eyes. "She's working as an exotic dancer at Caesar's Place."

Konan raised one clenched fist a few inches into the air, then smashed it down with such force that plates and cups jumped along the entire length of the counter, followed by muted complaints that Konan either ignored or never heard. "Such infamy shall not continue," he promised.

Rooms at the Slaughtered Smokie contained only the barest essentials, sleeping mat, chamber pot, and a weapons rack. There was a particularly raucous party underway in the courtyard so Konan decided to purchase a charm of silence from one of the dispensers he'd passed on the way in. Night had fallen with its usual suddenness in the desert, and no one had lit the outside torches yet, so he picked his way carefully across the grounds. As he did so, a flash of light from his right startled him, but when he turned to look, there was nothing there, although he thought he could hear a very faint growling from somewhere in the distance. A lesser man might have dismissed it, but Konan would not have lived so long if he hadn't been overly cautious.

He found the dispenser and fumbled in his belt pouch for an appropriately shaped coin. As he did so, another brief flash appeared on his left, blinked out almost immediately, and this time there was a very distinct grumbling sound, which died off after a second or two. There was a dirk in his belt, but he was acutely aware of the fact that his broadsword and battleaxe were both hanging over the back window of his cab at the opposite end of the parking area.

"They get pretty brazen if we don't light the torches." The voice came from close behind and Konan whirled, dirk out, to confront the source. A wizened man with a long beard and owlish spectacles stood in a pool of moonlight.

"Are you friend or foe?"

The stranger chuckled. "Neither, actually." He raised a hand and one of the sconces mounted on a nearby tree was suddenly filled with flame. "I'm the lamplighter."

Konan remained wary, but he put his weapon away. "What are they?"

Another wave of the arm and another sconce was illuminated. "Werechoppers. There's a whole pack of them living in a hidden garage somewhere. You know how it is. Some dirt biker has an accident, mixes his blood with enchanted transmission fluid, merges his soul with his bike. Attacks the unwary and contaminates them as well. Eventually someone will find the garage and send in a cleanup squad. If we get to them soon enough, a change of engine oil and a blood transfusion solve the problem, but sometimes it's too late and they're sent to the junkyard."

Two more torches ignited. "They won't bother us now, but I wouldn't go for a moonlight stroll. Good night, now."

The following morning, Konan delivered his freight, tied a bulging coin purse to his belt, and drove directly to the center of the town of Lesser Rizah, where he turned left at the main aqueduct and followed the watercourse into a rundown neighborhood whose streets were barely wide enough to accommodate his rig. Zembor had told him that Sonia rented a room at the Twisted Tailpipe Inn, and he found it with no difficulty. He had barely descended from the cab when two slender arms wrapped around most of his body from behind.

"Konan, you old gas guzzler! What're you doing here?"

Sonia must have recognized his rig from the window of her room and had probably come down to meet him because she didn't want him to see the seedy living quarters that were the best she could afford.

"Thought I'd look up an old friend and recall the good times while I was waiting for my next load of cargo." Despite his black mood, Konan's broad features assumed a pleased expression. "You're looking good, Sonia."

Despite the cool of early autumn, Sonia wore nothing but two crimson sashes, one high, one low, her smooth tanned flesh complemented by a long mane of auburn hair. "As are you. Is that a new scar I see?" She gestured with her chin and Konan immediately raised a hand to the short, straight crease on his temple.

"You always had a sharp eye. Got hit with a tire iron in a brawl in Zamora. The other guy looks a lot worse."

"You never could stay out of trouble."

Konan nodded and his smile faded. "I understand you've had some of your own recently."

Sonia nodded. "That I have. C'mon, let's go get ourselves a drink and I'll tell you all about it."

"So that's the situation," she finished a few minutes later. "Even if I could raise enough coin to cover what I originally owed, I couldn't buy back my rig from UPS. They want six sacks of gold coins, or the equivalent, more than I paid for it when it was new."

Konan leaned back so far that his seat wobbled. "Why don't you just take it then? These demon besotted laws don't hold any weight across the border. There's plenty of highway outside of Shadizar."

Sonia shook her head, but uncertainly. "Not yet anyway, but the old rules are changing. Queenie Zhuvana has been talking to her counterparts in Zamora and elsewhere. She's pushing for uniform laws on taxation, criminal justice, and other things. Wants to replace the C.R.O.M. with a more management friendly set of rules. I don't think she'll get her way on every issue, but there has been talk of a treaty on hot pursuit and extradition, and once they accept the principle that laws can extend across borders, it won't be long before the old freedoms are gone."

Konan made a dismissive gesture. "These are heat shimmers on the highway of life, Sonia, distracting but without substance." He slapped the handle of his dirk. "I'll take cold steel over cold print any day."

Laughing, Sonia leaned forward and patted his muscular thigh. "You old teamster, you're one of a kind."

Pleased but slightly embarrassed by the familiarity, Konan rose to his feet and stretched elaborately. "Time's wasting, Sonia. Do you know where they're keeping your rig?"

She finished the last of her beer and scrambled to her feet. "Of course I do, but do you really think this is a good idea? They won't just leave it parked by the roadway."

Konan frowned. "Is this the same Sonia who won the Triple Crown for the Tractor Pull, Demolition Derby, and Long Haul Racing three years running?"

"That was a long time ago," she protested, but her face flushed red. "I was younger then. We both were."

"People like us don't age, Sonia. We're archetypes."

The UPS terminal lurked at the end of a short stretch of dirt road. The weather had been so dry that they couldn't just drive up without advertising their presence with a cloud of dust, so Konan parked his rig behind a stand of tall cactus. He slipped a bright red tool box out of its place under his seat and they set off on foot.

Minutes later, they came within sight of a hurricane fence that stretched as far as they could see in either direction. The fence sparkled with the telltale signs of an alarm spell. Beyond was a complex of buildings, surrounded by clusters of cabs and trailers, all painted a uniform blood red, decorated with a distinctive symbol, crossed tailpipes with hood ornament rampant. There was no sign of life, but it was Sunday and they had counted on the terminal being deserted.

There was, however, a large sign attached to the fence.

## **WARNING! NO ADMITTANCE! GUARD DRAGON ON DUTY.**

Konan walked directly to one of the corner posts. From his toolbox he took a small goatskin pouch, removed a pinch of finely granulated dust, and tossed it onto the fence. Almost instantly, the twinkling of the alarm spell faded to nothing in a space wide enough for even Konan's broad shoulders. Satisfied, he grabbed the mesh with both hands, the bulging muscles in his arms knotting with effort as he exerted force along two different vectors, ripping the wire from its frame.

" If they've repainted your rig already, we'll have Baal's time finding it."

She shook her head. "I don't think they've had time. The day they moved it out of town, the AFLCIO went on strike, and they wouldn't dare work on it with non-Union labor. Their drivers would walk out in sympathy."

Konan frowned and glanced a question in her direction.

"The AFLCIO, you know, the Apprentices, Faith Healers, Levitators, and Clairvoyants Interkingdom Organization. No one is allowed to practice low level magic without a union card except full fledged wizards and sorcerers, and none of them would take on such a menial task as immortalizing paint jobs. I suppose they could have just painted it without the magic, but then they'd have to touch it up every time it weathered a little."

They were well inside the compound now, and Konan instinctively headed for the largest of the buildings, the one most likely to conceal a full rig from casual view. They were in fact very close to their goal when the guard dragon spotted them.

It was actually quite small as dragons go, barely ten meters in length; Konan had dispatched much larger specimens on numerous occasions, armed only with his short sword. But on this particular day, luck was not on his side. As the dragon roared and charged, Konan dropped the toolbox and drew his blade, stepping away from Sonia so that he wouldn't inadvertently wound her, but one foot came down on an oil slick. He threw up both arms in a desperate attempt to maintain his balance, and the back of his free hand struck Sonia under the chin, knocking her flat on her back, unconscious. The short sword slid out of his grasp and described a small arc before striking the ground and bouncing to one side, out of reach beneath a parked truck.

Fortunately, Konan's fall caught the dragon by surprise and the massive jaws closed with a cruel snap but on empty space. Konan rolled to his left, then scrambled past a clawed foot and out into the open.

Generally dragons aren't particularly bright, and this one was no exception. The giant reptile worked its jaws furiously, trying to chew the victim it had not yet realized was elsewhere. Konan sprang to his feet and waited for its next charge, and when the pointless mauling of empty space continued unabated, he finally had to resort to shouting to draw its attention.

Plainly confused but still game, the dragon turned slowly and arched its neck, preparing for a fresh lunge. This time Konan was better prepared. He ducked under the strike in a controlled roll that ended when he reached the toolbox. He flipped the catch and turned it over in a single movement, so that all of its contents were spilled across the sand.

Even the dumbest dragon catches on eventually, and this time it relocated its elusive quarry without assistance. Sand crunched as it advanced, determined to skewer Konan with those many, needle sharp teeth. Konan, however, had found what he was looking for, and he stood up just as the jaws opened. With both hands he thrust upward with his new weapon, bracing himself against the impact.

The dragon gave a strangled roar of rage as the truck jack between its jaws prevented it from devouring its prey. The massive head tossed so violently that Konan lost his grip and staggered back. Then blood lust rose in his mighty breast and Konan charged across the sand, lug wrench in one hand, tire pressure gauge in the other, screaming a battle cry at the top of his lungs. Leaping between those rows of teeth, he drove the sharp end of the wrench up through the roof of the mouth, twisting and pushing until it penetrated the creature's tiny brain, while his other hand drove one end of the pressure gauge repeatedly into a huge, gleaming, multifaceted eye. With a roar that was half rage, half dismay, the scaled monstrosity reared up, then fell back heavily, still alive but immobilized by pain.

It lay there panting, still pawing at its muzzle, while Konan helped a very groggy Sonia to her feet. She was able to walk unassisted by the time they entered the large building and her expression brightened as she spotted the familiar scarlet embellishments of her rig, parked at the opposite end.

"We'll be across the border before they know it's gone," Konan assured her, climbing into the passenger side of the cab as she reached under the dash and located her invisible spare ignition key.

"Let's just hope they haven't been working on her engine." But it caught on the first attempt and the locked gate didn't even slow them down.

Back at the main road, Sonia brought the truck to a stop alongside Konan's, then leaned over and kissed him fervently on the mouth before he realized what was happening. When she finally broke off, his pulse was racing.

"We shouldn't use the Crystal Band Radio until we're across the border. There might be a communications wizard monitoring the psychic waves and he could triangulate us."

"Where do you think we should meet?" Her eyes promised things her mouth hadn't spoken of.

"I thought Zingara. Rumor has it there's work hauling supplies out into the marshes. King Zoltan is building himself an Indian Summer Palace." And with a heated look that matched her own, he climbed into the cab.

The two trucks moved in tandem toward the Zingaran troll booths, their drivers already anticipating a less eventful term of employment.

Of course, they had no way of knowing that the king of Zingara had just been overthrown by minions of the evil sorcerer, Sidereal Distress, but that's another story.

# THE LIBRARY OF LOST ART

"All art consists of dreams given substance," my uncle told me during that wonderful summer when I briefly shared his home. "The best of it transcends the artist and takes on a life of its own."

I often wonder why he let me have a free hand in his library at such an early age. Perhaps it was because he'd never entertained even an overnight visitor prior to my arrival, and the sudden responsibility of sheltering and amusing an eleven year old boy must have caught him completely unprepared.

I wasn't exactly thrilled myself, although my mother assured me she would complete the assignment in Zurich in time for me to return to my regular school in the fall. I tried to view my temporary living arrangements as an adventure, but the prospect of spending three months in western Connecticut, which was after all even more provincial and therefore boring than Providence, did little to stimulate my imagination or my interest.

I had nothing against Uncle Dan, but I had nothing for him either. As far as I was aware, he'd only visited on two occasions, once to attend my father's funeral, and the only impression that remained was of a tall man in very dark clothing who spoke slowly and with a very deep voice.

My mother must have apologized a dozen times before letting me board the bus in Providence. She'd originally planned to drive me to Uncle Dan's, but the date of the initial conference had been moved forward and time conspired against us. I kept telling her not to worry, that I liked the idea of travelling by myself for the first time, but she insisted that I was a "brave boy" for trying to reassure her and that I shouldn't be frightened because the bus driver would help me if I had a problem.

The only "problem" I had was trying not to look too bored when the woman in the next seat insisted on telling me all about her grandchildren, illustrated liberally with pictures she kept in her bag. But I was determined that nothing should interfere with the pleasure of sudden freedom, and I did my best to act as I thought an adult might if caught in the same situation.

Uncle Dan had agreed to meet me in Tutford, and I had strict instructions to wait patiently until I was claimed. Mom's caution was unnecessary; I recognized him the instant I set foot off the bus, a tall, thin man with short black hair in a very dark suit, standing just inside the terminal door. He looked uncomfortable and out of place, and when he caught sight of me, the expression on his face was a blend of anxiety and relief.

"You're my nephew John, I believe. Or do you prefer Johnny or Jack?"

"John will be fine, sir."

"Then John it is. Shall we go?"

I pulled the baggage check from my pocket and held it up, a red and white strip of cardboard. He stared but made no move to take it, seemed to be waiting for me to explain further.

"It's my baggage check."

"Oh, of course." Uncle Dan, as I soon discovered, was woefully ignorant of the practicalities of everyday life.

The drive to his house should have consumed an hour, but took closer to two. His elderly Studebaker appeared sound, but I could tell the engine was laboring. The novelty of riding in what I recognized as a very old car wore off quickly, as did the scenery. I mean, how many picturesque farm houses and fields can you look at without getting bored?

Uncle Dan's home was a sprawling farmhouse so remote that as far as I was concerned, he had no neighbors at all. Certainly none within easy walking distance. The house was elderly but had been freshly painted and appeared to be in good repair. Adjacent and linked by a glass enclosed patio was a huge, modern barn, obviously of much more recent construction than the house. That seemed odd to me even before we got out of the car, because Mom had told me Uncle Dan wrote essays and poems for a living. Even to my unpracticed eye, it was obvious that the nearby fields were completely overgrown. There was no livestock, no farm equipment, and judging by the untrimmed rosebushes bordering the front of the house, it didn't appear that Uncle Dan did any gardening at all.

We each took one of my suitcases, and a minute later were inside. The front door hadn't been locked, and Uncle Dan later told me he didn't even own a key. "If someone wants to get in that badly, they'll do it anyway, so what's the use?"

It was like walking into a museum. The front room was filled with works of art, mostly paintings and sculptures, in bronze, clay, blown glass, carved wood, and every other medium imaginable. Some of the pieces were "found art", that is, images assembled from pre-existing objects like nails and belt buckles and small tools and stuff. The walls were covered from the chair rail to the ceiling, the individual frames interlaced like an intricate mosaic, with no space wasted. I couldn't even tell what color the wall might be underneath; it was nowhere visible.

Sculptured forms stood or lay on free standing shelving units, small tables and platforms. They ran the gamut from representational to surreal, as did the paintings and etchings. The disparate images were overwhelming not only in number but in variety. There was no segregation by school or subject matter or color or technique; cubist geometries were flanked by pointillist abstracts and surreal landscapes.

"Your room's this way."

I was too awestruck to respond, but I followed him up a broad stairway to the second floor and down a long corridor to a room that was four times the size of my bedroom back home. All of the walls we passed were similarly covered. An elaborately detailed representational landscape stood at the head of my bed, a skeletal church hovered in mid-air on the adjoining wall, and an armored knight wrestled with a red eyed dragon just opposite.

"We can swap some of the painting's around if you'd like. There are plenty to choose from."

Which was the understatement of the day, but I replied in as level a voice as I could manage, trying to sound mature and sophisticated. "No, these are just fine."

I didn't actually see the library until that evening. It was already late in the afternoon and by the time I'd gotten unpacked and arranged my clothes and things the way I wanted them, Uncle Dan was back asking me if I had any preference for supper.

I shrugged. "I can eat pretty much anything except broccoli."

"It's not one of my favorites either."

While he'd been speaking, his eyes slowly scanned the room, probably to see if I'd done anything to change the aesthetics. He spotted the neat row of paperbacks I'd lined up on the dresser, and without a word brushed past me and leaned forward, head tilted to one side. "Salinger, Baldwin, Sturgeon, Barth, Mrozek. I must say, my sister has cultivated excellent taste in you, John."

"Yeah, well, she doesn't really think I should be spending so much time reading. She's worried I'm going to miss out on being a kid or something."

"Well, then we won't mention to her the Selby and Miller titles. Somehow I don't think Alice would approve."

I flushed, having forgotten that I'd included those from my secret collection of books Mom would be happier not knowing about.

That first supper is still vivid in my memory. Uncle Dan set out a big salad made with fresh greens including raw spinach, with big white mushrooms cut in slices, pitted black olives, chunks of two or three different kinds of cheese, sprinkles of bacon, sliced radish red and white, and long thin strips of different colored peppers, red, green, yellow, and orange.

"A proper meal is a work of art in itself," he assured me.

He mixed the dressing in a decanter and it was sweet and spicy and so good I could almost have eaten it alone. Then he cooked up little cubes of beef with chopped carrots and onions and potatoes and leeks and some other vegetables in an oversized skillet and served it over fresh brown rice. It was the best meal I'd ever eaten. I loved my mother very much, but cooking was never numbered among her skills. An elaborate meal at home was having more than one vegetable with the meat course.

We didn't talk much while we ate. My mouth was too busy testing all those exotic nuances of taste and texture and I think Uncle Dan was still uncertain how to deal with me. He had seemed to relax a bit after seeing the books on my dresser, and I suppose I thought at the time he was just relieved to see I had something to do to keep me out of his hair.

"Would you like to see the library?"

We'd just finished eating and he was putting away the leftovers. The main course was completely gone; he'd cooked just exactly the right amount. "Sure."

He guided me to a sliding glass door, then through the enclosed patio I'd noticed earlier to a solid, wooden door. "I don't keep this locked, but it's best left shut, to keep the humidity out."

A moment later, I was in a dream world. The walls of the barn were lined with shelving from floor to ceiling, two and a half stories above, and there were freestanding units marshalled in tight ranks across the floor. A wrought iron spiral staircase led up to a mezzanine, and both levels were fitted with those sliding, vertical ladders that let you move them to wherever you need to climb to reach a particular book. There were paintings and sculpture here as well, but mostly larger pieces arranged on easels wherever there was enough open space. In one corner stood an enormous desk, and just to one side, a large screen television with a VCR.

"Awesome," I breathed. The rear wall was so impossibly far away, I couldn't believe this was the same building I'd seen earlier.

"Yes," he said softly. "It is that."

I walked around the perimeter, reading names off the spines of the books. Titles I'd never heard of, thousands of them, but many of the authors were familiar, even favorites -- J.G. Ballard, Carson McCullers, Ibsen, Eliot, and Faulkner, novels, short stories, essays, plays, and poetry. After a few minutes, I realized I had not yet seen a single title that I'd read, and the sheer volume overwhelmed me.

"Feel free to borrow anything you'd like to read. Just be sure to return everything when you're done. Most of these are very rare editions."

Rarer even than I imagined. I passed *When You Care, When You Love* by Theodore Sturgeon, *Whispers of War* by Ernest Hemingway, and a set of plays by Shakespeare that included *Love's Labour Regained* and *Simon of Syracuse*. While I browsed, Uncle Dan touched a switch on the wall and an unfamiliar orchestral piece reverberated through the room, one which I later learned was Beethoven's Tenth Symphony. Several times I reached out to select a volume, *The Compleat and Wondrous Narrative of A. Gordon Pym* by Edgar Allen Poe, *The Hampshire Horror* by Saki, *Crimes and Chaos* by Avram Davidson, or Jules Verne's *The Wonderful Journey to Mars*, but each time my fingers hovered, then moved to another shelf.

"You'll be here all summer, you know," Uncle Dan said softly, and with a note of quiet amusement. And sympathy as well; I could sense it distinctly. We'd only been together a few hours, but there was already a resonance between us that was beyond anything my eleven year old mind could reduce to words. "There's plenty of time."

He was standing beside a convoluted piece of sculpture that reminded me of a Moebius Strip, something called "Internal and External Forms" by Henry Moore. "The first version," he told me several days later, when I asked about it. "Moore was dissatisfied and had it destroyed, then started over from scratch."

"If it was destroyed, how did it get here?" I asked. Uncle Dan just smiled mysteriously, his usual response to questions he didn't care to answer.

You might imagine that we had little in common, an aging bachelor and a precocious youngster. He spent the mornings writing in his study, using an old fashioned manual typewriter whose keys were so worn that the finished copy invariably looked smudged no matter how carefully he handled it. I spent that time reading, and around noon we'd have a light lunch, then talk for a while, usually in the library.

"Did you buy all of this?" According to my mother, Uncle Dan just barely scraped by financially.

"No, John. None of what you see could be bought or sold. It's beyond value."

"Then where did it all come from?" I flushed, afraid I was being impertinent.

He was silent a moment before answering, and I had a sense that I was about to share in a great secret. "Art is alive, John, and like any other living thing drawn to those who truly welcome it."

Sometimes we played chess using a set sculpted by Max Ernst, sitting in front of a panorama from Paul Klee's "Scenes from the Botanical Gardens". Although paintings had never previously interested me, I soon learned to distinguish between Leger and Braques, developed respect for the subtlety of Seurat, and puzzled over the emotions in Edvard Munch's woodcuts.

At other times we watched classic films, like Lon Chaney's 1927 silent horror movie, *London After Midnight*. That one I'd heard of at least, although I didn't know any copies had survived. But there were others whose titles and casts amazed me, with stars like Bogart and Karloff and Garbo and Fay Wray.

"If you didn't buy any of this, where did it all come from?" I asked once, after we'd just finished viewing a 1931 version of *Frankenstein* with Bela Lugosi playing the monster.

"Here and there." Uncle Dan was always vague when I questioned him about the source of his collection.

"But shouldn't they be in a museum or someplace where they couldn't burn up in a fire or something."

Uncle Dan was silent a moment before answering. "Art is immortal, John. It has an existence independent of the physical world. Once a work has been imagined, it can never be destroyed, even if the artist fails to transform thought into action. What has been conceived of, is."

The summer sped past, Mom came home, and before I knew it I was being bundled onto the bus at the Tutford depot.

"You'll have to come back and visit sometime. There are lots of things you haven't read yet, things that deserve to be read by someone who appreciates them." It must have been the light, but it looked as though my uncle's eyes were gleaming in the pale light.

"I will," I promised. It was only one of many promises I never kept.

Mom was transferred to California and we moved during the Christmas holiday. I wrote to Uncle Dan a few times, but the letters kept getting shorter until they would have fit on postcards. He responded to each with long, thoughtful discussions of everything I'd said, but adolescence sneaked up on me when I wasn't looking and while I never lost my fascination for reading, the greater obsession of sex pre-empted it for several years, By the time of my marriage, my only communication with Uncle Dan was a terse note scribbled inside a Christmas card once a year. By the time of my divorce, I wasn't writing to anyone. Not that I blamed Lisa; she was so emotionally committed to motherhood, she just couldn't accept that I was infertile. That wasn't the only problem, of course, but it was the core, and our attempts to deal with the fringe issues only exacerbated the central failure of our relationship.

A year later, my mother and Uncle Dan both died within the space of three months, Mom from undiagnosed cancer, Uncle Dan from an unspecified heart condition.

It was a complete surprise to me to discover that I was his sole heir. The deep sense of loss was even more of a shock.

Although Uncle Dan had diminished to an abstraction, the realization that he was gone forever penetrated the armor of indifference I'd worn since the divorce. I am not embarrassed to say that I cried as much upon learning of his death as I did when my mother passed away.

After several lengthy telephone conversations with the lawyers in Tutford, I decided to fly back east and close out Uncle Dan's affairs personally. That night, I woke in the hours just preceding dawn, realizing that there was nothing to keep me on the West Coast any longer. Lisa and I were quits, Mom was dead and buried, and the job I was holding at Lewis Aerotech was boring and a professional dead end.

I handed in my resignation later that day and arranged for the proceeds from my profit sharing to be mailed to me at the Connecticut address.

If I had any concrete plans for my life when I boarded the plane for the flight east, they were a secret even from me. I had some vague idea of selling off part or all of my uncle's property in order to support myself while I looked for a new job, but frankly I wasn't certain what I wanted to do with the rest of my life. In Tutford, when I realized that as literary executor of my uncle's estate I would be able to live modestly on that income, it was a revelation that verged on the religious.

In my uncle's study, I learned that he had inherited the property himself, forty years earlier, from a woman named Claiborne. Pamela Claiborne had eked out a precarious living writing advertising jingles while trying unsuccessfully to interest someone in the elaborate symphonies she had composed. The name was familiar, however, and when I checked the library, I found several recordings of her work.

I moved into the farmhouse and decided to see if the novels and stories I had bottled up inside could be coaxed forth. I used my uncle's aging, manual typewriter, and the manuscripts always looked smudged no matter how careful I was.

The years passed with surprising swiftness. Every so often, a new title would appear on a shelf, or a new painting on some previously vacant section of wall. I never saw how they arrived, and surprisingly enough, lost any interest in that knowledge very early.

Suffice it to say, the collection continued to provide a haven for those works which deserved to be included.

I sold a few stories during the next decade, but to no great critical or reader acclaim. After four years, *Dangerous Dreams* was completed and started making the rounds of publishing houses. Sometimes the rejections which followed were brusque: "Not suited to our program." Sometimes they were sympathetic: "Fascinating but not commercially viable". Rejection followed rejection, fourteen in all over the course of the next decade.

I celebrated my forty-fifth birthday today by sitting and rereading the only novel I have ever completed. It was returned a week ago, with deep regrets and considerable admiration according to the editor at Proscenium Press. "In another time, I'd be proud to publish this fine work, but contemporary tastes being what they are..." There are still places I could send it, both commercial and university publishing houses. But I won't. I know now that it will remain unpublished.

I was walking in the library first thing this morning, searching for something to read, and my eyes trailed past *Three More Lives* by Gertrude Stein, *Potpourri Planet* by Stanley Weinbaum, and *The Teapot Testament* by Charles Dickens. And there, in among the books I'd set aside to read, was *Dangerous Dreams* by John Cosgrove.

I am content that the child of my imagination has been judged and accepted by whatever profound powers decide these things. When the time comes for me to pass the custodianship on to my successor, whoever he or she might be, I hope that it will at last find an appreciative audience.

I moved it to another shelf, though, and now it sits next to *Wavering Images*, the collection of poems Uncle Dan had just started to write when he passed away.

We are best judged by the company we keep.

# THE SEEDS OF SAFARIAN

When Niki and Aly decided to abandon their farm to the encroaching desert reaching out from Cincor, they had no clear destination in mind.

"Beyond Zhel," Niki told her younger sister. "We'll buy a small farm in Tasuun or perhaps Dhir."

Aly had nodded and made no protest, keeping her doubts secret. Their father had been the last in their village to abandon his holdings in the face of the growing western desert, refusing to relinquish his grip on the land until the coughing sickness took his life. The sisters had begun packing for their trek the same day they buried him, recognizing what their father had refused to accept - that crops could not grow in soil that held too little moisture.

It had been Aly who suggested that they cut their hair and dress as young boys for the trip, for she had heard stories of desperate men turned bandit in the hilly country to their east. As Cincor had fallen to the dust and sand and heat, so also would Zhel and perhaps even Tasuun in its turn. Niki had been reluctant to trim her long hair, preferring to trust to her skill with sword and bow, but Aly had persevered with her usual quiet patience.

They had found it surprisingly easy to part with most of their personal possessions, and the contents of the bundles strapped to the pack beast trailing their mounts were carefully chosen. There was a small stock of gold coin, a few precious gems, bags of seed, and a handful of other items of value. It was with these that Niki hoped to secure a new living for them both. Aly remained skeptical. Their neighbors had long since moved east, and if there had been land available, it would most likely have been snapped up long before. With the blighted land already licking at Zhel's borders, it was probable that the eastward migration had already started there as well, and in fact two years earlier, a traveling tinker had spoken of refugees flocking to Ustaim on the coast. But she had no better suggestion, and in any case was in the habit of following her sister's lead.

The road east was exhausted by the passage of so many feet and so much sand had blown across it in places that they had to look smartly about to avoid losing their way. "Not that it makes much difference," Niki remarked. "With the hills of Zhel marking the horizon, it would take a conscious effort to miss them."

"But we'll miss the wells if we lose the road."

"Such as they are," Niki answered, but she paid more attention to their path thence forward.

They reached the foothills on the sixth day and sheltered in a narrow ravine while a fierce wind threw half the desert in their direction. They resumed their march the following morning, but at a slower pace. The convoluted trail wound perpetually upward and their mounts were more suited for the plow than for long journeys. The sisters rode in silence, neither willing to give voice to their discomfort, both aware of the fact that there would be many more nights spent sleeping in the open, and days riding under the hot sun, before their journey ended.

The attack came on the thirteenth day.

They had passed the unmarked border of Zhel two or perhaps three days previously. Their path had leveled out and wandered through a maze of jagged peaks and dark chasms, their vision frequently obscured by clumps of wizened trees with crooked branches that seemed to be reaching for them as they passed. They were nearly at the bottom of an usually long downslope when Aly spotted something moving at the edge of her vision and heard Niki's short sword rasping against its sheath.

There were two men on their left and two more on the right, each emerging from cover to run toward the two travelers. One weapon showed the glint of metal but the others were all wooden cudgels. The sisters nudged their mounts forward, but more men appeared ahead of them, dragging a coarse net down from above to block the trail. There was a hoarse shout as one of the men closed with Niki and found her not unable to defend herself. He reeled back with a pierced shoulder and fell to one knee.

Aly ducked under an assailant's swing and pinked his arm with her dirk; he retreated a few steps but was clearly not out of the fight.

"Back!" Niki parried another blow with the clang of metal against metal, while Aly wheeled her mount abruptly to the side, knocking a man to the ground. The pack beast tugged at the lead, eyes wide with alarm, as Aly tried to turn its head back the way they'd come. A sudden scream made her heart stop for a moment and she turned to see Niki's mount collapse on its forelimbs, hamstrung by the attacker's blade. Niki leaped to the ground, landed well, and swept her own weapon around to disembowel the swordsman.

At least a half dozen more figures were emerging from hiding, some of them women, all brandishing cudgels. One of them caught the pack beast's lead rope and severed it with a knife. Aly hesitated, then turned her mount again.

"Climb up!"

For a second, Niki seemed more inclined to fight than flee, but there were at least a dozen bandits in sight now, not including the two wounded ones. With a muttered curse, she mounted behind her sister, who immediately urged their mount forward. One of the women snatched up the gutted man's sword and swung at them as they passed, but Aly ignored her and concentrated on escaping back up the steep slope.

Near the top of their rise, their mount missed a step and went down, throwing both riders to the ground. Aly was the first to rise, and the first to see the gaping wound in their mount's side. Then Niki was grabbing her arm.

"Hurry! They're coming after us!"

Aly didn't look back, followed as her sister scrambled up the remainder of the slope. Angry shouts and howls chased them, and when she took a second to glance back, she saw that four of their attackers were in hot pursuit. There was a sudden turn in the trail and they were hidden from sight. Niki darted to one side, into a narrow defile thick with vines that hung down from a jutting promontory. Without hesitation, Aly followed, brushing aside the vines and stumbling forward until they were concealed from their pursuers.

The shouting voices passed by, faded slightly, then returned muttering. Aly clutched her dirk nervously, but no one attempted to explore their hiding place, and eventually all was silent.

"Do you think they're gone?" Aly's whisper was hoarse with tension.

"Maybe." Niki moved for the first time since they'd taken shelter. "Let me take a look."

She slipped through the vines and was gone for only a moment or two. "They've butchered the animals and have a fire going. I think we can get away if we don't make any noise."

"Where can we go?" It was a good question. Without their supplies and on foot, they had no chance at all of reaching their original destination. Game was scarce in the heights, and they'd found water only twice since leaving the lowlands, one stagnant pool covered with greenish scum, and one narrow stream that smelled like metal and tasted worse.

"We can't stay here," Niki answered unnecessarily. And so they went.

They retraced their steps until they felt safely out of the hunting grounds of the bandits, then struck off cross country, hoping to bypass their enemies and find the trail further along. Unfortunately, there was nothing even approximating a clear path, and they had to make so many detours in heavily overgrown country that they became thoroughly lost on the second day. Fortunately, they did find palatable water and Aly managed to stun a tree rabbit with a thrown stone which provided a small but tasty supper.

They slept in the shelter of a jagged rock and woke in the morning to find their arms and legs pockmarked with insect bites that itched furiously until well into the day. Most of the afternoon's progress was wiped out when they found themselves in a narrow culdesac whose walls crumbled into powder when they tried to climb out. They had nothing to eat that day and their only water was what they managed to extract from leaves they chewed as they walked.

The following morning they discovered a valley.

The sun had risen reluctantly, its dull red light barely piercing heavy clouds that hung low in the distance. They were following the ridge of a humpbacked crest when Niki stepped on a stone that turned under her foot and lost her balance. She slid down the bare rockface and ended up in a thorny bush that shredded her left sleeve and scratched her flesh. Aly was looking for some clean, broad leaves with which to swab her sister's arm when she discovered a notch in the rocky barrier surrounding them, beyond which she could see a wedge of lush grassland.

More from curiosity than hope, the sisters slipped through the gap. Their efforts were almost immediately rewarded by the discovery of a small pool of clear water, from which they drank deeply before shedding their clothes and bathing. Aly lashed her dirk to a long pole and speared three fish in the waist deep water, while Niki gathered dry wood for a fire. After they'd eaten, they washed their clothing and napped naked in the sunlight while it dried. They didn't wake until a dozen paralopes came to drink from the pool.

"There's game here, as well as water," Niki observed. "If we can find salt, we could prepare enough meat to last us for a week."

"Better to trap some of them alive. They'll answer to a tether and we can use them to carry skins of water." The paralopes were, unfortunately, not sturdy enough to be ridden.

"Then we'll stay here for a while."

The following morning, they set out to explore the valley. It was narrow enough that they could see both sides from anywhere within its confines, but much deeper than they had expected. By midday they still had no idea where it ended. And by shortly after mid-day they knew they were not alone.

They found a cultivated field.

The ground had leveled out and the low scrub growth that covered much of the valley was thinning. They walked around a stand of wide boled trees and saw ahead of them neat squares of crops both familiar and unfamiliar, grains and vegetables and fruits all planted in neatly tended rows. The sisters exchanged looks but neither spoke as they continued to approach.

From closer proximity, they could see further squares, some of which had been tilled but not yet seeded. Aly approached one of these and crouched, running her fingers through the soil.

"It's just as dry as back home," she remarked with considerable puzzlement. "How can they grow so well?"

"They must irrigate." But even as Niki spoke, she was observing the absence of any visible signs of such activity. "Underground pipes, maybe."

Aly rose and brushed off her hands, then crossed to another square where beetwheat grew in sheathed stalks higher than her head. Here she thrust her fingers into the ground again, digging a small trough with her hand. "Nothing. The ground is completely dry. How can they grow plants without water?"

Niki had been staring into the distance as her sister spoke and now her lips thinned and she drew her sword. Immediately sensing danger, Aly scrambled to her feet and placed a hand on the hilt of her smaller weapon.

In the distance, something was moving in their direction. It was half hidden by the intervening brush, but enough of it was visible for them to discern its shape. It appeared to be a malformed spider with a massive central body studded by entirely too many legs. At first it seemed to be heading directly toward them, but as the gap narrowed they realized its course was slightly offset, that it was headed toward one of the as yet unproductive squares. Still cautious, they moved closer and noticed for the first time that only six of its many limbs touched the ground. The others terminated in three of four distinct appendages, each suited for a different purpose. Upon reaching the fallow field, it began using some of these to turn the soil while others removed seeds from cavities in the creature's side, burying each in a tiny cone of earth. Other limbs remained idle, apparently intended for other duties, perhaps involving weeding and harvesting.

"Is it some kind of machine?" An itinerant entertainer had once demonstrated an ancient machine in their village, an arrangement of wheels and levers which moved by themselves with tiny whirrings, but which seemed totally devoid of purpose.

"I don't know." Aly had noticed metal bands around many of the creature's joints, but for the most part it appeared to be covered with natural chitin. She could also see a scar on one side that had healed badly.

Whatever it was, it appeared oblivious to their presence. Niki wondered aloud what would happen if they stood directly in front of it, impeding its progress, but Aly dissuaded her from experimenting. "It's not a risk we need to take."

"Where do you suppose it came from?"

"Maybe we can find out." Niki pointed to the ground where the creature had passed; it was pockmarked by divots where the oversized feet had touched the ground.

They traced it back for some considerable distance, until the cultivated fields were lost from sight behind them and the valley wall loomed high above. Then the ground turned hard and rocky and it was increasingly difficult to find any sign of recent passage. When they finally admitted to themselves that they could trace it no further, they were standing on a barren hill of bald rock surrounded by a thick wall of brush.

They were debating whether or not to return to the pool at the high end of the valley when several figures emerged from behind a pillar of stone. There were half a dozen men and women wearing drably colored but presentable smocks and a much taller man with a dark beard and even darker eyes whose light blue robe seemed to shine with an inner light of its own. The sisters were instantly on their guard, but the newcomers made no threatening moves and all but the robed man stopped at a reasonable distance. He continued forward until just beyond the reach of their arms.

"Welcome, strangers, to our valley." His speech, though intelligible was thickly accented, resembling somewhat that of the sea traders from Cyntrom. He smiled behind his beard and seemed relaxed, but Aly noted that his eyes watched them steadily and with great intensity. "My name is Safarian."

"We didn't mean to trespass." Niki spoke slowly and cautiously, and Aly noticed that her hand never strayed far from the hilt of her sword.

"Please, feel welcome. It isn't often that we have guests here."

"What is this place?" asked Aly, still on her guard.

"This?" Safarian swept one arm to indicate the entire valley. "This is a refuge from the decay, an island of life in a sea of death. But I confess that I sometimes miss the outside world and would gladly trade you food and shelter for a few words of news, and the pleasure of your company."

Although Aly remained suspicious, Niki seemed to relax and before long they were accepting Safarian's invitation.

Safarian and his people lived in an enormous cavern whose entrance was masked from the outside world by a wall of immense trees that challenged the cliffs themselves in reaching for the sky. Aly found their presence puzzling because they were so completely out of place. They were of a type she hadn't seen since leaving the lowlands and they appeared to thrive in an area where smaller, hardier growth normally struggled just to survive. Each was evenly spaced in an arc that enclosed the cavern entrance and beyond, and their lower branches were lush with leaves even though little light could reach them.

Within the cavern was a small town, row after row of identical dwelling places snuggled against the walls, common areas including a bathing pool, a storehouse, and a carpentry shop located more centrally. Safarian dwelt alone in a much more impressive dwelling place at the very rear of the cavern. His rooms were more lavishly furnished than that of the people he apparently ruled, though not particularly opulent even by rural standards.

The villagers brought food - roasted meat and boiled vegetables and candied fruits and coarse heavy bread with a strong flavor - and drink - a delicate but slightly sour wine - but withdrew immediately, leaving Safarian alone with his guests. From them he plied information about the outside world, and they set about dredging their memories for every bit of news, and rumor, that had come their way in the past two years, for that was when Safarian had last entertained a visitor.

"He died shortly after arriving despite all my medicines," Safarian said quietly and with a sigh, picking up his fifth slice of bread. "The solution to every problem lies within its roots, and I was never able to delve that far into his illness."

"How long have you lived here then?" asked Niki.

For the first time, their host seemed uncomfortable. "I tend to lose track of time. The seasons are all beginning to run together even in the outside world and within this valley, they are almost indistinguishable. I was much younger when I stumbled upon this place than I am now, and I will be much older yet before I leave."

The villagers continued to bring food until neither sister could find room for more. "I haven't eaten this well, or this much, in more than a year," admitted Niki.

"We are blessed with bountiful crops."

That gave Aly an opening for the question she'd wanted to ask for some time. "We saw your fields. How do you grow such fruitful crops in such dry soil?"

"And what manner of creature is it that tends them for you?" added Niki. "Is it a living being or a machine?"

Safarian laughed softly. "As to the latter, why it is something of both. I acquired some wisdom before my self-exile, including the gift of wedding flesh to metal, and bending both to my will. As to the former, I would be happy to show you." And so saying, he rose from his pillowed seat and the two young women followed suit.

He led them to a small building adjacent to his dwelling, which he identified as his workshop. It consisted of one large room filled with a bewildering array of boxes and canisters, bottles and flagons, lengths of glass tubing and retorts and other instruments to which neither sister could put a name. One wall contained row after row of wooden boxes, each filled with seeds, each labeled in characters which the sisters could not read. From one of these, Safarian took a single seed and handed it to Aly.

"The soil here is much too rocky for ordinary cultivation, but it will serve our present purposes. If you would be so kind, please plant this as you would any other seed."

Aly turned it over in her hand. It was a fairly large seed, covered with a thin coat of tiny hairs, but was otherwise unremarkable. She squatted and excavated a small hole in the earthen floor, inserted the seed, and covered it up.

"Now what?"

Safarian smiled. "Let's wait a few moments, if you please."

Niki spent the time looking through the paraphernalia piled nearby but Aly merely stood in place, her face impassive. After a not particularly long interval, Safarian spoke again. "If you would unearth the seed you just planted, I think your questions will be answered."

With one finger, Aly cleared the soil away from the seed, which appeared to her completely unchanged. She glanced up questioningly.

"Remove it, if you would be so kind."

She endeavored to do so, and discovered that the seed would not easily budge. When she wrapped her hand around it and exerted greater force, it came loose with a slight sucking sound, but she could only raise it a hand's width from the ground. From its lowest side, several strands of dark fiber penetrated deep into the earth.

"By now it will have penetrated to a depth equal to the height of a man. By morning each strand will be many times as deep and will have extended subsidiary threads in all directions. The farther you descend, the more moisture remains in the soil; it is simply a question of designing a plant which can adapt to those circumstances." He withdrew a small knife from within his robe, bent low and slashed through the fibers.

"Where did you find these seeds?" For the first time, Aly forgot her distrust of Safarian. Here, she realized, was possible salvation of their fortunes.

"Alas, they do not grow naturally. Nor do they breed true. The process by which ordinary seeds are transformed is complex and arduous. Fortunately, the plants which spring from them are sufficiently hardy that they rarely need to be replaced. Isolate them from light and open air for a moment or two and they begin to search for sustenance, drawing water and nourishment from their environment. If there is any trace of it nearby, they grow at quite an amazing rate to exploit the resources available. And now, if you're satisfied, I believe it is getting quite late. We have several unoccupied houses in the village, and I would be delighted to have you as our guests for as long as you're willing to visit with us."

The sisters quarreled mildly the following morning. Aly remained suspicious of their host, not least because no one else in the community would speak to them. They'd answer direct questions and were uniformly polite, but not one of them initiated conversations, and they never volunteered any information. When one of the women brought a plate of fresh fruit for their breakfast, she asked her outright if she was happy living in the valley. The woman merely shrugged, looked uncomfortable, and hastily left.

Niki thought Aly was being unfairly suspicious, and announced her intention of searching for their host as soon as she'd had an opportunity to bathe. Aly suddenly realized the truth, that Niki's fondness for male companionship was clouding her judgment as it had more than once in the past. She realized as well that there was no point in arguing; Niki became as firmly rooted as one of Safarian's plants when she'd set her eyes on a man she wanted.

So when Niki went off in search of Safarian, Aly tried to make friends among his people.

She wasn't very successful. No one was unfriendly or rude, but no one met her eyes either, and she had the distinct impression that something was lurking just beneath the surface, remaining just out of sight. This was finally confirmed for her late in the morning when she was returning to their temporary quarters to see if Niki had returned.

Someone touched her arm from behind. "Don't turn around!" It was a harsh whisper, so muffled that it could have been either a man or a woman.

"All right. What do you want?"

"You and your friend should be very careful. Sometimes he gets angry and punishes us. He can be very cruel."

"Then why do you continue to serve him? There are many of you and only one of him."

There was a short, humorless laugh. "Try to leave the valley and you will find out. And look behind the broken tree downstream."

"And what will I find there?" But there was no answer, and when Aly turned, she found that she was alone.

Niki didn't return for lunch and Aly discovered she had little appetite. Instead, she set out to hike back to the head of the valley, passing the cultivate fields where two of the spider things were laboring. One of them hesitated as she passed, but then continued its work, methodically removing weeds from around the stems of small larksfruit trees. Nothing seemed amiss until she turned to her left and reached the upslope down which they'd descended the previous day.

Two more spider things emerged from the brush ahead and stopped directly in her path. She angled to the right to bypass them and a third popped up directly in front of her. After a moment's pause, she returned to her original course, closing to within a short distance of one of the creatures. As she did so, it straightened its main legs and began waving its lesser limbs in what she interpreted as a warning. Deliberately she started forward again, and this time the other two creatures moved to flank the third, presenting an impenetrable wall.

Thoughtfully, she turned back toward the cavern.

The stream ran close by the entrance, and she followed it with no trouble. When she came to the broken tree, she recognized it immediately. Apparently struck by lightning, it had split into two roughly equal halves; one had fallen to the ground, the other leaned drunkenly against the next in line. Aly picked her way across the water, climbed over the fallen trunk, and found just beyond it a deep ravine.

At the foot of the ravine she found a dead body.

It was a young male, probably her own age, and in life he must have been quite handsome. Now his neck was broken so that his head lay at a bizarre angle. His arms and legs had been split open right to the marrow of his bones and his entrails had been drawn out of his body and tied to several saplings. It must have been a very ugly death.

Aly turned away in revulsion and was about to climb out of the ravine when he spoke.

"Would you turn my head?"

Aly's legs trembled and she almost fell. "You're alive?"

His eyes were open now. "For the moment. Could you turn my head please? When it rains, the water pools up and I choke on it."

She knelt beside him and gently turned his head, and he thanked her.

"Why?" she asked.

"Because a girl favored me over him. Or perhaps he just didn't care for me. What does it matter?" The voice seemed infinitely sad.

Aly forced herself to look at his mutilated body again. "Would you like me to...end this for you?" She still had her dirk.

His laugh was a bubbly, unpleasant sound. "Don't bother. He'd just bring me back to die again. He's done it several times before."

She thought about it, then drew her dirk. "Not this time, he won't."


Aly sat in the center of the town for the rest of the afternoon, stirring only when it was obvious that the evening meal was being prepared. Niki did not appear at all during that time, which only hardened Aly's resolve. She approached Safarian's hut and waited outside while his people brought meat and soup and skewers of vegetables. Then a woman approached with a broad platter of the coarse bread, and Aly intercepted her.

"Let me take this in."

The woman looked dubious, but eventually acquiesced. A few minutes later, Aly entered Safarian's home.

"Ah, your sister is back from her wanderings." Safarian lay on a bed of cushions, his body partially covered by a saffron robe. Niki lay just beyond, wearing a garment of similar color and skimpier proportions. Her eyes were unfocused and she seemed to have trouble recognizing her sister, as though she'd been drugged

Aly set the platter of bread down and seated herself on a cushion. "I tried to walk to the end of the valley today," she said quietly. "I was prevented from doing so."

Safarian sat up and casually selected a slice of bread. "You must mean the guardians. They wouldn't harm you; they're supposed to keep children from wandering away and sometimes they can't distinguish between children and adults." He took a bite of the bread.

"Then you don't have any objection to our leaving."

"But surely you aren't tired of my company already." He glanced to the side. "Your sister certainly isn't." He ate some more of the bread.

"You didn't answer my question."

He finished the bread and selected another piece before answering. "I get the impression that you're angry with me about something. Have I displeased you in some fashion? I believe I've been quite generous."

"I saw an example of your generosity in a ravine downstream of us. It was quite enlightening."

Safarian set aside a half eaten slice of bread and his expression hardened. "He was a criminal and deserved to be punished. There must be order if our community is to survive."

"Perhaps it shouldn't survive."

"I intend that it shall." All pretense of friendliness vanished with those words and Safarian glared at her angrily.

"It is doomed already. The seeds of its destruction have already been planted."

Safarian threw his head back and laughed. "Little girl, you have no idea who you're dealing with. I was once the greatest sorcerer of Naat. I have lived more lifetimes than you have years. Kings have tried to defeat me and all have failed. What makes you think you can fare better than they?"

"Simple observation."

He raised an eyebrow. "Perhaps you'd deign to explain that to me." He shifted uncomfortably and blinked, suddenly distressed.

"I observe that you've eaten two slices of bread. And since I put two of your seeds in each slice, I imagine that they're going to be drawing quite a bit of nourishment from your body very soon now."

Safarian's eyes widened and his mouth opened in a shout of rage and he lunged forward, hands reaching for her throat.

They never made it.

Aly and Niki left the valley two weeks later, leading several paralopes laden with flagons of water and bundles of preserved fruits and vegetables, and leaving behind a people who were slowly regaining their self confidence. One two of the paralopes were large bags of seeds with very unusual properties that could provide bountiful crops from even the most depleted soil, and which eventually made the sisters the most successful farmers in Dhir.

# MR. BOTTLE

Neither family nor friends would speak to me during the days immediately following my death, so with few regrets I decided that it was time to find a new place for myself. I left the large house on the West Side feeling considerable pique even though I knew that the situation was not entirely their fault. They simply weren't aware of my lingering presence, except perhaps for my granddaughter Alicia, who kept glancing in my direction with a rather puzzled expression on her face, as though something tickled her senses without resolving itself into an actual presence. It had never occurred to me that there was some special bond between the two of us, no more than that which existed with my other five grand children, but perhaps Alicia was fonder of her aging and somewhat crusty grandsire than the others, or perhaps she is just of a more sensitive nature. It is possble the others might have seen me also, if they had wanted to, but I observed nothing that told me my passing brought them any great sorrow.

I left through the front door, which had been left propped open to facilitate the entrance and egress of the mourners, of whom there were fewer than I would have expected. I felt a flash of resentment that so few of my business associates had taken the time to pay their last respects and I wished them mild ill will as their faces flashed past my inner eye. Already their names were fading from my memory, however, and by the time I reached the park at the corner of our block, I could almost feel my old existence sloughing away. It was rather liberating but also somewhat frightening. I had no idea what to expect or where I should go, although my feet seemed untroubled by my doubts and kept moving briskly toward the center of the city.

It was dark and foggy and the streetlamps clutched their light to themselves, making only tentative efforts to disturb the shadows. I encountered occasional pedestrians, none of whom gave me a second look and all of whom I assumed were just as unaware of my presence as were my sons and daughters. When a particularly hurried young man made a slight detour to avoid me, I thought it might just be some form of instinctive aversion, but then two well dressed gentleman passed close by and one nodded hospitably in my direction and I wondered if they, like myself, were some form of revenant intelligence until they hailed a passing cab, which swerved obediently to receive them and carry them off into the distance. I had no immediate explanation.

Having died while my wristwatch was on the dresser, I could not gauge the passage of time as I walked, obliquely cutting across the now dormant commercial district into a part of the city which was as foreign to me as the markets in Casablanca or the promenade in Hanoi. The deterioration set in almost immediately, abandoned shops giving way to abandoned warehouses followed by vacant, trash strewn lots, dilapidated tenement buildings with doorways boarded over though still home to a few residents who slept on piles of newspapers. Then I was at the river's edge and over the pedestrian bridge into Cloversdale.

While alive, I had of course known that the borough of Cloversdale existed and it is even possible that I passed through it at one time or another, my eyes fixed on some financial report or prospectus, or perhaps while staring sightlessly into the distance as I spoke on the car phone to my broker or my lawyer or my executive administrative assistant. But in all those years, I'd never actually been aware of its existence as anything other an abstract concept, though I understood it to be a community made up predominantly of retirees not sufficiently affluent to relocate to a more luxurious and trendy location. I looked upon it now with fresh eyes, and even in the darkness and from a distance the town houses with their faux brick fronts and high gabled windows seemed pretentious and false and even a bit ugly, but it was a good natured illusion that fooled no one and I knew that this was my goal even before my feet turned from the highway.

There is no clover in Cloversdale, at least none that I've ever seen. Perhaps there was at some time in the distant past and that inspired the original developers. Today there are only a few patches of reluctant grass fighting losing battles against dandelion, violets, and Queen Anne's Lace. There are a handful of small gardens, but most of these live in window boxes, and even fewer trees, although the decaying stumps of elms destroyed by the blight in years past still punctuate the sidewalks of almost every block. I became completely disoriented once the lights and spires of the city center were hidden from view by these darker artificial canyons, but my feet seemed to know their way and I gave them their head, so to speak. I was used to streets arranged in a grid, north-south or east-west, with names ending with street or boulevard or avenue. Cloversdale, like nature itself, seemed to abhor a straight line, and I found myself traversing lanes and circles and even a concourse. There were few streetlamps, and only half of those which did exist actually worked, but the sky had cleared, the moon was near full, and I had no difficulty examining my surroundings.

I had just turned onto a narrow, cobblestoned roadway called Camber Lane when my feet suddenly came to a halt, leaving me standing in front of a three story structure of mixed architectural styles that even sported a pair of diminutive gargoyles alongside the front walk. A hand painted sign drawn in quite artful calligraphy indicated "ROOM TO LET" and it occurred to me that I really needed to find a place to spend what remained of the night, although the chill and damp no longer discomfited me and I felt no need to sleep. The habits of a lifetime are hard to discard even in death, so I swung open the wrought iron gate and passed through a small but well tended yard. My foot was on the first of the five concrete steps when it suddenly occurred to me that – even supposing that anyone inside would be physically aware of my presence – it was certainly an inappropriate hour to be inquiring about the availability of lodging. I hesitated, uncharacteristically indecisive, and at that very moment, the door was thrown wide and a cadaverously thin man emerged, clutching two empty milk bottles to his chest.

"Oh! There you are!" He almost flowed down the steps, moved the two bottles to the crook of his left arm, and reached out with the other to grasp my hand before I realized what he intended. I half expected his arm to pass right through me, but his grip was firm and felt entirely natural. "I expect you're here about the room." He nodded over his shoulder toward the sign.

I found myself nodding as though this was all perfectly ordinary.

"Well, come right in, Mister…? I didn't catch your name."

I opened my mouth to tell him, but curiously enough I discovered that I couldn't remember my name at all. I felt a flash of panic as I cast my thoughts back and realized that the details of my former life were receding from me as though I'd just wakened from an unimportant dream, leaving only bits and pieces of residue behind. I remembered my office, but I wasn't sure exactly where it was located, and the name of the company I once directed eluded me entirely. The faces of my family all seemed to merge into one generic form and I couldn't bring to mind any of their names except for one grandchild, Alicia, and even in her case I could not recall the family name or from which of my own offspring she had sprung. I'm not sure how long my funk lasted before I realized that the cadaverous man was still waiting for an answer. Frantically I reached out for something, some handle I could attach to my personal identity, and I saw what he was holding and the name came out before I consciously planned it. "Bottle," I told him. "My name is Bottle." And so it now is.

"Pleased to meet you, Mr. Bottle. My name's Lacking and I'm the manager. Please come in. I'm sure you'll like the room. It's one of our finest."

We passed through a pair of heavy oak doors with inset beveled windows into a narrow, poorly lit, but immaculately clean foyer. An equally circumscribed hallway led to a staircase with polished mahogany handrails. The overhead light was one of those ridiculously intricate chandeliers with myriad dangling crystals and glass balls which I normally detest but which looked entirely appropriate there. The walls were hung with dark tapestries depicting fox hunts and sailing ships and people tilling fields and others fighting epic battles.

"It's on the second floor, at the rear of the building where it's quieter." Still carrying his milk bottles, Mr. Lacking led the way up the stairway to a landing, then down a shadow strewn corridor to a door embellished with a very elaborate brass numeral three. He opened the door, which was unlocked, and I followed him inside.

It wasn't at all what I'd expected. The apartment was completely furnished and consisted of four rooms, bed, bath, kitchen, and a sitting room large enough to accommodate no more than two couples comfortably. The furniture itself was of uniformly good quality, old but well cared for, not anything I would have chosen for myself under ordinary circumstances but certainly more than adequate for my current needs and inoffensive to my taste. More importantly, it felt right to me. When I sat in the plush chair in the drawing room, the cushions seemed already to have been molded to fit my body, and I knew how the kitchen utensils and supplies would be arranged even before I opened the cupboard doors for confirmation.

"Is everything satisfactory?"

I'd almost forgotten about Lacking, who had followed me silently as I toured the rooms. I turned now to find him standing directly behind me, still clutching his glass totems, face radiant with anticipation.

"It's really very nice."

"Then it's settled. Welcome to Crestwell." He shifted his burden and shook my hand again. "I'll just leave you to settle in. If you need me, I'm in apartment zero on the ground floor." He retreated from my new quarters so quickly that it was almost as though he's simply blinked out of existence.

It never occurred to me until later that we'd never spoken about rent or other terms.

Although I no longer feel fatigue, I find that I still require periods of inactivity during which I am no longer aware of my surroundings. I experience this as a sudden jump in perception. When Lacking left me, I walked into the bedroom, wondering if I would ever need to use it for its intended purpose, and between one thought and the next it was morning and bright sunlight streamed in through the crack between the drawn curtains. I threw them wide and looked out onto a tiny patch of lawn, completely surrounded by a stockade fence, with a well tended and quite colorful bed of flowers tucked into the corner where they were most likely to feel the sunlight.

I spent the morning exploring the apartment without finding anything remarkable. It felt almost as though I had lived here in a previous life. When I experimented by rearranging things, I always returned them to their original position. It was some time in the afternoon before I ventured out into the hallway and downstairs. I knocked on the door of apartment zero but there was no answer, although I heard stirring in other parts of the building. I stood in the foyer for a long while with my nose pressed against the beveled glass, staring out into the street where occasional pedestrians went about their business without glancing in my direction, and even less frequently automobiles drove past slowly and disinterestedly. My hand moved to the doorknob and I felt, not panic exactly because my emotions were still peculiarly muted, but an uneasiness, and I retreated upstairs, drawing the perimeter of my world in around me. I spent the rest of the day and all of the night that followed sitting in my room, although most of the latter elapsed during one of those instantaneous blackouts I had already experienced.

It occurred to me on the following morning that I hadn't eaten since my death and I inspected the pantry even though I still felt nothing akin to hunger. There was tea and coffee, sugar and salt and various spices, a few canned goods. The icebox was empty and in fact not even plugged into the wall socket, and I left it that way. Feeling restless, I ventured out into the hall where I met the first of my fellow tenants.

I would guess her age to be in the early forties. She was shorter than I and a bit heavy, though by no means obese, and she was wearing a pale gray sweat suit that was at least a size too large for her. "You'd be the new tenant, I take it?" She had a deep, mannish voice and the faintest trace of an English accent.

Reassured that she could actually see me, I nodded. "My name is…Bottle. Bernard Bottle," I improvised quickly as I extended my hand.

"Eva Harbinger. I live at the other end of the hall in apartment four, by myself now that my husband's gone. Welcome to Crestwell, Mr. Bottle." Her tone was neither warm nor cool, but hinted of both. Her approval was restrained and conditional.

"Thank you. I'm glad to be here." And I was actually, but I was also puzzled. Somehow I had come to believe that everyone in Crestwell, except possibly Mr. Lacking, would be like me, a malingering spirit, but I recognized immediately that this was not the case with Mrs. Harbinger. I was trying to think of something appropriate to say when she glanced at her wristwatch.

"Heavens! I'm going to be late. It was nice meeting you. We'll talk again, I'm sure." And then she was descending the staircase with an awkward rolling gait and I stood above, one hand on the railing, watching her go.

I met most of the others at Crestwell over the course of the next few days, and they were a strange and disparate lot, although none as strange as I. They all seemed to accept me without reservation, and if any of them noticed my peculiar condition, they had the good manners not to comment. Mr. Dour in apartment one was the least outgoing; his conversation was limited largely to grunts and shrugs and his eyes were always skipping away as though he was searching for an escape route. Apartment two held the Teller Twins, Ava and Agatha, two aging spinsters who seemed ridiculously happy all the time. Only Mr. Dour seemed immune to their infectious cheer.

Mr. Short lived in apartment five, and appropriately enough he was a midget, or perhaps a dwarf, I've never understood the difference. His legs were disproportionately short and his shoulders disproportionately wide, but he had a handsome face, a pleasant disposition, and one of the Teller Twins told me that he supported himself by writing, although she had no idea what the subject matter might be. And finally there was apartment six, taking up two thirds of the top floor, and there lived Jessica Warren. I was in my early seventies – or at least I had been at the time of my death – but Jessica was at least two decades my senior. Her skin was dry like old leather but it fit her like a tailored suit. She was taller than I and must have been taller still before the calcium had begun leaching from her bones. Her hair was as white as polished bone and fell to her shoulderblades in a style that might have been thought inappropriate for a woman her age, but which suited her perfectly. She was deliberate in her speech, as though she was choosing each word carefully, interested without being too inquisitive, and had a mind still as sharp as a cat's claw. She was also the first of my neighbors to invite me into her rooms.

It was about a week after I'd moved in to Crestwell, or at least I think that's right. I was starting to have trouble keeping track of time. There were no clocks in my new apartment. Fortunately, I no longer felt the need to divide the day or night up into distinct slices. I had no appointments to keep, deadlines to meet, schedules to maintain, or anniversaries to commemorate. Ageless, unsleeping, unemployed, and disconnected, I felt wonderfully liberated, with no obligations, no dependents, no employees. I had no friends in this new existence, at least not yet, but when I stopped to think about it, I couldn't remember having had any real friends in the old life either, and although I may have forgotten them just as I was slowly forgetting everything from that earlier existence, somehow I knew this wasn't just a product of fading memory. I had never really acquired any true friends; there was no one for whom I'd have honestly mourned, just as none of them had honestly mourned for me.

I was descending to the first floor when I heard the crash. Curious but not alarmed, I quickened my pace and spotted Jessica Warren crouched in the foyer, slowly collecting a spray of groceries that had erupted from a tear in the bag tucked against her shoulder. "Here, let me help you." I stooped and gathered up bay leaves and cinnamon, bird seed and maraschino cherries. She was using one hand to hold the tear shut but it was obvious that she wouldn't be able to carry the entire load upstairs to the third floor without assistance.

"Let me help you with these."

"Oh, just put them on the stair there and I'll come back for them. You're obviously on your way out."

"Not at all. I was just going to see if Mr. Lacking was in."

She glanced at the door to apartment zero. "Did you need something?"

I shook my head. "No, not really. But I haven't spoken to him since I arrived and we never actually discussed payment."

She laughed, and it was the sound of a delicate wind chime disturbed by a gentle breeze. "No one pays rent at Crestwell, Mr. Bottle. No one ever has. The Owner takes care of all our expenses. And Mr. Lacking is only at home when one of us needs him."

"I don't understand."

"You don't need to, Mr. Bottle." She started up the stairs and I followed, bearing condiments. "If you're coming up, I'll make us both some tea."

I followed, bewildered by her explanation and pleased by her invitation. She opened the door to her apartment without unlocking it and I realized for the first time that there was no lock on my door, and no indications of locks on any of the others, or the front entrance either for that matter.

Her apartment was easily twice the size of mine, a maze of rooms and furniture that seemed to double back on itself and extend into the indefinite distance. There were mirrors on every wall, which exaggerated the effect, but I could have sworn her apartment extended beyond the exterior walls of the building itself. And she had birds. Large birds and small, parakeets and lovebirds, a toucan and a pair of mynahs, a cockatoo and a parrot and canaries and exotic birds I could not identify. Their cages stood on tables, hung from the ceiling, jutted out from the walls. They were square and oblong, round and oval, tetrahedrons and at least one that had branching arms. Some of the cages were fitted with small swings, others with fake tree limbs, ornate perches, and bird feeders of various sizes and shapes. Outside of the cages, there were small tables everywhere and shelves jostled the mirrors on the walls. Each and every horizontal surface was used to display delicate figurines, most of them sitting on elaborate crocheted doilies that sometimes dripped over the edges of the surfaces they protected like spilled molasses.

"This is my family now," she explained. "Make yourself comfortable, Mr. Bottle, and I'll put on the water for tea."

When she returned after several minutes, bearing a tray with cobalt blue teapot and matching cups, I experienced a sudden moment of doubt. Was I still capable of drinking tea? I felt neither thirst nor hunger, and I hadn't opened my bathroom door since the first night's inspection. With no help from me, my jacket and pants retained their crisp cleanliness and my skin and hair still seemed freshly bathed, brushed, and lotioned.

"Mrs. Warren, I'm not exactly what I appear to be." I felt awkward and a bit anxious. I liked the woman and would have felt terrible if I had alienated or frightened her.

"No, of course not, Mr. Bottle. You're dead. But I don't see why that should prevent us from being friends." She arranged the tea things on the low, glass topped table in front of me while I mulled that one over.

"You know then," I said at last, admittedly a weak and altogether unnecessary rejoinder.

"Oh, yes. When you've lived as long as I have, Mr. Bottle, you learn to size people up very quickly. I've spent many years within reach of my own death, so it shouldn't be at all surprising that I've learned to recognize it." She poured tea and nodded toward the sugar and cream. I shook my head and reached out, took the cup, and raised it to my lips. It smelled wonderful and I took a tentative sip. It tasted like tea, but with a sharper, more distinctive spiciness than anything in my previous experience.

"It's my own blend. I hope you like it. The Twins found it a bit strong."

"No, it's delightful." And it was. I took another sip. "I just didn't expect that I'd be able to, well, appreciate it. How did you know that I could?"

"You're not the first dead person I've had to tea, Mr. Bottle."

"But you're not...?" I was unable to finish the sentence; it caught in my throat like an unchewed cracker.

"Dead? No, of course not. Not yet. You're the only one of your kind living here at present, although poor Mr. Dour enjoys life so little that he might as well have passed on, I'm afraid."

"It felt almost as though I was expected," I confessed. "Mr. Lacking wasn't at all surprised to find me on the doorstep."

"No doubt Mrs. Harbinger told him you were coming. She always seems to know when things are going to change around here."

"Can you tell me anything about what's happened to me? Why I'm still here? What I'm supposed to do with myself?"

She shook her head and drained half of her own cup before answering. "I'm afraid I don't know any more than you do. Mr. Swift, who had your apartment until last month, had also passed on. He was with us for almost a year. A nice man, but very impatient. He always wanted to know what was coming next and when we couldn't tell him, he got quite out of sorts."

"What happened to him?" I finished my tea and set the cup down, and she immediately refilled it.

"I don't know the answer to that either. One morning we woke up and he was gone. I knew the moment I passed his door that the room was empty, that we wouldn't see him again, but I have no idea where he went. Another world? Heaven? Hell? Or just to different lodgings? We never solve all the mysteries in our lives no matter how long we live, or linger on. Why should death be any different? There are more questions in the world than answers."

"I see." I stared down into my cup, watching a thin wisp of steam curl slowly up and fade away. The birds had begun chirruping and rustling their wings when we'd first arrived, but by now they had subsided. "There has to be some reason why I'm still here, Mrs. Warren."

"Perhaps. A task yet to be done, a lesson to be learned, a prophecy to be fulfilled. Or maybe it's just a clerical error, a glitch in the system, a soul misfiled. And please call me Jessie, Mr. Bottle."

"Of course, Jessie. And you can call me…" I struggled to remember what I had told Lacking. "Bernard. My name is Bernard."

"No, it isn't, but that's what I shall call you." We chatted a while longer, but I remembered such a small portion of my past now that I had little to contribute, so I listened instead as she told me of her family, or rather families. Two husbands and four children, but only one grandchild. All dead now. She had outlived three generations and was the last of her line. Her tone was regretful but without self pity. We finished the pot of tea and she offered to make another, but I stood up instead, thanked her, and retreated to my room, where I had much to think about.

Although I had little awareness of the passage of time, I lived in this benevolent purgatory for several weeks without gaining any insights or acquiring a sense of purpose or direction. I eventually found the courage to leave the house, and discovered that I could interact with the physical world just as I had in life. No one in Cloverdale had known me before, so there was no difficulty in that regard. On one occasion I found a coin lying in the grass and took it to a telephone booth. I could no longer bring to mind the faces of any of my relatives, and their names were as lost to me as my own except for Alicia. I sensed her presence every once in a while, often at the oddest moments, and I fancied that this was when she thought of me. If so, she was apparently the only one of my relatives who spared the time to remember. I could even bring to mind the appearance of the house where she lived, the street out front, the park at the corner, although I could not recall the address. Oddly enough, the telephone number was distinct in my mind, and I took my quarter to a public telephone booth one block from Crestwell.

Someone answered, a young girl, a voice immediately familiar. "Alicia," I said softly, "It's grandfather." It was foolish of me, of course. She would either be frightened or interpret it as a cruel trick. But neither event came to pass.

"Hello? Is anyone there?"

I responded again, more cautiously this time. "Alicia? Is that you?"

"Hello!" Her voice was raised, impatient, and I realized that she couldn't hear me, A second later, she broke the connection.

I am lost forever to everyone who knew me. Only strangers can see or hear me now.

During my lifetime I had traveled over much of the world, countless cities about which I could remember little if anything. I had visited them so that I could say that I had done so, or to meet with other avaricious men and women in surroundings so indistinguishable from the ones that I had left behind me that it seemed at times as though I could walk through a door and emerge in another office half a world away. Now my world had become more circumscribed. I rarely ventured outside of Crestwell, and never more than a block away. I wasn't afraid of the larger reality beyond, but it no longer held any relevance for me. I spent countless hours sitting on the front stoop, watching the ebb and flow of traffic, remembering from somewhere the inaccurate adage that if you stood for long enough in Times Square, you would eventually see everyone you had ever known. The currents of humanity that flowed past our door did not approach the volume to be found elsewhere in the city, but they were just as deep and broad and passed by as quickly and I never once saw a familiar face.

I also began a detailed exploration of Crestwell, at least those parts which were accessible to me. I had catalogued every object in my apartment early in my stay, even committed to memory the web of tiny cracks in the ceiling, but I had not visited any of my fellow tenants other than Jessie, although I had caught tantalizing glimpses through briefly opened doors. I explored the tiny garden at the back of the house, maintained fastidiously by the Teller Twins with occasional help from Mr. Short. I devoted a great deal of my time to the elaborate tapestries on the ground floor, taking each in turn and pressing my eye close to the weave, running my fingers lightly over the surface, once even tasting one of them with the tip of my tongue.

There were seventeen of them in all, each dealing with different subject matter – agriculture, war, exploration, childhood, nature, and other elements of human existence. The last one I examined was located just behind the base of the staircase, and was harder to discern because of the heavy shadows that lay across it like drapes. Its subject was aging and death and I spent more time studying it than all the others combined. The figures depicted were invariably elderly or already dead. Some strode through a graveyard, others hovered in the sky with elaborate white wings to support them, and still others lay quietly in coffins which were visible through a cutaway portion of the ground. It was curiously bland, with no overtones of horror, dread, sadness, or celebration. The angels and the buried dead all bore neutral expressions, neither happy nor sad.

I was trying to puzzle out its meaning when I noticed that it didn't lie flush against the wall as the others did. Curious, I lifted one corner and discovered that it concealed a nondescript, unmarked doorway. It was the only door in Crestwell that was fitted with a lock, and the lock was engaged.

Quite intrigued by now, I approached apartment zero and knocked on the door. I had seen Mr. Lacking only once since the day I arrived, as he accompanied Mr. Dour to his apartment speaking cheerily about air bubbles trapped in the water pipes or something of that nature. There was no answer so I tried again, more forcefully. "Mr. Lacking? Are you there?"

There was still no response and I had half turned away when some impulse made me stop. I grasped the doorknob firmly and turned it; there was of course no lock. A moment later I was staring into Mr. Lacking's quarters.

It was by far the smallest apartment in Crestwell. From the doorway I could see into all three rooms, the largest of which held two chairs, a small table, and a narrow brass bed set at the far end. A tiny bathroom and minimal kitchen facilities were appended to it, and the doors to each were open. There was no other significant furniture, no pictures on the walls, no rug on the floor, no quilt on the neatly made bed, no books or vases on the shelves. And no Mr. Lacking. Feeling mildly guilty at invading his world with my eyes, I gently closed the door and turned away.

Agatha Teller was standing at the foot of the stairs.

"Did you need Mr. Lacking for something?"

"No, not really. I just wanted to say hello, but he isn't there."

"Of course he isn't. He's only there when you need him."

It wouldn't be true to say that I forgot about the mysterious door, but neither did I dwell on it. Several days later I had tea with Jessie, this time accompanied by delicate pastries that crumbled if I held them too tightly. They were delicious and they were the first solid food I'd consumed at Crestwell. We were talking about one thing and another, nothing of consequence, and I remembered the door and asked about it.

"That's the door to the basement. No one ever goes down there, not even Mr. Lacking."

I raised an eyebrow. "Why? Is it dangerous?"

She paused briefly, thoughtfully. "As a matter of fact, I have no idea. The subject has never come up. We just don't go down there."

I'd like to say I rebelled at the thought of leaving a mystery unsolved, but the truth is that I nodded and reclassified the door as an oddity of no consequence and of no further interest. In that I was totally mistaken.

Mrs. Harbinger was the first to be affected. I was downstairs at the time, had in fact just peeked into Mr. Lacking's room on one of my periodic attempts to speak to him. Everything appeared exactly the same as when I'd last seen it, the rooms still betrayed no evidence of their tenant. I had just closed the door when Mr. Short came down the staircase with uncharacteristic haste.

"I need to see Mr. Lacking right away!" He was quite animated, not at all the calm, thoughtful man I'd spoken to in the past.

"I'm afraid he's not in," I blurted out as he rushed past me, his knuckles rapping against the doorframe.

To my utter consternation, the door opened immediately and Mr. Lacking was standing there, his face twisted in concern. "Whatever is the matter, Mr. Short?"

"It's Mrs. Harbinger! Something terrible has happened!"

The three of us went back up to the second floor as a unit. The door to apartment four was open and even from a distance I had a feeling of emptiness. "She invited me to lunch and wasn't at the door, so I just pushed it open. She always knows exactly when I'm coming, so I knew right away that something was wrong."

Mr. Lacking was the first to enter, and he let a low hiss of breath escape through his teeth. Mr. Short turned away from the door, his face an exaggerated mask of dismay, and I stepped quietly past him and looked inside. Mrs. Harbinger had always been pleasant to me, but I'd never actually been in her apartment and I sensed that I made her slightly uneasy, as though my existence implied a future she didn't want to face. I had looked in from time to time, because she frequently left the door open, and I remembered it as a brightly illuminated place with potted plants in neat little rows under fluorescent bulbs against the rear wall. Her furniture had sharp, almost gaudy colors, mostly reds and yellows with other colors present only as accents. She was a bit disorderly and there would almost always be magazines or knitting or discarded clothing on the sofa or draped over the arms of a chair, but everything was spotlessly clean, dusted or washed or vacuumed or swept.

It had a very different appearance today, so much so that I felt more disoriented than at any time since I'd left my old home on the West Side. The furniture was still placed exactly as I remembered, but the colors were faded, the fabric worn and threadbare and streaked with grime. Patently dirty clothing was heaped on the sofa and had overflowed onto the carpet, which was torn and discolored. The lights were off, and what little came in through her small window seemed to do so reluctantly. The neat rows of plants were now a wasteland; all wilted and dry, some so desiccated that they had already begun to lose their shape. There were cobwebs in the corners of the room and some large insect scurried out of sight when I glanced toward the archway to the kitchen.

"Mrs. Harbinger?" I was surprised to hear the tremor in my voice. I thought that I had lost the capacity for strong emotion, but it seemed that was not the case.

We found her in the bedroom. She was lying on her bed, on top of the covers, and she wasn't breathing. But she wasn't dead either. Her skin was warm to the touch and her eyes were open, but there was no light in them, no pulse in her veins. There was a cobweb in her hair and dirt under her normally immaculate fingernails. I was stunned by the sight of her, moving only when Mr. Lacking touched my arm.

"We should leave now."

He was right. I felt as though I had invaded her privacy like some obscene voyeur. We returned to the hall and Mr. Lacking gently closed the door.

"What happened to her?" My voice was as thin and dry as the air in Mrs. Harbinger's apartment.

"I don't know," he said simply. He turned to Mr. Short, whose expression was twisted in shock, his shoulders shaking violently. "When did you talk to her last?"

"This morning, when I went out for the paper. She was fine then." He paused and moistened his lips with his tongue. "I stopped by her apartment to say hello and everything was just the same as always."

The blight, as we called it, was the main subject of conversation in Crestwell that afternoon. Mr. Lacking thought that all the other residents should know what had happened, and when we finished telling the impassive Mr. Dour of our discovery, Lacking was suddenly gone as though he'd never been there. Even Dour overcame his usual reclusiveness and left his room to listen in on the hushed conversations that continued in the stairwells. I was actually the one who sneaked off to be alone. I felt a vague sense of guilt, as though Mrs. Harbinger's life had been brought to a close in order to compensate for the fact that my own had continued beyond my death. It was patently absurd, of course. My predecessor at Crestwell had been no more alive than I and nothing like this had happened during his tenure. Emotions aren't susceptible to logic however. When the residents of Crestwell retired to their beds that evening, I wonder how many of them wished that there was, after all, a lock fitted to the their door.

The Teller Twins were next, and I was the one who discovered them. I had just emerged from my nightly blackout and was leaning out of my window to feel the morning breeze. I glanced down at the garden almost casually and frowned. Something was wrong. Ordinarily I could see almost the entire flower bed, but today it was partially obscured by intervening branches. It looked as though a large section of climbing ivy had detached itself from the rear wall of the adjacent building and was now hanging awkwardly blocking my view.

I heard no one else stirring as I descended to the ground floor and used the rear exit to investigate.

It was ivy, all right, but it hadn't fallen from above. Rather, it had sprung up from the ground, turning and twisting to completely encircle the Teller sisters, who were standing side by side, hand in hand. The ivy wound in and out of their clothing, around and around each limb and through the strands of their hair, and lay like heavy drapes across their shoulders. They were both smiling and their eyes were open, but they weren't breathing and when I touched the back of Agatha's hand, it felt like wax.

Mr. Lacking had nothing to suggest this time either, and wandered off, leaving me to tell the others what had happened. Mr. Dour harrumphed and nodded, Mr. Short looked immensely sad and mildly frightened and retreated into his apartment without saying a word. Only Jessie hastened down to the garden to see for herself, circling the two silent figures with the back of one hand pressed against her lips, the other clutching the side of her skirt as though it was a life vest.

Afterward we sat in her apartment and drank tea, but I had to pour because her hands were shaking so badly.

"I'm not afraid of death, Philip. I've lived in its presence so long that it's almost like an old friend. But this isn't death. It's something worse."

"They didn't look unhappy. Neither did Mrs. Harbinger." It was the only comfort I could offer.

When our tea was done, Jessie told me that she was tired and wanted to nap for a while so I left, although I stood just outside her door for a long time, lost in unconstructive thought. I decided to look in on Mr. Short, who had always struck me as having the quickest mind of any of us, but when I knocked on his door, it swung open onto silence.

I poked my head inside and called his name, but I think I already knew something of what I would find, or not find. His apartment seemed completely unchanged from the last time we'd played chess. The walls were all lined with books, row after row of them, nonfiction and fiction carefully separated and arranged by subject or author as appropriate. They were mostly hardbound and mostly old, and each and every one looked as though it had never been opened, although if you chose one at random, Mr. Short could summarize its contents and usually offer a quotation or two.

His typewriter was on the coffee table just where it always was, flanked by two shallow wooden trays, one with blank paper, the other with error free typed pages. A half filled glass of beer stood on a coaster, still cold enough that beads of moisture glistened along its base. I called out several more times, but it took only a few seconds to assure myself he was not present. It was possible that he'd just stepped out for a moment, was visiting Mr. Dour or had run down to the corner market for some peanuts to go with his beer. But I knew none of those explanations would prove true.

I sat down awkwardly in his custom made chair and stared at the typewriter, but it was several minutes before my eyes focused enough to see what was written there. Two words only, all in capitals, centered in the middle of the page.

VICTOR SHORT

I walked down to apartment one. Mr. Dour's door was closed and I did knock, but perfunctorily. I already knew that he wouldn't be there. Or at least, not as I had always known him. His was the only room I had never seen clearly. He was a large man and always held the door partly closed when he spoke to others, his body blocking most of the view beyond. Only Mr. Lacking had actually been inside his apartment, and Mr. Lacking never spoke of it. So I was curious.

Clutter. If ever a scene deserved a one word description, this would be the one. Given his size, I was surprised that Dour could manage to fit down the narrow aisles that separated enormous piles of…stuff. There were piles of newspapers and magazines, boxes of tools and toys and canned goods and old clothing. There were file cabinets with drawers so full they didn't close properly, and more stuff was piled on top of them. There were books and cooking utensils and old VHS tapes in boxes that had never been opened. Four television sets clustered together in one corner, none of them plugged in, and there were large clear glass jars filled with pencils and coins and rubber bands and nails and paper clips.

But when I peered into his bedroom, I found something else, something I would never have expected. The bed was neatly made, though vacant. The walls of the room were lined with wooden shelves, and arranged in an orderly fashion on those shelves were several dozen wooden sculptures. They were delicate, intricate things, carved with infinite care, sometimes all in one piece but more frequently assembled from separately created components. I saw clipper ships and articulated skeletons and buildings and trees and flowers and birds and machines and creatures from mythology. No subject was repeated but no subject was neglected either. I felt suddenly as though I was looking at another man's soul and I retreated hastily from the room, feeling guilty about intruding.

Mr. Dour's apartment was otherwise a treasure house of junk, and I had the feeling that if I looked long enough, I could find anything I could possibly want in one pile or another. Everything, that is, except for Mr. Dour. I'd been alarmed when I'd entered, but now I felt saddened and disinterested. At first I thought it was a reaction to what had happened to my fellow tenants, but then I realized that my perception of them had altered. Mrs. Harbinger's friendly overtures were suddenly revealed as noisy and incessant irrelevancies. Mr. Short was a caricature of a man, and the Teller Twins were so wrapped up in one another that they had no feelings to share with anyone else. Worst of all, Jessie Warren was a dried up prune who didn't know when it was time to die and move on and make space in the world for those who still had a life to lead.

That was what I was thinking, but they weren't my thoughts.

Horrified at these perverse images, I bolted from Mr. Dour's apartment, and as soon as I was out the door, the mood lifted and I realized the truth. Mr. Dour was still in his apartment, or at least a significant part of him. It just wasn't the physical part.

The pace of events had obviously accelerated, and I ran up to Jessie's room in near panic, pounding on the door with a clenched fist. I'm not sure what I intended to do, probably insist that she pack up and go someplace else until we could figure out what was happening. Oddly enough, I felt no fear for myself. I was dead, after all, and supposed nothing worse could happen. How naïve.

Jessie didn't answer, even though I knew I'd made enough noise to waken her. I leaned my forehead against her door and sighed, then turned the handle and stepped inside.

I didn't know exactly what to expect, and at first I thought it was a repeat of whatever had happened to Mrs. Harbinger. The apartment was darker than I remembered it, but it remained clean and orderly, no cobwebs, nothing out of place. The birds were all silent, which wasn't entirely unusual. They seemed to sense Jessie's moods and rarely made noise when she was pensive or sleeping. When I looked into the first cage, I realized there was another reason for their silence this time. All that remained of her parakeets were two perfectly articulated skeletons.

That alone would not have upset me. Now that I was dead myself, death no was no longer a particularly fearsome specter. But this was different. Those two little skeletons were moving back and forth on their perch just as they had in life, and when I glanced into the next cage and then another, I saw that the same was true in every instance. Aghast, I almost bolted from the room, but I had to know what had happened to Jessie, so I turned and stumbled blindly toward her bedroom.

She was lying on her bed, in almost the same position as Mrs. Harbinger downstairs, with her hands clasped on her breast, still wearing the clothing she'd worn during our last tea together. But her flesh was completely gone; only polished bone remained, and when she lifted one arm and gestured for me to come to her, I felt a rush of shameful panic, ran from the room and the apartment without even pausing to close the door behind me.

I don't even remember descending the staircase, and my next clear thought came as I stood in front of Mr. Lacking's door.

There was a lock on it, and the lock was engaged.

I must have stood there staring for some considerable time, because when I finally recollected myself, the streetlamps were lit outside. It wasn't one of my blackouts either; I'm quite sure of that. And it was only then that I saw the plain white envelope taped to the outside of Mr. Lacking's door, an envelope with my name on it.

The envelope contained a key and nothing else, and the key wouldn't open Mr. Lacking's door.

But there was one other lock in Crestwell. I turned and walked behind the staircase, lifted the tapestry aside, and tried the key again. The lock clicked cooperatively but the door itself scraped tightly against the frame when I tugged on it, as though reluctant to give up its final secrets. But then it was open and I found myself standing at the top of a very narrow and poorly lighted staircase.

There was no light switch but I started down anyway.

The staircase was much too long. I must have descended the equivalent of three stories before I saw the bottom, and a fourth before I reached it. The steps were completely enclosed until the bottom, undecorated tarpaper walls to left and right, neatly tacked in place, close enough that I could touch either without changing position. Too close, if anything. But when I reached the bottom I found myself in what looked very much like what I would expect of an apartment house basement. A huge, very dirty furnace huddled in a corner, silent and radiating no heat. Just beyond it were two oil tanks, arranged in parallel, draped heavily with cobwebs. A heterogeneous collection of wooden and cardboard crates and boxes were stacked up under the staircase, to either side, and in uneven rows as far as I could see. There were no windows and I was puzzled about where the light originated until I peered around a corner and saw two fluorescents unhappily fighting a losing battle against the darkness.

"Hello?" I called out, and there was no echo but the sound of my voice, altered by the acoustics of the place so that it sounded alien. "Is anyone down here?"

The floor was covered with cement dust and dirt and crunched under my feet. I advanced cautiously, not so much because I was afraid of what I might find but because whenever I could not trace a direct line to the lights, I could barely see where I was going. The shadows were not just dark; they seemed to cling to everything they touched, like a shroud of soft velvet with plush so deep you thought you might fall into it and be lost forever. The shadows moved as I passed through them, but not the way I expected, not because I altered the flow of light, but more as if they were recoiling slightly, withdrawing from my path so that I wouldn't tread on them.

The basement extended much further than should have been possible. I tried to orient myself but I had rounded so many corners that I couldn't be sure of the direction in which I faced. I was either under the street now or below one of the adjacent buildings. The rows of boxes and cartons and crates and barrels and drums and pails and bags and burlap sacks seemed to unfold and expand with each step I took, each corner revealing new shadowy vistas and more possible pathways. I found side lanes and intersections and places where I had as many as six paths to choose among, and I never hesitated, choosing one or another at random, knowing instinctively that whichever way I chose to go would ultimately lead me to the same destination.

Eventually the basement accepted its defeat. That's the only way I can describe it. The myriad paths dropped away and I no longer had any options. A single pathway lay ahead, and when I glanced back at the last intersection through which I had passed, it was no longer there. I could not be distracted and drawn away, my unliving flesh did not feel fatigue, and I had acquired in death a patience that always eluded me in life.

My surroundings began to look familiar. No, the crates and boxes and other debris were not transformed. It was not the details of their appearance that touched my memory. It was their organization, their positions relative to one another. The way in which a barrel snuggled up between two boxes struck a resonant chord somewhere and it wasn't until I had walked another score of paces that I realized what it was.

I had just walked into the front room of my apartment.

Not literally, of course. I was still in the basement and I was still surrounded by trash and wreckage and things long since discarded. But two boxes of disparate size pushed together reminded me of a cane backed chair, and a row of pails with a large sheet of masonite leaning against the back was a faulty replica of my sofa. I looked around in wonder and growing insight, and then I sensed movement where the doorway to my bedroom would have been and I turned and greeted my host.

"Hello, Mr. Swift. I think we need to talk."

I had realized long before that Swift and I were very much alike, even though we were superficially very different. Jessie had described him to me, a fairly large man, tall and broad in the shoulders, with a thick neck and a sharply chiseled chin. Swift had been a common laborer of some sort during his lifetime, but like me he had forgotten the details. He had changed since abandoning his apartment – now my apartment – on the top floor in favor of this musty, crowded, limitless basement. But I wasn't sure if he chosen to leave of his own free will or if had he been locked in down here by Mr. Lacking, perhaps to protect the other residents, although if that had been the reason, it had only deferred things for a while.

He still looked like a man, but only approximately. His edges were blurry and the underlying shape was in constant motion, constant change. One moment he was taller than I, the next I looked down at him. He was broad and muscular, then graceful and fragile. He moved forward confidently and shrank back in fear. I caught glimpses of his face and it looked familiar, but only because his features were drawn from among those of the people in Crestwell. I saw nothing that reflected the underlying man. My recognition of his identity had no basis in his physical appearance.

We faced each other for an endlessly short moment, then he retreated back the way he'd come, inviting me to follow and warning me off simultaneously. I never hesitated, followed him deeper into this version of our bedroom.

He had redecorated.

A half dozen wooden barrels were scattered around, each with staves missing so that they looked like bird cages. Indistinct things moved inside them, fluttering presences that weren't quite birds and weren't quite solid, but which managed to convey their terror and panic. Three rows of identical cardboard boxes had been arranged into a block where the bed should be, all covered with a moldy, soot stained, ragged blanket. Something moved there as well. Two amorphous shapes, elongated forms even more tenuous than Swift, each struggling to rise, neither succeeding, and the feeling of panic was even stronger from that direction.

More cardboard boxes had been torn apart and cut into rectangles, each eight and a half by eleven, stacked neatly in two piles at opposite ends of a black, brass clad trunk that had been laid on its side. One stack was untouched, but the other had been inscribed with precise rows of dark printed characters, words and phrases, although it was all senseless gibberish. I sensed another presence there as well, but nothing of Mr. Short was visible. Smaller pieces of colored cardboard decorated a stretch of otherwise bare wall in shapes that might have been flowers, but flowers seen through the eyes of a madman. Finally, against the far wall where a window should have been, there was a row of what I suppose were sculptures of some sort. Pieces of wooden crate had been torn apart, splintered, and reassembled in elaborate constructions that not only failed to represent anything real, but which seemed to connect and diverge at angles not always confined to three dimensional space.

"You have to let them go," I said softly.

I sensed something pressing against my eardrums, not sound exactly, but something that wanted to be sound. Swift hovered just beyond my reach and I felt him watching me.

"You're using them to stay, aren't you? You're holding onto them because it's the part of this world to which you feel closest. They're your anchor."

This time I thought I almost heard a voice speaking. "Too soon," it said. "Afraid."

I thought about it. "I understand. Sometimes I'm frightened too. But you have to let go, Swift. You can't stay here and you can't take your friends with you."

"Afraid," the voice repeated, and it was a voice this time. The bond between us was strengthening. "Made mistakes. Hurt people."

The names and places and details of my life had long since faded away, but I knew what he meant. I could remember things that I'd done, people I had used ruthlessly and sometimes unfairly, words I had spoken that were meant to sting and even if they were true and sometimes even deserved, I regretted them.

"That was the person you were then. What matters is the person you are now. It's time to stop using other people, Swift."

The amorphous, ever changing shape pulled in on itself, becoming smaller and denser. "Afraid," it said for the third time. "Come with me."

"I would if I could, but I don't know how. I think this is something we all have to do alone." Just as I had spent all my life alone, I realized. I was no more isolated in death than I had been in life, less so, in fact, because I felt closer to Jessie and the Teller Twins and Mr. Short and Mrs. Harbinger and even Mr. Dour than I had ever felt to anyone in life, not even to Alicia who loved her grandfather and still thought of him from time to time.

"Lonely."

"Yes," I sighed. "We have been lonely, you and I. But we don't have to be any more. Wherever we are, wherever we go, that's where we start again. You have to let go of the past before you can touch the future, Swift."

He didn't answer, or perhaps he did but only after he had started to move on and the words couldn't cross back. The swirling, metamorphosing shape continued to shrink in upon itself and the agitation grew less, and around us the phantom shapes faded away from the bed and from inside the cages, and the elaborate sculptures and bizarre flowers all began to fall apart, breaking down into dust and splinters, and the neat little lines of print slowly faded from the cardboard sheets and then I was alone in the basement and it was just a basement, and when I turned around the stairs were only a few feet away, and I went up them, but I didn't lock the door behind me.

No one in Crestwell will speak about what happened, not even Jessie. But Mrs. Harbinger has warmed to me and I have been invited to walk with her in the mornings, and Mr. Short has allowed me to read some of his work, most of which consists of very clever little tales for children, and the Teller Twins are always inviting me to come sit in their garden while they weed and prune, and they talk to me constantly about things that don't matter, and I find that very soothing. Mr. Dour has disappeared back into his cave, of course, but the other morning I found a very delicately carved statue of a knight in armor sitting in the hall outside my door, and it now has an honored place in my sitting room. Mr. Lacking is back, of course, and the lock is gone from his door. I still don't understand Mr. Lacking at all, but it doesn't seem to matter anymore.

So what have I learned from what happened? Precious little. If this phase of my existence was intended to further my education, then I may have flunked the course even if I didn't fail the residents of Crestwell. But perhaps it is just as big a mistake to search for a purpose now as it was in my former life. Maybe existence is just a series of states of being, culminating in something we cannot conceive, and maybe we don't always travel there by the same path. Most people believe in some ultimate fulfillment – Heaven, Valhalla, the perfect incarnation, or Oneness with the Universe.

But I don't think so. If we have a purpose at all, I can't believe it's to strive for some mystical goal where we will be rewarded or punished as appropriate, after an evaluation of our accumulated sins and virtues. This has to be more than just an elaborate game. I no longer think that the destination is of any consequence. I think it's how we make the journey that matters.

# THE KALEIDOSCOPE

Ted Croner never realized how unhappy he was with his life until he found the kaleidoscope in a box in his basement. Beth had been after him to clean out the trash left by the previous owner for almost a year, and he'd actually taken a few cartons out to the curb from time to time. Unfortunately, Ted was a dreamer and had visions of finding some forgotten treasure hidden within the trash, a rare stamp from British Guiana, forgotten jewelry, private correspondence between Thomas Jefferson and Alexander Hamilton. He sorted through each box very carefully before abandoning its contents to the trashmen, and so far the only item he had valued enough to rescue was an elderly radio that might, if he invested a couple of hundred dollars to have it repaired, fetch almost that much from a collector.

But then he found the kaleidoscope.

He identified it immediately, although it was unlike any he had ever before seen. Fashioned of some lightweight metal, now heavily tarnished, it had an unusually long shaft and supported a prism barrel fully twelve inches in diameter. He cleaned matted dirt off the eyepiece and tried to look through it, but the light in the basement wasn't strong enough to project a clear image. Ted threw open the bulkhead door and climbed up into the backyard, then raised the kaleidoscope to eye level.

It was the most beautiful thing he had ever seen. The facets were tiny and complex, the images sharp, brightly colored, and surprisingly detailed. Although they were too small for him to make out the individual shapes clearly, they seemed less random than the usual colored stones or pieces of translucent plastic, almost seeming to have discernible, specific forms.

Ted reached around to the barrel and gave it a turn. Or tried to. It wouldn't move, even when he exerted considerable pressure, and he lowered it from his eye, regarding it with undisguised venom. The two metal surfaces were so close together that he couldn't examine the space between, but surely it was meant to turn so that the pattern inside could be altered. He set the shaft between clenched thighs and used both hands, hoping to break the seal of grease and time and free the mechanism. It surrendered, but only by the tiniest fraction of an inch, locking in place once more despite every effort he made to turn it further.

"Ted? Is that you out there?"

He turned, saw Beth staring down from the second floor window, waved diffidently.

"As long as you're outside anyway, would you mind going next door for me? Karen said she'd loan me her roasting pan and I need it for tonight. And check the mailbox on your way back, will you?"

"All right," he answered sullenly, setting the kaleidoscope down on the wall of the brick patio. But despite the show of reluctance, he was secretly pleased. Ted's opinion of their next door neighbor had quickly moved from admiration to lust, and the fact that they both taught at Managansett High School, although in different departments, had added fuel to the fire. He had recently talked her into carpooling, and thought he'd done an excellent job of concealing his frequent, covert appraisals of her legs and breasts. It was hard to believe she had two kids, and that the older, Joe Junior, was almost a teenager.

Karen Pereira was in her kitchen, emptying groceries from a row of paper bags, when he knocked on the side door.

"Hi! Beth said something about a pan I'm supposed to borrow?"

"Oh, sure. Just a sec." Karen gestured for him to come inside and pulled a step stool out of the corner, used it to retrieve a stainless steel roasting pan from the top of a cupboard. She was wearing a very short skirt and Ted averted his eyes quickly, lest he be caught.

"Say, it looks like the Prescott's cat sneaked in when you weren't looking." The tabby's left ear had long since been torn into an instantly recognizable shape and it was staring at him balefully from its perch on a nearby counter.

Karen descended and handed him the pan, but her expression was puzzled. "What do you mean, the Prescotts' cat? Boots has belonged to us since she was a kitten. Andy and Samantha have that awful dog they bought for the twins."

Ted tried to cover his frown with a laugh; he was <u>sure</u> that the Prescotts owned a cat and the Pereiras a dog. "Sorry, I wasn't thinking."

He was still worrying about the exchange when he walked out to the street to check the mailbox, wondering if his memory was failing him or if he'd just been made the butt of some obscure joke. Andy Prescott's van was parked in front of the Pereira house, he noticed, and for some reason Joe Pereira had left his pickup truck across the street in the Prescotts' driveway. A moment later, Prescott himself came out through his front door, climbed into the truck, and backed it into the street, waving briefly before driving off.

Ted was surprised to see that Andy had shaved off his moustache.

The mail was depressing, a handful of circulars and an even larger handful of bills. He left it on the hall table and carried the roasting pan into the kitchen, set it on the table.

"Here you go, dear. Where do you want it?"

Beth glanced up from where she was relining the lower cupboard shelves with contact paper. She had gathered her waist length, bright red hair up into a bun and pinned it in place, out of her way.

"Just put it anywhere. I hope you're making progress with that mess in the basement."

"I'm working on it." But instead of returning to the task, he retrieved the kaleidoscope and carried it into the small, windowless room he called his "office".

Ted used an unbent paper clip to scrape along the inside, clearing away several small clumps of unrecognizable matter that had been lodged between the inner surface of the barrel and the outer perimeter of the shaft. After finishing one complete circuit, he braced the shaft between his legs and tried once again to turn the mechanism, this time with slightly more success. It rotated perhaps an eighth of an inch before stopping. Ted glanced through the eyepiece, thought he could see changes in the revealed pattern, but only in some of the peripheral details.

Frustrated, he set it aside, decided to walk next door and see if Joe Pereira had an aerosol lubricant he could spray inside. Joe would be home, sitting in front of the television in all likelihood. It was baseball season and he was an avid Red Sox fan, nor was he willing to stir from the house while his right arm was still in a sling. He'd broken it a week earlier in a fall from the telephone pole where he'd been stringing cable and was still embarrassed by his clumsiness.

"Joe, you in there?" He rapped on the sliding glass door to the Pereira's family room, trying to see through a crack between the drawn bamboo drapes.

"Hey, that you Croner? C'mon in; my hands are full."

Ted obediently slid the glass door open, stepped into the air conditioned interior. The television was off, but Joe Pereira was standing at the far end of the room, arranging sixpacks of beer in a small refrigerator. That was surprising, since Joe had never been much of a drinker, despite Andy Prescott's many attempts to entice him into a night of barhopping.

"No game today?" Ted nodded toward the silent television.

Joe straightened up, looked momentarily puzzled. "Oh, is it baseball season already?"

"Has been for two months."

"Yeah, well, I've never been much for sports. You know how it is." But Ted didn't, and he was becoming very confused, particularly since he'd just watched his next door neighbor swing the refrigerator door shut with an arm which had suffered a compound fracture only a few days before.

"What can I do for you, neighbor?"

Ted blinked, having completely forgotten why he had come over in the first place, improvised feverishly. "I just wanted to check with Karen and see if we can switch off in the carpool next week. I need the car during the day on Monday."

The other man's eyes narrowed. "Why would you and Karen be carpooling? She's all the way the other end of town from the high school."

Ted was definitely confused; he'd been very careful to suggest trading off the driving in front of Joe right from the start, and hadn't pressed seriously until he was sure the man wouldn't object. "Did Karen quit her job?" His heart sank; one of the high points of this year had been discovering that his and Karen's free periods coincided, and that she invariably spent the time in the faculty lounge.

"No way. She's hoping the Callanders will make her a full partner eventually."

The Callanders were brother and sister, owners of the most prestigious (actually, the only) accounting firm in Managansett. In fact, Andy Prescott had worked for them for several years, and was in line for a partnership himself.

And when had Joe Pereira found time to grow himself a moustache?

Ted was never quite sure how he managed to extricate himself from the conversation.        He walked home in a fog of confusion, not even noticing when Samantha Prescott walked out to bring in the mail, carefully holding her broken arm pressed against her side.

Back inside his own house, Ted stumbled into the living room, slipped behind the bar, and poured himself a few fingers of brandy, downing it so abruptly that it burned the back of his throat and he began coughing uncontrollably. Alarmed, Beth came running in from the kitchen, pounded his back and steered him over to the couch.

"What in the world?" She sat beside him, watching closely as he regained his composure, drew a deep breath, and sat back.

Beth's long red hair was suddenly blonde, and barely reached her shoulders.

Ted Croner lay awake for a long time that night, long after his wife's breathing had evened out and the traffic noises from outside had weakened and finally ceased almost entirely. He lay with his eyes open, staring up into the darkness, wondering if he'd lost his mind. Everything had been quite normal this morning, but now things were all mixed up. His wife and neighbors remembered a different past than his, had mysteriously exchanged pets and interests and who knew what else.  And since that was clearly impossible, he must have gone crazy.

A passing car's headlights played through the branches of a tree just outside the bedroom window, throwing a crazy quiltwork pattern on the near wall. Like my sanity, he thought, shattered into myriad pieces and rearranged, the way colors and shapes were altered in a kaleidoscope.

The kaleidoscope.

He sat bolt upright, his forehead suddenly covered with perspiration. Could it be? No, that was crazy. But he'd already decided that he was crazy, hadn't he? And if that was the case, then why not indulge his insanity a bit further?

Quietly, not wanting to waken Beth, Ted slipped out of bed, tiptoed out of the room and down the stairs to the ground floor. He almost expected the kaleidoscope to be gone, but when he flicked on the overhead light, it was right where he had left it.

He picked it up tentatively this time, as though it might be dangerous. And if his insane idea was right, it probably was. This time he examined every inch of its surface, searching for some legend, some inscription, any mark which might help to identify it or its origin. But other than a few scratches and gouges, there were no distinguishing features whatsoever.

After several minutes of concentrated effort designed to find significance in the current pattern, Ted decided to try moving the barrel again. As before, it resisted his efforts, but he continued to strain until his hand slipped and he scraped his palm badly along one edge. Frustrated, he stood up, weighed the kaleidoscope thoughtfully in one hand, then carried it downstairs to the basement.

Ted wrapped the shaft with an old towel before placing it between the jaws of his vice, then wrapped a second loosely around the barrel to protect his hands and improve his grip. Even with this increased leverage, he thought he had failed, but just before he abandoned the effort, there was a tiny sound, metal sliding on metal, and the barrel turned a quarter inch before once more refusing to budge. He released it from the vice, examined the new and now noticeably different pattern, then carried the kaleidoscope back upstairs.

The house was the same. He looked out the windows on either side and couldn't spot anything changed in either direction. Back in his bedroom, he briefly turned on the light; Beth slept peacefully, her shoulder length blonde hair twisted beneath her head.

"You are going crazy," he whispered to himself, turned off the light, and went to bed.

He felt much better in the morning, even though Beth's hair was still blonde and Joe Pereira's truck was once again parked in the Prescotts' driveway. It was Sunday, and no one seemed to be up and about. Obviously he'd had a brief lapse of memory, disorienting and undoubtedly upsetting, but everything seemed to have settled down now and Ted felt quite certain he could reconcile his erring memories with reality.

It felt even more unreal later, while he was sitting on the front porch, reading the Sunday paper. Oddly enough, nothing he found there conflicted with his memories; the strange discontinuities seemed to have confined themselves to details of his immediate suroundings. He'd half expected to discover that Dukakis was President, the Soviet Union had remained intact, and Martians were invading.

When Joe Pereira came outdoors wearing a tee-shirt and shorts, and began washing the pickup truck, that should have been a sign that things were returning to normal. Except that he came out of the wrong house to do it. And when the Prescott twins started to play on their swing set, they did so in the Pereiras' yard, or what should have been the Pereiras' yard. The newspaper fell from Ted's limp fingers.

Later, after he'd regained the ability to move and talk, he explored his newly rearranged environment by encouraging Beth to talk about the neighbors, a subject she was willing to discuss with minimal encouragement. From her freely offered store of rumors, facts, theories, and speculation, he learned several things that contradicted his memories.

The Prescotts and Pereiras had switched houses, obviously, and Andy was no longer an accountant but a real estate agent. When he cautiously asked Beth how her own work was going, Ted learned that rather than work for Catterall Realty, she was now an employee of Callander & Callander Accounting Services. The Prescotts still had the twins, Cindy & Julie, but now there was a third as well, another girl, Felicia. Felicia had been the Pereiras' daughter, but Joe Junior was now apparently an only child.

Karen Pereira was a teacher again, currently on a short medical leave because of the skydiving accident that had left her with a broken arm. Ted remembered Andy Prescott's fascination with skydiving, but apparently the closest he now came to participating in sports was his fanatical devotion to the Red Sox. Beth also made a passing reference to a miscarriage he was quite certain she had never had, at least not before, and wondered from which of his neighbors that particular attribute had come.

Nor was Ted himself immune from the changes. He found a scar on his arm that was an exact match to one he'd seen before, but it had belonged to Joe Pereira at the time. He'd gone to bed needing a haircut and wakened with a crewcut. And when Beth made lunch, linguini in a spicy sauce, he disocvered that he had somehow managed to shed his allergy to tomatoes.

He might still be crazy, he realized, but Ted decided that a more satisfying, if less plausible, explanation was that the mysterious kaleidoscope was somehow changing reality, shifting bits and pieces of the lives of the three families back and forth. If he could somehow learn to control the process, pick the best parts of each for himself and Beth, he'd have it made.

And then he thought of something else. If the kaleidoscope could shift a child from one family to another, why not a wife? He no longer loved Beth, hadn't thought of her in those terms for years now. She was still attractive in an undistinguished sort of way, but she'd put on some weight over the years, and her idea of good sex was conservative, predictable, and as brief as possible.

Karen on the other hand...

But how could he control it? Even if he could somehow free the barrel so that the mechanism turned freely, how choose a single attribute to change? Perhaps everything was reflected in the new patterns formed in the inner chamber, but if so, he hadn't the faintest idea how to interpret them.

After lunch, he walked into the study, closed the door, and spent nearly two hours staring through the narrow eyepiece, fancying he saw human forms, houses, pets, trees and vehicles and abstract forms all mixed together. But even if his eyes and imagination were not seeing what he wished to find rather than what was actually there, he still had no way of manipulating the discrete parts of his reality.

Except by trial and error.

Ted spent much of the afternoon on the back patio, watching the kids play in the adjacent yard and across the street, noticing that the dog and cat had switched back to their original houses, although they were still with the wrong families. Felicia Prescott was a precocious seven year old, and when she came outside to play with the twins, he discovered where Beth's red hair had gone. Andy

Prescott had his moustache back, but now it was Karen who insisted on watching the Red Sox.

"Ever since she went to work in field maintenance for the phone company, she's been interested in sports," Joe confided when he wandered over to visit his neighbor late in the day. "I guess she picked it up from the guys she works with."

Ted ignored the kaleidoscope, trying to work out the implications in his mind. There had been so many rapid changes, he wasn't sure he remembered the original configuration of the neighborhood well enough to set things back, even if he could figure out how. Was it Andy or Joe who had originally sported that pencil thin moustache, for example? And had Samantha Prescott always worn glasses?

He was also bothered by the fact that only he seemed to recognize that things were not as they had been before. Of course, he was the one operating the kaleidoscope, but the scar and his absent allergy demonstrated that he was just as vulnerable to the changes. But unless his wife and neighbors were extraordinarily good actors, none of them suspected anything was amiss. Ted also entertained the possibility that despite all the evidence, he was actually experiencing some weird variety of breakdown, that he was either imagining the changes or creatively re-editing the past in order to convince himself that magic was at work.

Ultimately he decided to accept as his working hypothesis that the kaleidoscope was genuine, that the changes were real, and that further alterations were possible. If he was in fact crazy, it could do no harm, and if he was sane, he had a chance to substantially improve his situation, to say nothing of acquiring Karen Pereira as his wife. Karen Croner...he liked the sound of it.

The kaleidoscope proved to be as stubborn as ever when he finally picked it up. Frustrated, he carried it down to the basement, where he discovered that he now owned the fully equipped workshop that Joe Pereira had proudly shown off shortly after the Croners moved into the neighborhood. A quick search revealed an aerosol lubricant spray, which he used liberally around the circumference of the shaft. This time, when he tried to turn the barrel, it moved freely, a full half turn before he stopped.

The pattern had changed significantly, but he still couldn't interpret the shapes and colors. Setting the kaleidoscope down on the workbench, he walked upstairs to explore his new world.

Samantha Prescott met him at the top of the stairs. No, actually it was Samantha Croner who stood there, wearing her waist length red hair loose across her back.

"There you are!" Her eyes flashed angrily. "Would you please talk to your daughters about their behavior? They've done nothing but fight since they got up this morning."

Stunned, Ted turned toward the living room, his feet moving automatically, found the twins sitting sullenly at opposite ends of the couch. Julie's right arm was in a sling. He glanced out the front window, noticed a pickup truck parked inside his carport, then jumped as a tabby cat ran across the floor practically under his feet.

"No, this isn't what I wanted," he whispered to himself, then turned and bolted back to the basement door, brushing past his new wife so quickly that her jaw dropped in amazement. Ted practically ran to the bottom of the stairs, snatched up the kaleidoscope, and gave it a full turn without even coming to a stop. A discarded rag shifted under one foot and Ted lost his balance, threw out both hands automatically to break the fall, and lost his grip on the kaleidoscope.

He hit the floor hard enough to take his breath away, slowly found the strength to roll over onto his back, drew deep, ragged breaths until the pain subsided. A few seconds later he sat up, then stood, then began to search for the kaleidoscope. But not only was it no place to be found, he quickly realized he was no longer in his own basement. The workshop had been returned to the Pereira house, and he along with it.

A sudden premonition chilled him and he raced upstairs, not even nodding to his wife, Karen, before rushing out the front door.

As he had suspected, he lived in the Pereira house now, although the mailbox read Croner; at least he hadn't swapped identities. To his right, in his original yard, Beth...Pereira?...was working on hands and knees in the flower garden that Samantha Prescott had planted in the yard across the street early in the spring. Andy Prescott was outside, meticulously trimming weeds from the streetside edge of his property, using the weedwhacker Joe Pereira had bought at Sears the previous year.

Ted started down the front walk, just as Joe came out through his own front door, with a familiar object cradled in one arm. "Hey, Andy! Come see what I found!" As he stepped down from the porch, Joe was already attempting to turn the barrel of the kaleidoscope.

"Oh my God!" Ted wasn't sure if he had said the words aloud. He started across the lawn, trying to figure out how to convince Pereira to surrender the kaleidoscope, never even noticed the delivery van whose driver vainly slammed on the brakes when Andy Prescott blindly and foolishly stepped into the street without looking for traffic. There was a thud audible above the screech of tires on asphalt and Prescott flew twenty feet through the air before slamming down onto the pavement, where he made feeble efforts to move. At the very same instant, Joe Pereira used his well muscled right arm to turn the kaleidoscope's barrel.

Ted stared up into the sky, feeling the pain of his broken body as an abstract thing, no longer a part of his personal reality. Faces came into view, Joe Pereira, Andy Prescott, a stranger wearing a uniform cap of some sort. In some remote, emotionless corner of his mind, Ted realized that he was dying and wished that there was some magic device he could use to change the world, to erase his foolish lack of attention, to preserve his life.

But there was no such thing, of course.

# KINGDOMS GREAT AND SMALL

The kingdom of Meadow, as you might expect, was a quiet land of farmers, fishers, and woodsmen, surrounded by equally peaceful neighbors with whom they traded across loosely defined borders. King Volis, like his father and his grandfathers before him, ruled with a hand so light that his people barely felt it. He dressed like a commoner except during affairs of state and visited every town at least once a year to hear the grievances of his people, which were few. His castle was beautiful but small, the only army was a small honor guard, and as a consequence the taxes were so low that the people almost didn't mind paying them.

The only problem that vexed his subjects was that King Volis was well past middle age and still hadn't married. This was particularly serious because he had no brothers or sisters, and his only uncle had died in a hunting accident years before. Unless the king took a bride and fathered a child, it would be the end of a line of kings that extended back so far that not even the histories recorded a time when they had not sat on the throne.

Some worried that Volis lacked the capacity to truly love another individual deeply because he loved all of his people so much that his affection had become attenuated. These people suggested that the King should choose a wife from a list of nominees generated by the wisest people in Meadow, purely as a matter of policy. They had no doubt he would be kind to his queen, even if he didn't love her, just as he was kind to all of his subjects. Others believed that Volis simply hadn't met the right woman, and if that woman could not be found in Meadow, then perhaps she lived in Glade or Seaside or even in Crag. They urged the king to travel, and invited highly regarded women from those lands to pay visits to the court of Meadow, which many of them did. They were all well pleased by the manners and appearance of King Volis, but none of them truly caught his eye.

The truth was that King Volis already was in love, more so every day in fact, but none of his subjects had ever met the object of his affection because she only appeared in the King's Private Garden. The King's Private Garden lay at the very heart of the palace. It wasn't very large, because the palace itself wasn't very large. It was open to the sky above but there were vine covered trellises overhead arranged to block the view even from the battlements at the four corners of the castle. The garden was forbidden to all but the king himself and was maintained by a magic spell so old that its origin had long since been forgotten.

There were no windows and a single door, and one of the sternest rules in the entire kingdom of Meadow was that if the king was inside, he was not to be disturbed lightly. In the event of an emergency that required the king's immediate attention, there was a bell that could be rung to summon him, but it had never served its purpose during Volis' life, or that of his father, or even his father's father. Under no circumstances could anyone but the king pass through the door.

King Volis visited his garden at least once a day when he could, usually in the morning, and often again in the afternoon. He stayed about an hour each time, and no one ever saw what happened during that time, and he never spoke of those visits to anyone else. He had first come there as a boy of nineteen, the day after his father's heart failed and Volis assumed the throne, but it had been no more than curiosity and he had not returned for almost a year.

It was on his second visit that he met Lysandra.

Lysandra was a pixie, small enough to stand in the palm of his hand, but even at that size she was a beautiful woman. Pixies were not unknown in Meadow, although they generally kept to themselves, and there were only occasional complaints about their pranks, which were almost always good natured. Lysandra was in self imposed exile, she explained, because by nature she was solemn and that made other pixies decidedly uneasy in her presence. The magic that prevented human beings from entering the garden didn't apply because she, obviously, was not human. Her people had never suggested that she take herself away, had always been very kind to her, but she could perceive that there was something just slightly different in her nature, something that set her apart from the other pixies, and she knew that they felt it as well.

King Volis commiserated and casually promised to visit her again, but that night, in his bedchamber, her words rolled around inside his head and he sat upright suddenly, completely awake, and realized that she had revealed a truth that he had hidden from himself. The people of Meadow loved him, he was sure, and they ostensibly treated him as a friend rather than a ruler. But there was always a hint of hesitation, of distance, because even though he had never treated a subject unfairly, there was always the chance that he could, and no one would stand against him because he was, after all, the king. And that meant that he was just as alienated from his people as Lysandra was from hers, except that she could go off and live by herself and no one would object, while no similar escape was available to Volis. He felt too strong a sense of duty to abdicate until he had a competent heir to rule in his stead.

And so he began visiting with Lysandra almost every day, because she understood him and she was the only one he could talk to about his loneliness. As time passed, he began to love her as a friend, and then as a woman, and even though he could hold her in the palm of one hand, so too could she hold his heart in hers.

The years passed and Volis grew older. Pixies age only if they allow themselves to do so, and at first Lysandra remained unchanged from year to year. But eventually her love for Volis became so great that she began to age along with him, although she was no less beautiful as a woman than she had been as a girl.

And then one day something marvelous happened.

King Volis arrived as always, made his way through a swarm of flutterbies and around the central fountain to the bench where they always met. Even as he took his usual seat, Lysandra emerged from a cluster of ornamental shrubs and jumped lightly up onto his proffered palm.

And he dropped her. Never, not once, in all the years since they'd met, had anything remotely similar happened.

"My dear, I apologize. I must be getting old if my arm grows so weak."

"You're not that old, Volis," she answered quietly as she settled on his knee. "Have you been ill?" He had not, and soon their conversation turned to other things.

Several days later, Volis noticed something else. "I think you're growing taller, my dear. I don't have to lift you nearly as high to talk to you as I did before."

Lysandra insisted that such a thing was impossible, but Volis demonstrated until she was forced to admit that he was right. "I don't understand it. I can use pixie magic to change my appearance, but I can't change my real self."

But change she did. By the autumn, she came up to his knee, by winter his waist, and by spring she could rest her head on his shoulder when they stood together. At first the change frightened Lysandra, and Volis spent more time with her and felt greater love than ever before, and that accelerated the change. He called upon the wisest man in Meadow, the philosopher Wedicon, whose knowledge of the ways of magic and legend was without parallel. Wedicon, sworn to secrecy, was told all and after many days and nights of feverish research, he ventured an opinion.

"It's the touch of a loved one that does it, my liege. When the two of you clasp hands, you become for a moment a single being with a single will."

On one bright spring morning a short time later, King Volis emerged from his garden hand in hand with another, an event unprecedented in the history of Meadow, and introduced her to his court as their queen-to-be. There was considerable consternation as you might expect, but the people of Meadow were so happy at the prospect of the continuation of the royal line that they treated Lysandra with kindness and respect and soon came to love her almost as much as they did their king.

There was only one small problem. A year after their marriage, Volis embarked on a visit to some of the farthest towns in his realm. Lysandra had always accompanied him in the past, but she was involved with preparations for the annual festival and decided to remain behind just this once. Volis was to be gone for seven days, which was the longest they'd been apart in a very long time.

On the third day, Lysandra tripped over the hem of her gown. On the fourth, she could not wear much of what hung in her wardrobe because everything was too large for her. She was shrinking. A messenger was sent to the King, who rode through the night to return, convinced that she might die in his absence. He found her lying in bed, distraught, and wrapped his arms around her childlike form and whispered soothing words and they fell asleep in each other's arms.

The following morning, her clothing fit perfectly.

They were never apart for more than a day after that and less than a year later Volis and Lysandra had a son. They named him Volysan and presented him to the people of Meadow as their next king, and there was considerable rejoicing. Volysan grew up straight and tall, a handsome young man who was blessed with his father's strength and his mother's beauty, who was prone to practical jokes, though only of the gentlest kind, and whose sense of justice was every bit as solidly based as that of his father. Volysan trapped game with the hunters, cut trees with the woodsmen, planted and harvested with the farmers, cast nets with the fishermen, and even sold little loaves he'd baked himself in the marketplace from time to time. He loved his parents and they loved him, and the bonds among them were so strong that they had never been separated for more than a ten day.

The years passed and the people of Meadow were content and hoped that life in their land would never change. But everything changes eventually.

Volis developed a cough one winter that lingered into the spring and then the summer. Physicians were summoned from across Meadow and elsewhere and they prescribed nostrums and sweatings and poultices and charms, and Volis seemed to take some comfort from their ministrations but his cough grew no better. Lysandra resented every moment when she could not be at her husband's side and their son was always hovering, offering to run errands, to close or open windows, to prepare cold tea or hot rum or whatever else might help. Volis thanked them constantly and insisted that they had made him feel much better, but he died in his sleep anyway, the day after Volysan's twentieth birthday.

Lysandra was crushed by the loss and only the devotion of and her devotion to her son prevented her from following Volis into oblivion. At first she feared – indeed expected – that her stature would rapidly decline, both metaphorically and physically. Oddly enough, neither happened. Thirty days after Volis was in his grave, ten days after the crown had been officially placed on the head of King Volysan, Lysandra stood at his shoulder, as tall as she'd been the day she brought him into the world, still as popular with the people of Meadow as she had been in the past.

Volysan wanted to continue in the manner of his father and rule with a gentle, almost imperceptible hand. But fate conspired against him.

The weather became uncertain during the second year of Volysan's reign. Crops didn't fail, but yields were down. A volcanic eruption in Crag poured lava into the sea, and the changing temperatures drove the fish along the coast of Meadow farther from shore. Ships returned with holds unfilled and prices rose. The shortages made hunting more profitable, but the increase in hunting led to a shortage of game.

Times were difficult in Meadow and Glade, very difficult in Seaside, and almost impossible in Crag. Kracellus, the ruler of Crag, was overthrown and Corbin assumed the throne. Within a year, Corbin had annexed the northern third of Seaside and the eastern half of Glade. The Regent of Glade began quietly raising an army and he approached Volysan, suggesting an alliance. Seaside would cooperate as well, but only if Meadow – the most populous of the four kingdoms – agreed to participate. Volysan consulted with his people, both those who studied such matters and those who did not. Arguments could be made for either position. The only universal agreement was that it was up to Volysan to decide and that his people would support his decision.

So Volysan held council with himself, and sometimes with his mother, and after a ten day in which his people never saw him at all, he emerged from the King's Private Garden and issued a proclamation. Meadow would join with the others in a joint effort to deal with the problems facing the four kingdoms, but he insisted that Crag be invited to participate as well.

There was much opposition in Seaside and Glade, but Volysan was adamant and at last an emissary was sent to invite Corbin to a meeting in Meadow where all grievances would be presented and addressed. King Hadok of Seaside predicted that there would be much talk and little movement, and Volysan agreed. "But if Corbin spends his time in argument, he will have less to spend on war." King Dell of Glade protested that Volysan would feel differently if his people were living under a foreign ruler, but Volysan pointed out that the borders had never been sharply defined and that more than half the people in the disputed area had been settlers spreading westward from Crag.

And so they met, and talked, and talked some more. Corbin steadfastly refused to withdraw his army, but was made to understand that any further advance would be met with superior force. Corbin was not a stupid man though he was equally not a wise ruler. Less than a year passed before supporters of a surviving niece of Kracellus named Kyrillis rebelled and seized the northern half of

Crag. The invading armies were withdrawn to deal with the new threat and the borders returned to their previous muddled state.

It was not an unmitigated success for Volysan. When Corbin's power was broken at last, he and a considerable body of followers fled south, carving a path of fire and blood across Glade, an arrow of death pointed straight at Meadow. Volysan rallied his diminutive army, kissed his mother goodbye, and led them to meet and hopefully crush the outlaws. It was the first time he'd been away from her side for more than two consecutive days and he missed her almost from the moment of departure.

They rode for three days and made camp just inside their own border. Intelligence suggested that Corbin's band would cross somewhere close by, possibly as soon as the following afternoon. Volysan set pickets out to watch every possible river crossing and told the balance of his soldiers to sleep as best they could. Then he disappeared into his own tent to set an example.

It was hazy the following morning and fog drifted through the encampment like clouds of smoke. Volysan himself walked among the tents, rousing his followers, then listened to the reports from the pickets, one of whom was his close friend Tiburon, whom he'd known since childhood. Tiburon was describing some furtive movement he'd detected on the opposite bank when he noticed that Volysan was frowning and blinking.

"Is something amiss, my liege? Are my words not clear?"

"Clear as the purest water, my friend. But tell me, have you grown taller since the winter?"

Tiburon faltered. "Why, no, my liege. Not that I'm aware of."

Volysan sighed. "Ah, then it must be that I am grown shorter."

And so it was.

Two days later Volysan commanded his small army from a platform built into a tree overlooking the battlefield. He was the size of young child and lacked the strength to raise his sword. Corbin's forces, already weary and confused, were defeated with surprising ease, the survivors taken away for medical treatment and judgment, the rest buried in a mass grave. Corbin was among the latter.

The returning heroes were greeted with joy by the people of Meadow, but the celebration became muted when news of Volysan's plight was revealed. By the time he reached home, his head was level with Tiburon's knee. Lysandra greeted him with love and understanding and they went to the King's Private Garden to be by themselves for a long time.

The following morning, Volysan seemed the same, but two days after that, he was noticeably taller and a few more sunrises more saw him restored completely. Wedicon was summoned again and there was much consulting of ancient tomes and an envoy was sent to find Lysandra's people and solicit their help. It soon became evident that just as King Volis had transformed Lysandra through his touch, so too did Volysan require periodic contact with his mother to retain his normal size. Ordinarily this would have posed no problem, but Lysandra was aging quickly now, no longer able to retard time's advance or restore her previous longevity. Wedicon announced that she had become completely human at last, and that this also explained why she hadn't begun to shrink along with her son during their separation. But he was unable to explain why Volysan had done so.

"Perhaps there is a part of him that remains Pixie."

Volysan accepted the situation tranquilly, and insisted that since his mother was unlikely to die soon, it was of little consequence. Lysandra was less sanguine and sought to make provision for her son. Experimentation showed that if he carried a lock of her hair with him, the transformation was arrested even during prolonged absences. Unfortunately, the shorn lock lost its efficacy after several months and had to be replaced. While Lysandra still lived, it allowed Volysan a freedom of movement that he actually never required, but there was still no answer to the eventuality of her death.

Wedicon suggested that if Volysan were to have a child, he might pass along the same magic he'd inherited from his mother. The only problem with that was Volysan's continued bachelorhood. "I have only so much love within me," he insisted, "and I have expended that on the people of Meadow." But in truth, he was reluctant to risk passing on what he privately thought of as a gentle but persistent curse to yet another generation. Better, he thought, that the line end with me.

But eventually matters of state came to outweigh personal considerations. Lysandra had grown frail with the passage of years, and this time the shrinking of her body was an entirely natural process. The people of Meadow became restive – or at least as restive as was possible given their settled nature – and wanted to know that provisions were being made to preserve stability and continuity. They wanted Volysan to have an heir.

He tried to oblige them. He sponsored balls and festivals and danced with every unmarried lady who attended. He visited remote villages and small holdings and introduced himself to every eligible maiden in the land. He armed himself with fresh locks of his mother's hair and traveled to Glade and Seaside and even to Crag to meet more potential queens, and many of them both at home and abroad were smitten with him.

But, alas, Volysan found none to love and when Lysandra finally breathed her last, his people had become resigned to the fact that he never would.

Volysan may never have loved another woman with the intensity that his parents felt for each other or for him, but he loved his people no less and his heart was torn by the prospect of abandoning them without leadership. And so he proposed an idea that was new to his people and to his world. The people should rule themselves, said Volysan, and no longer be dependent upon the whim and wisdom of kings and queens.

"But who will tell us what to do?" his people asked, and he told them they would decide for themselves, individually and in council.

It had never been tried before but Volysan vowed to have a system in place before he died. To that end, he announced the creation of a governing council to be elected by every adult citizen who chose to cast a vote. There would be fifty delegates and during the first year they would each have one vote, but the king would have fifty to balance them. If all went well, he would absent himself from their deliberations after that, and his authority would expire when he did.

Wedicon had found a way to prolong the effect of Lysandra's locks of hair, but even his skill had its limits. By the time the council completed its first year, Volysan was shrinking again. He wasn't entirely unhappy. His had been a busy, productive life and he was tired and looking forward to being reunited with the people he loved, if such reunions were in truth possible after death.

And so it was announced that King Volysan would be spending the remainder of his life in seclusion in the King's Private Garden. A great festival was announced, the last he would attend, and his subjects were warned that this would be their final opportunity to pay their respects to their king. Volysan, who was now the size of a particularly healthy squirrel, was installed on a raised platform on the main square, raised not to pander to his vanity but to make it unnecessary for those who came to see him to bend or squat uncomfortably.

Volysan's advisors had expected a formidable turnout, but they were unprepared for the reality. It seemed as though the entire kingdom was on the move. People waited in long lines from dawn to dusk just to touch Volysan's hand and perhaps say a few words. Even when the sun was hot, or the rain fell heavily, they continued to come and in such numbers that the resources of the capital were sorely strained. The ten day festival was extended and then extended again.

On the morning of the twenty-fourth day, Volysan asked for a new seat. The old one chafed, he insisted, even though the cushions were freshened daily. He had the same complaint the following morning, but this time a child in the crowd revealed the truth, calling out loudly, "The King is too big for his throne."

It was true. Volysan was growing again. And as the days passed, and as he touched the hands of his people, the incremental love that they provided restored him to his previous stature.

Volysan never shrank again. Despite his new circumstances, he decreed that the council should continue to govern Meadow. He spent the following years traveling among his people, and until he was no longer physically able to do so, he planted with the farmers, hauled nets with the fishermen, and baked bread to sell in the marketplace. When he died, the ashes from his pyre were blown into the King's Private Garden, which was then closed up, never to be used again.

The people of Meadow never forgot him, however, and there were likenesses and statues of Volysan displayed throughout his former kingdom even many generations after his death, but in every case these reproductions have honored his final request – that the single largest of those statues should stand in a place of honor in the Council Chamber.

It would fit quite comfortably in the palm of your hand.

.

www.ingramcontent.com/pod-product-compliance
Lightning Source LLC
Chambersburg PA
CBHW072055170626
46813CB00004B/1368